FITNESS CAN KILL

PATRICIA FISHER SHIP'S DETECTIVE BOOK 2

STEVEN HIGGS

Finding people to dedicate my books to has always been a tough gig, which probably just means that I haven't worked out how to do it yet.

This book, just because I was beginning to write it at exactly the moment she happened along, is dedicated to Debbie De Winne. Debbie stopped what she was doing for a few minutes to listen as I bored her with talk of my books. She was even good enough to pretend to be interested.

Thank you, Debbie.

1

WILD WEST MONKEY

How many people does it take to catch a monkey? No, that's not the start of a terrible joke, it's a genuine question.

"Come along, Buddy," I cooed. "Come and get the nice banana from Patricia, pretty please."

Buddy the monkey, so called because I felt it was easier to give him a name, was, so far as we knew, the last Gibraltar Rock Ape on board the Aurelia. His family and friends boarded the ship en masse when we docked in Gibraltar, but we enticed them back to the quay-side with a glut of fruit and other treats.

Buddy had other ideas and seemed quite content to remain on board. I wasn't sure if monkeys got homesick or lonely, but thus far Buddy appeared to be having the time of his life.

The ship was parked … um stationed? I really need to read a handbook or something for all the right nautical terms. Whatever, we were in Lanzarote, another place I rather fancied visiting if I got the chance. However, in a moment of infatuation-induced stupidity – my boyfriend had just bought me a huge sapphire - I volunteered to deal with the rock ape infestation and that meant the one monkey still on board was my problem.

Going back to my question about how many people it takes to catch the monkey, the current count of crew members involved in the roundup was just short of twenty, more and more unwitting crew members finding themselves drawn into my ridiculous escapade as they happened by.

"Has anyone got eyes on the ape?" asked Lieutenant Commander Baker, his voice coming over the radio.

I raised my left hand to my mouth, pressing the send button on my own radio with one finger as I peered under a sun lounger. "He was here with me a moment ago," I replied. "I saw a flash of his tail."

"Can you give us a precise fix on your location, Mrs Fisher?" Baker requested.

Coming out of my crouch, but keeping my eyes very much peeled for the elusive primate, I signalled to my assistant, Sam, who was just a few yards away and thoroughly enjoying the search for the ape.

"Go left," I mouthed, indicating that Sam should circle around because I thought perhaps Buddy might be behind the cocktail bar. To reply to Lieutenant Commander Baker, I said, "We are on deck eighteen, portside end, midships by the transoms." I wasn't sure I had all the terminology right, but no one radioed back to question it, so my description had to be close enough.

No one else had seen Buddy for several minutes, so since mine was the most recent sighting, Baker was coordinating the rest of the round-up party to come to me. They had nets and a few blunt instruments like broomsticks or paddles with which they hoped to humanely capture the little brown rock ape.

Not that he was all that little, and I had to wonder how dangerous he might be when cornered. My mind recalled wildlife documentaries where Sir David Attenborough or others talked about the relative strength of different creatures when compared to a man. I had no desire to test any such theories by getting one of my arms torn off.

"Buddy? Buddy, are you there? It's your friend, Patricia." I kept my voice light, hoping this would make me seem more friendly. For his own good, Buddy needed to be returned to his colony, but the real drive to capture him was due to his continual need to terrorise passengers. It had only been two days since he arrived, and we had forty-seven reported sightings and incidents.

To be fair to Buddy, I don't think he was intentionally scaring people, but he was happily scaling the sides of the ship and using balconies to access cabins. Imagine coming out of the shower to find a primate rummaging in your fruit bowl. He was finding food everywhere, including fruit from cocktail glasses on the sundecks during the day.

Eating vodka-soaked chunks of pineapple was undoubtedly messing with his head and he wasn't one of those nice drunks that just went to sleep. Oh no, he was the other kind entirely.

Alistair, the captain of the ship and my boyfriend, had all but begged me to catch Buddy when the ape got spooked and threw poop at some kids playing in the pool on the upper deck sun terrace. Apparently, this is not the sort of thing that happens on board the Aurelia.

Baker's voice boomed over the radio again, "We are on route to you, Mrs Fisher. ETA thirty seconds."

Lieutenant Commander Baker is the man in charge of a small team of security officers from the ship's crew. They were assigned to support me in my role as the ship's detective. The team of four comprised Lieutenant Commander Baker and three lieutenants. First was an Austrian giant called Schneider - he had a first name, but no one ever used it and he much preferred to be addressed by everyone using his last name. Then there was Deepa Bhukari, a former Pakistani infantry soldier who also happened to be Baker's wife. That was a recent development and something of a whirlwind romance. The youngest member of the team was a South African called Ander Pippin.

The four of them were complemented by a fifth member, sort of like D'Artagnan to the Musketeers, in my assistant, Sam Chalk. Sam is thirty-one years old and has Downs Syndrome. It is hard to find him without a smile on his face and Purple Star Cruise Lines, the joint conglomerate who own the cruise ship and others like it, afforded him the rank of ensign so he even gets a uniform.

As a team, we do our best to keep crime onboard the ship to a minimum and swiftly resolve crimes when they inevitably occur.

Buddy was not, of course, a criminal. Nevertheless, and due to my big mouth, we were stuck with trying to round him up.

Sam made it to the other side of the sun terrace cocktail bar where he peered behind it hopefully. Unfortunately, he then turned my way with a disappointed expression because Buddy was not there after all. I discovered in the next heartbeat that Sam could not see Buddy because Buddy was on top of the bar, scaling it quickly when we were not watching.

I got that sense of being watched and looked up to find the Gibraltar Rock Ape looking down imperiously upon me.

"Hello," I offered the primate my cheesiest grin and wondered if I should add a thumbs up for good measure. Settling upon a cheery wave, I produced a banana. "Are you hungry? I asked. "Patricia has a nice juicy banana just for you. Wouldn't you like to come down here to eat it while the rest of the crew sneak up behind you?" I continued to coo in my babyish voice.

In answer to my question, and not for the first time, Buddy extended toward me the middle finger of his right hand. I found myself questioning where an ape might have learned such a gesture, but then remembered he lived on a rock at the end of Spain which was largely inhabited by British soldiers and sailors – a population demographic not known for its decorum.

"That's not very nice, Buddy" I found myself berating the monkey.

His expression darkened a touch, a frown dropping his eyebrows as he squinted menacingly in my direction. The middle finger went away, and I saw his right hand begin tracking a path behind his back. Flipping me the bird, as I believe the Americans like to call it, was not Buddy's only trick. He was also rather fond of flinging his own faeces. Having been the victim of such an attack once before, I had no intention of there being a second incident.

Like two Wild West gunslingers facing off, our eyes were locked on each other watching for any sign that the other was going to make their move. With my fingers twitching, I inched my right hand towards my handbag.

I knew from previous experience, that attempting to run away in such circumstances would result in the poop peppering my back, so I had devised an alternative solution to prevent the horrible little ape from ruining another of my outfits. He watched me and I watched him, each of us daring the other to move first.

We remained frozen like that for several seconds, until the squawk of my radio, when Baker announced he was just about to arrive, broke the spell.

Buddy's right hand shot behind his back where presumably his weapon of choice was loaded and ready. In a frantic burst of motion, I thrust my hand into my handbag, grasping my unpatented, yet genius, poop defence device. As the ape's right hand came swinging around his body in an arc, my hand whipped out of my handbag and upwards. I had already pressed the button on the pop-out umbrella, but my heart caught in my chest as I questioned whether I had been fast enough.

A blob of something unspeakable came winging in my direction. It was aimed directly at my face, and it was going to strike home.

My mouth opened – not the best plan, I know – as I screamed my horror, and I fell backward as my legs attempted to propel me away from the brown missile. At what seemed like the very last moment, the spring of the umbrella burst into action, popping the clear plastic shield in front of my face with a *fzzzzzt, pop!* sound.

The poop splattered right in front of my eyes, but I could still see Buddy's disappointed face through my umbrella and thus I was watching when the net landed on top of him.

I've heard people referred to as going crazy ape in the past, but I can assure you, until you get to see a real ape going crazy ape, the expression really doesn't have any meaning.

"Get him down from there quick!" Lieutenant Commander Baker shouted. There were crew members converging on me from both directions. Buddy hadn't seen them, because he had been so focused on me.

The rock ape leapt from the roof of the bar with the net covering him, but when he landed, found himself to be entangled. He was two yards from my feet and thrashing around like an alligator in a shopping bag. Perhaps though, a better analogy might be to describe him as an ape in a net.

No one wanted to get too close, but someone had to. The net was followed up with a bed sheet, Lieutenant Schneider arriving at speed to engulf the ape. Right on his heels was Dr Hideki Nakamura, the junior doctor on board and the one who got volunteered to administer the sedative when we caught the ape.

We do not have a veterinarian onboard the Aurelia, but a call to one in Gibraltar had been sufficient to be sure that the dose being administered would do the trick safely.

Getting my breath back, the shock of playing quick-draw with the rock ape having ratcheted my heart rate up close to its maximum, I threw the umbrella to one side - I wasn't going to clean it and use it again, that was for certain.

My assistant, Sam, was laughing and clapping, enjoying the show as much as anyone could.

"He almost got you, Mrs Fisher," Sam chuckled, offering me a hand up from the deck.

The struggling shape under the bed sheet had grown still, the sedative taking swift effect. All around me, crew members I had commandeered to aid me and my team in corralling the primate were looking to sneak away now that the task was complete. They didn't need to sneak, but I couldn't let them go without passing on my thanks.

"Thank you, everyone. Thank you for helping out. I think that's it now." Turning to look at Baker, I asked, "I assume we have a suitable cage ready for him, yes?"

The sound of something heavy being wheeled along the deck caught my ears and I turned to find two stewards hauling a pallet truck on which a large crate was loaded.

I breathed a sigh of relief. Truthfully, I felt a little sorry for Buddy. He appeared to be having the time of his life running free onboard the Aurelia, but he was a bit of a rascal, and it wasn't as if I could allow him to continue his reign of terror over the passengers.

Thankful that Buddy was no longer my problem, my thoughts turned to what else I needed to do today. A quick mental check confirmed that I had no ongoing investigations and would be able to go ashore.

Well, there was the one case of the stowaway. The body of an as yet unidentified man had been found way down in the bottom of the ship where no passenger ought to ever find themselves. He had been murdered, the knife employed in the task still embedded in the poor man's chest, but that wasn't why he was still in the cold storage in our morgue.

No, he was still on the ship because I hadn't yet figured out what to do about the uncut gems we found in his stomach. Diamonds, rubies, and other stones, undoubtedly worth millions, were safely hidden in the man's gut until Hideki found them during the autopsy.

I would work out how to identify him soon enough, but it wasn't a case that was pressing me to investigate it at this very minute. So I had a free day and that was great news; the chance to explore a place I had never been to before as exciting today as it had ever been.

I knew Alistair would join me – he loved showing off how much he knew about all the places the ship stopped, but my relief at having a clear caseload proved to be quite short lived.

2

THE MYSTERY METER

Before we were even able to disperse, the dreaded sound of a coded message echoed across everyone's radios.

"Secretary, secretary, secretary. Cabin 1215. Assistance required immediately, over."

Lieutenant Commander Baker and I exchanged glances as he leaned his head towards the radio pinned on his lapel and pressed the send switch.

"Lieutenant Commander Baker here. Responding. ETA three minutes. Out."

I felt like grumbling my displeasure, falling into line with Baker, Schneider, and the others, as we all made our way back inside the ship. Why couldn't passengers have the decency to drop dead when we were at sea? At sea there was far less to interest me. Yet they always seemed to time their demise for when we had arrived some-where new and interesting.

Obviously, I kept my thoughts to myself - no one likes a whiner.

Just as we came through the door to re-enter the superstructure of the ship our radios crackled once again.

"Secretary, secretary, secretary."

I was just about to comment that there is no need to deliver the message a second time when the person at the other end added something most unexpected.

"Forward gymnasium on deck sixteen, over."

Everyone's feet stop moving, and the group turned inward to look at one another. We each bore the same concerned look on our faces.

Deepa spoke first. "Two bodies in separate locations at the same time? I don't like the sound of this."

Baker attempted to instil some calm. "It's probably just a couple of elderly passengers. It's barely breakfast time, so the one on deck twelve probably passed away during the night and has only now been discovered."

Schneider frowned. "So what about the one in the gym?"

Baker did not have a ready answer to explain that one, so he hazarded a guess. "Perhaps it was someone getting a workout who did not realise they had an underlying heart defect," he suggested with a shrug.

Whatever the cause, we had two bodies demanding our attention, so we were going to have to split up.

Placing a hand on Lieutenant Commander Baker's arm, I suggested, "Why don't you take Deepa and Pippin to the gymnasium? Schneider can accompany Sam and me to deck twelve."

No one saw a need to put in a counter proposal, so that was the decision made. We shook hands and went separate ways. Though actually, we all went to the same elevator bank and only then did we split up.

Schneider knew precisely where it was that we needed to go to find cabin 1215. Like all crew members, he had been required to memorise the ship's layout. I was required to do that as well, but was taking a rather lazy stance on the subject, largely because my plate was already filled with cases to investigate. In my opinion, I could do one or the other and since I was aiming my argument directly at the captain while we were in bed together, well ... I am sure you can imagine who won.

Arriving on deck twelve, it was a trek from the elevator to the cabin in question. I wasn't paying attention to the cabin numbers as we passed them, but knew we were there when I spotted the white uniform of a member of ship's security positioned in the passageway ahead. I didn't recognise her at first, but noted that she was short and petite. The epaulettes of her uniform bore the rank of ensign, the same as Sam's, which I knew to be a probationary rank that few security officers wore for very long. It meant the young lady had to have come aboard very recently and explained why I didn't know her.

Approaching the cabin, and just about to introduce myself, my eyes jutted out on stalks when she turned to face me.

"Molly!"

It's not so much that I had forgotten the housemaid from my mansion in England, it had just never occurred to me that once she had finished her training, she would arrive back on the Aurelia. I hadn't seen her in months. I brought her onto the ship with me to protect her from the clutches of the Godmother, but exposed to a lifestyle infinitely different to any she had imagined for herself, she had elected to join the cruise line's security team.

Molly tilted her head up to meet my smile with one of her own.

"Hello, Mrs Fisher."

She wasn't getting away with that though. I didn't slow down, closing the final yard between us to pull her into a hug.

"I had no idea you were coming back to the ship. When did you come aboard?" I was about to berate her for not coming to see me, expecting to hear that she had been on board for a week or more.

However, she said, "I arrived last night, Mrs Fisher." She spotted Sam behind me and nodded her head in his direction. "Hi, Sam."

In his normal goofy manner, Sam replied, "Hi, Molly," giving her a wave at the same time.

"In truth, it was the early hours of this morning. I haven't even had time to unpack yet," Molly admitted. "Not that I'm complaining," she added quickly. "I had orientation two hours ago, including a speech from the captain." A yawn split her face which she fought and then tried to hide. When it subsided, she said, "Whew! Sorry about that. I didn't get a whole load of sleep last night and the jetlag is kicking my bum." I remembered her training had taken place in America.

"And you're straight into the thick of it," I remarked.

"Yes," she replied, her tone making it clear she could not be happier. "Thankfully, all I have to do is stand here. I got sooo lost last night trying to find my cabin. Everyone else found theirs and I was roaming the decks getting more and more confused. I might still be down there now if this girl hadn't come along to point me in the right direction. She even helped me with one of my bags despite clearly being on her way back from the gym."

The door behind Molly opened, the head of Lieutenant Kashmir poking out to see who was there.

"Ah, Mrs Fisher. I think you'll find this one scores a ten on the mystery meter."

I had no idea what that meant, but I rather liked the idea of having a measure for how mysterious and uncontrived some of our cases were. Making a mental note to use the term 'mystery meter' in conversation, I followed Lieutenant Kashmir into the cabin.

Kashmir wasted no time in getting down to business, escorting Schneider, Sam, and me through to the bedroom. Crossing the cabin's threshold, I mentally prepared myself to deal with anything from an elderly person who had passed away in their sleep leaving a bereaved spouse behind to a brutally murdered person who had fallen foul of a lover's tiff. Then I remembered Kashmir's words about how this case was particularly strange and adjusted my expectations.

I still wasn't prepared for what we found.

Lying across the bed was a man in his early thirties. He was facing away from us, a small mercy because I don't like seeing the faces of dead people. However, there could be no question that he was just sleeping. He had been strangled, or possibly the correct word was garrotted because it looked more like a rope burn on his neck than the bruising a pair of hands might have left.

What Lieutenant Kashmir had been referring to was the climbing gear the victim was wearing. He had on shorts and a t-shirt, but also climbing boots, gloves, a full harness, and a helmet.

Since I know for absolute certain that there are no climbing walls anywhere on the Aurelia, his outfit begged the question what on earth he was doing in the gear.

Not only that, cabin 1215 is one of those that is inboard of the ship, and thus did not have a porthole to look out to sea. Any thought that he had been planning to climb up or down to someone else's cabin with thievery in mind could not be considered.

"Now that is not something one sees every day," Schneider remarked.

"He's dirty," Sam pointed out, extending the index finger on his right hand in the direction of the man's knees.

I would have noticed myself, but Sam got there first, and he was absolutely correct. The man had grime on several parts of his body, some of which had been ground into the bed sheets. I ran a scenario through my head, picturing the man in the climbing gear fighting back while being pinned to the bed.

It made his killer another man, and not someone small, for the victim had muscle and girth plus youthfulness on his side. Of course I could not rule out a woman as the killer, but she would need to be hellishly strong.

I continued to visually examine the victim. His arms and elbows, the outer edges of his shoulders and down his back were all dirty and through the dirt one could see tracks where sweat had run. He had been exerting himself quite strenuously.

"His name?" I asked, the question aimed at Lieutenant Kashmir though I didn't name him or look his way.

Kashmir said, "We're still looking into that, Mrs Fisher. I wanted you to see the body and the crime scene as it is first. Once you are satisfied, we can turn him over and get a proper look at his face."

I turned my head to look at Lieutenant Kashmir for a moment, confusion dominating my features until I reached an obvious conclusion, "He's not the resident of this cabin?" That had to be the case or the man's name would be known already.

Kashmir shook his head. "No, Mrs Fisher. There is a couple from Ghana staying in this cabin. They found him this morning having spent the night ashore. They came back to collect a few things and discovered this gentleman almost by accident. It was the wife, Mrs Teresa Boateng who discovered the deceased. I believe she is still being treated in the deck ten medical centre by Dr Davis." Kashmir named the ship's senior physician. "I believe it came as quite a shock."

I was beginning to understand why Lieutenant Kashmir had introduced the mystery meter.

Tending to formalities first, I asked, "Has death been pronounced?"

Kashmir nodded. "Yes, Dr Davis had to come here to revive Mrs Boateng and was good enough to attend to that minor detail at the same time."

I confirmed that pictures had been taken, but decided that it was appropriate to perform a full crime scene job - as full as we could manage on board a cruise ship with our limited resources, that is - so we were not going to touch the body just yet.

I didn't have to worry about keeping the Boateng's out of their accommodation - finding them an alternative cabin, probably one with higher grading - would happen without the need for my involvement. I would, however, need to speak with them.

When Schneider left the cabin to fetch crime scene equipment, Kashmir went with him. His duty was done, and he had other places to be. Now that it was quiet in the cabin, I took out my phone. I could have used my radio, but I wanted the conversation to be as private as possible.

"Patricia, darling," Alistair purred in my ear when he answered the phone.

"Since you are not where I am, my assumption is that you are with the other deceased passenger in the gymnasium," I replied, getting straight to the point. As captain, unless he were otherwise detained, in which case he would send his deputy, Alistair always went to the scene of a deceased passenger.

His voice was more solemn when he replied. "I am, yes. However, it's not a passenger, Patricia. This is a member of the crew."

Automatically, I gasped in shock, dreadful thoughts filling my head when I asked with trepidation, "Who?"

"Nicole Tibbett. She's a yoga instructor. Was a yoga instructor, I guess I should say," Alistair corrected himself and I could hear the sadness in his voice. "I remember when she joined the crew – it was in Miami just more than a year ago. She is twenty-six years old. No age at all."

"How did she die?" I pressed him, hoping to hear her death had been natural. It would be tragic nevertheless, but a peaceful death from an undiagnosed medical condition would always trump a suicide at the end of a miserable fight with depression.

Alistair made a sort of tutting sound before he spoke. It was only afterwards that I figured out he was disappointed to have to tell me the next bit and had been trying to figure out how.

"She was murdered, Patricia, I'm sorry to say. There is no doubt at all."

I closed my eyes and hung my head. Two murders? After taking a second to draw a breath and give the righteous detective at my core a jolly good kick in the pants, I flicked my eyes open again. My purpose and motivation were renewed, a fire started in my belly – someone had killed that poor girl and I was going to find out who it was.

I was going to find them, and they would face justice.

The climber – intriguingly mysterious though he was, wasn't going anywhere. I had no idea who had killed him either, but possessed a strong suspicion that he had been up to no good. His death, therefore, while also tragic, had probably come at his own hands.

Either way, he would get my full attention once Schneider had done the crime scene thing. I was going to leave Sam in the cabin to guard the body and would come back later.

To end my call with Alistair, I said, "I'll be right there."

3

FITNESS CAN KILL

The gym was closed when I arrived, the door guarded by yet another of the new ensigns taken on board last night. They were getting a proper indoctrination of fire.

I got halfway through introducing myself, because I look like a passenger to the uninitiated, when Deepa arrived to explain things.

"This is Mrs Fisher," she said, gripping the tall, but young man's shoulder. "Learn her face, you will see it a lot and hear her name even more. Mrs Fisher is the ship's detective."

"Ship's detective?" The young man repeated her words in a puzzled tone.

Deepa nodded in my direction with a smile.

"Yes. Things happen on board and ... well, sometimes it's a little tough to figure out what the heck happened. That's where Mrs Fisher comes in. Be respectful," she administered a final piece of advice as she held the door open to let me in.

Nicole Tibbett had been killed by a blow to the head. She was in the fitness suite, splayed on the exercise floor as if dropped from a height. Her skull was the wrong shape, that was the first thing I noticed. She was facing away from me – a mercy because I didn't wish to see her face.

Dr Hideki was on the deck next to her. Seeing me approach, he stated he would need to perform a more complete autopsy, but he was confident Nicole had died from a single blow to the right side of her skull.

There wasn't much blood – a massive relief to me. I mean, who's a fan of blood? There were a few drops though.

Lieutenant Commander Baker came to my side.

"If you are wondering about the murder weapon, there is a twenty-pound dumbbell suspiciously missing from the rack."

I glanced across at the rack of weights lining one wall. The gap where one of a pair was missing its twin – the dumbbells were arranged in ascending order – was starkly obvious.

When I glanced at Hideki, he said, "Maybe." It was the best response I was going to get until the autopsy was complete.

Baker continued his report. "There's no sign of forced entry to the gym, and the door was last opened when Miss Tibbett used her key card to open it at 0256hrs this morning."

"That's too early to be setting up for even the first session of the day," I remarked, my eyes still glued to the terrible sight of her body.

Baker nodded. "There's more."

His comment got my interest, but I knew my team was efficient so it was no surprise that they were already digging into what might have happened to her.

"There are some threatening messages on her computer," he revealed.

"With names attached?" I questioned instantly, a tremble of excitement in my voice. It was the thrill of the chase when one really wished there was no killer to chase in the first place. I held my breath waiting for his response.

Baker didn't give me a name though, instead, he said, "There's more than one person involved. It's a group chat with multiple persons arguing."

I blinked, getting ready to jab him in the ribs if he didn't stop being cryptic – that was my job. "What are you saying? That fitness can kill?"

Seeing my expression, Baker swiftly added, "I believe we have uncovered some gym related rivalry between the different academies of thought on board, Mrs Fisher. The threats against Miss Tibbett could be construed as harmless when viewed from one perspective, or as harassment when viewed from another."

Not understanding, I frowned in confusion and asked, "What do you mean?"

"Okay," Baker cast his eyes upward as he tried to figure out how best to explain what he wanted to say.

Deepa joined us, interjecting, "Would Barbie threaten to kill someone?"

Deepa was best friends with Barbie, who until very recently, was living in one of my suite's spare bedrooms. Barbie is a California blonde bombshell and the master of torture in the upper deck gym.

Without needing to think, I said, "Of course not."

Deepa gave me a lopsided grimace. "Weeeellll, she did."

I found myself caught between wanting to snort derisively and straight out denying it could be true, but Deepa was still talking.

"It was last night and well ..."

Baker finished his wife's sentence, too eager to get the words out to wait for her to say it. "Barbie wrote that she was going to smash her on the head with a dumbbell. Miss Tibbett was arguing that crossfitters like Barbie end up looking too masculine because of all the time they spend lifting weights."

I was knowingly dismissive when I said, "Okay, we can talk to Barbie, but what's the big beef here?"

Deepa answered, "That's something we need to get to the bottom of, but it looks to be some fitness camp rivalry between the crossfitters like Barbie and the yoga masters like Nicole. There were other voices involved – Andrea Bassinet-Blatch, she's another yoga queen, came out on Nicole's side but argued for diet and cardio. The dancers were getting involved saying all a person needs is an active lifestyle. They burn enough calories just doing their jobs that they don't need to think about exercise."

In my head, I was arguing that none of the dancers were in their fifties because all that dancing killed the cartilage in their knees, and they would all be giving it up in their thirties if not before. Whatever the case, there was no question in my mind that Barbie could be involved. She just didn't have it in her.

"So we have some banter between crew members that could be construed as outrageous."

"That might be true," announced Alistair loudly as he came back into the exercise room from one of the offices. "If I didn't now have a murdered crew member." He was tucking his phone away so must have been taking a call in private – it explained why he wasn't visible when I arrived. "Since Nicole Tibbett is very definitely dead, and I believe she was murdered, there needs to be a full investigation. I truly hope it was not another member of the crew who chose to take her life."

I went to him, touching his arm with my hand. He took too much responsibility for events that were far outside his ability to control. He could not have foreseen or prevented Nicole's death, yet I could see on his face that he was carrying the blame.

"I will get to the bottom of it, Alistair," I promised.

"You will need to look very closely at Miss Berkeley," he replied flatly.

"Barbie had nothing to do with this," I assured him, being dismissive again. There was just no way she could be involved, and any time spent exploring the concept was going to be time wasted while the real killer got to cover their tracks or escape.

Alistair nodded his head in understanding, but said, "I can see how this will be difficult for you. Perhaps it would be wise to take a backseat on this investigation. Lieutenant Commander Baker can head it up instead, darling. You have another case to focus on, after all."

I did my best to stop my eyes from narrowing when I looked up to meet his gaze.

"I can manage to separate my feelings from the facts, thank you, Captain Huntley." I growled.

Just beyond Alistair, Lieutenant Deepa Bhukari made a face that said no one else on the whole ship could get away with talking to the captain in such a tone. She backed away rather than remain in my vicinity – just in case I had just lit the fuse to a powder keg.

Alistair is a passionate man – trust me on this, I know what I am talking about – but he is also one who keeps his emotions on a tight leash ninety-nine percent of the time. I am yet to see him angry, but I have heard tales of him cracking the whip and bringing righteous justice down on members of the crew when he felt it was necessary.

All I got in response was a mild twitch of his lip.

"Please make sure that you do, Mrs Fisher." We were almost-glaring at each other, and I wondered for a moment if we were about to have a fight with a body lying just a few yards from us.

"I am needed ashore," he remarked almost absentmindedly. "I have a meeting with local dignitaries."

I remembered now that he had told me about it several days ago. It was one of those schmoozing things that the cruise line expected of their captains. As one might imagine, arriving with ten thousand passengers and crew provided a fat blip in the local economy – politicians liked to be seen shaking hands with the captain and the cruise line wanted favourable docking rates.

I could have accompanied him, but even if I wasn't going to be up to my neck in an investigation, it was not an occasion that interested me.

Alistair departed, the young ensign at the door snapping out a crisp salute as his captain went by. It left me with Baker and the others and poor Miss Tibbett.

Whispering to myself, I stared down at her face and said, "Tell me your secrets."

I had no idea how difficult they were going to be to unpick.

4

AN UNWELCOME PRIME SUSPECT

I was still staring at Nicole's body when the sound of somebody getting loud in the corridor caught my ears. I was not the only one who heard it, Lieutenant Commander Baker was already on his way to see what the commotion might be. Leaving him to deal with it and assuming that whoever was outside would be sent away with a flea in their ear, I started to think about all the things I needed to do.

We would shortly be taking a close look at Nicole's life. Was she involved romantically with anyone? Did she have anyone in particular who might have wanted to do her harm? Was there a person who would tangibly benefit from her death? My team and I would minutely inspect the contents of her cabin, her movements in recent days or even weeks, and through that we would build a picture of her life. Someone had chosen to end it, but they would not have managed to do so without leaving clues to their identity.

Clearly, I needed to look at the rivalry between Nicole and other members of the health and fitness fraternity. That the argument could have become so heated it resulted in murder seemed ridiculous, yet Nicole's body suggested otherwise.

My train of thought was interrupted by the gymnasium door

opening and a very familiar voice echoing in from outside. I snapped my head and eyes around to confirm what I already knew: the person making all the noise outside was Barbie.

"It's true, isn't it?" she all but wailed.

I could hear the anguish in her voice and was not surprised when Baker let her enter the gym. Barbie, so far as I was concerned, was another member of the team. She had helped me solve more cases than anyone back when I was just a passenger on the ship and still discovering that I was also something of an amateur sleuth.

The commotion outside had been Barbie attempting to get past the young ensign stationed there specifically to prevent people coming in. Baker nodded to let her through, and Barbie stepped into the gym, her eyes going immediately to the limp form on the floor. Not that a person could miss Nicole's body - everyone else in the room was standing around it.

Barbie was clutching either side of her face, her complexion uncharacteristically pale in reaction to the shock of seeing someone she knew come to such a terrible end.

"Oh, my God. Oh, my God. Oh, my God," Barbie repeated the words over and over as if it were some kind of mantra. "Who would do this? Nicole was such a sweetie."

I rushed over to her, pulling her into a hug and making her look away.

"She was your friend?" I asked.

Barbie nodded, her head tucked into my shoulder though she had to bend or crouch a little to do so. When she pulled away a moment later, wiping the tears from her cheeks and out of her eyes, she had to focus her gaze away from the body.

"We were only chatting last night," Barbie confirmed what I already knew. "There's this silly rivalry going on between some of the girls …" Barbie abruptly stopped speaking mid-sentence, her eyes widening to twice their original size as her hand went to her mouth.

She could see how Baker and Bhukari were looking at her – a mix of curiosity and anticipation because we all wanted to ask her the same question.

"Oh, no!" she gasped. "No, you can't think I had anything to do with it! What I wrote was just the two of us messing about. We always talk like that."

I held up a hand to stop her. "I believe you, Barbie, please don't spiral."

She took a deep breath and looked about with eyes that spoke of panic and doubt.

"You do understand we have to explore such an obvious clue," I continued.

Barbie nodded her head vigorously, but did not reply.

Deepa came around to place a hand on Barbie's shoulder.

"We will have time of death confirmed by the doctor shortly, but I expect it will be somewhere between three this morning and maybe five. She was found just after six by Omar Obligate," Deepa named one of the other crew members who worked in this gym. "She had been dead a while by then."

Barbie was still trying to get her breathing under control but managed to stammer, "You're about to ask if I have an alibi for that time, aren't you?"

We all looked at her, expecting she was going to say she was with her boyfriend, Dr Hideki Nakamura, and that would be the end of that. She didn't though.

"Well, I don't," she replied, her eyes nervously twitching from me to Deepa and then on to Baker.

I blinked in my confusion.

"What do you mean, Barbie?" I wanted to know, my concern deepening. "Where were you? What were you even doing out of bed at that time?"

"I … I can't tell you," she stammered, her words blurting from her mouth in a torrent that was beginning to sound guilty.

"No." I put my foot down. "I don't want to hear it, Barbie. You tell us what you were doing right now so we can move on with our investigation. You had nothing to do with what happened to Nicole Tibbett – we all know that. Just tell us where you were so we can rule you out of our enquiries."

My radio made its usual squawking noise right before Schneider's voice echoed inside my handbag.

"Mrs Fisher are you coming back? I'm about done taking pictures of the victim and the stewards are here to take the victim away, over."

I wasn't finished grilling Barbie, but she wasn't talking, so with an annoyed hand, I snatched the infernal radio from my bag and held it to my lips.

"I will be there shortly. Out." I never took my eyes from my blonde friend, refusing to let her escape my gaze as I tried to comprehend why she was being so mysterious.

Barbie was biting her bottom lip, a sure sign that she was worried, and she had good reason to be. I hated myself for it, but if she wouldn't tell me what was going on, or provide me with an alibi, I had no choice other than to have her taken into custody.

Battling mixed emotions as anger at her for making me do it vied with sympathy because she must have a really good reason, I squared up right in front of her face.

"Last chance, Barbie. Tell me where you were. Give me something, please," I begged. "Otherwise …"

"It's okay," she interrupted me in a quiet voice. "You can have me taken to the brig. I know this is difficult for you, but I don't want you to feel bad."

The disbelief I felt caused my head to shake from side to side of its own accord.

"I can't believe this. What is going on, Barbie?"

My blonde friend, who had already moved out of the royal suite we shared because there was someone on board attempting to mess with my life, turned away from me and held out her hands toward Deepa.

"I don't think there will be any need for restraints," said Baker, stepping forward to recite Barbie's rights as he performed the arrest.

I could hear what he was saying, but my head felt like it was under water. Was this how Alice felt when she went through the looking glass? Everything was back to front somehow.

Barbie left the gym without once looking over her shoulder at me. She would be taken to the brig, and we would need to question her again later. Whether she was more forthcoming once she'd had some time to think, I could not guess.

A lance of decisiveness shot through me. Like a steel bolt down the length of my spine, I felt myself grow an inch as I resolved to solve the crime and clear Barbie's name. There was no chance she was involved, so all I had to do was prove it.

With that in mind, and with Lieutenant Commander Baker setting up to manage the crime scene before Nicole's body was taken away, I set off back to cabin 1215.

There were two mysteries to unravel, and I was going to ace them both in record time.

5

THE BOATENGS

Back at the cabin on deck twelve, I found Molly still guarding the door though she was holding it open for me when I got there. Or so I thought. Arriving at the cabin's entrance, I discovered my mistake – there were stewards inside with a stretcher trying to get out. They had the body of the deceased loaded onto a gurney in a black bag to keep it from the sight of passengers and strapped down to ensure it wouldn't fall off.

I stepped back to allow them egress from the cabin, hugging the portside bulkhead until they were able to manoeuvre their load around and begin making their way along the passageway. The victim was heading for the morgue and an autopsy, but I assumed Schneider had been able to identify him before letting him go.

"Yes, Mrs Fisher," he replied when I posed the question. "Sam did it, actually."

Sam beamed at me from the corner of the room where he sat playing with Schneider's palm top tablet. With it the officers were able to access the ship's central register where all the passengers' information was retained.

"His name is Vincent Pompeo, an American who boarded the ship in Naples and was supposed to get off in Gibraltar."

I took a second to absorb the information before saying. "He's hasn't been dead that long, so he chose to not get off."

"So it would seem, but …" Schneider pointed a hand at Sam and clicked his fingers to cue my assistant in.

"But according to the computer, he got off when he was supposed to," Sam said with a broad grin. He loved having a part to play and everyone in my team was great at including him. It wasn't a sympathy thing, letting him join in so he had some input, Sam genuinely added value – his uniqueness allowed him to see things the rest of us might never notice or consider.

"Another stowaway," I remarked. The ship hadn't recorded one for years – a different statistic to not having one since a good stowaway would never get caught – and now we had two in just a few days. Both dead too.

Schneider was nodding his head. "The Boatengs are coming back now that the body is gone. I have more stewards coming to shift their things to a new cabin on deck seventeen."

That would be nice for them. They would find they had almost twice as much space in their new cabin and would be much closer to all the activities. That wasn't my first thought though. Nor was Schneider's efficiency, though it crossed my mind to comment. Instead, the thought crashing through my brain to be at the front of the queue was to do with what was special about the Boatengs? Their cabin had been targeted, but was that coincidental or deliberate?

A man died in their cabin, and while I could believe they were not responsible for his murder – they were alleged to have been ashore at the probable time of his death, I suspected they had been in possession of something that caused Vincent Pompeo to invade their accommodation.

Vincent hadn't strangled himself so whatever it was he came in here for, his partner/killer almost certainly made off with it.

Schneider said, "I expressed that we need to go through their things and be sure nothing was taken."

"You've been through the cabin already, yes?" I sought to

26

confirm, certain the tall Austrian would have tackled that as a priority.

"Of course, but I could not find anything that appeared to be an obvious hole in a drawer where something had been taken, and there were no signs that the drawers had been tossed. If Vincent and/or whoever killed him were in here looking for something, they are the tidiest thieves I have ever heard of."

Right, well that didn't give us a lot to go on.

I began to look around for myself, but I only got as far as crossing the room to the closet when I heard Molly speaking to someone in the passageway outside – the Boatengs had returned as requested and it was time for me to quiz them.

I needed to do so really rather gently. If they were innocent, and I had to proceed as if I believed they were, then they had suffered a terrible shock this morning and as passengers aboard the Aurelia, needed to be treated with the utmost respect. If I could prove they were lying about whatever they told us, then I would get the chance to tear into them.

Just as I was about to turn away from the closet, I noticed a small mark on the carpet. I stopped to inspect it, finding what appeared to be sawdust. It was wood grains for sure, but I got no time to put further thought to what it meant or where it might have come from because the passengers were now inside the cabin and Schneider was already leaving their bedroom to head them off.

Moving fast to catch up with him, I started speaking, "Mr and Mrs Boateng, please accept on behalf of the Aurelia and Purple Star Cruise Lines my most sincere apologies for what you have experienced today. My name is Patricia Fisher ..."

Mrs Boateng interrupted me, "Yes Mrs Fisher," she replied with an enthralled expression, "we heard you would be heading up the investigation. I must tell you that I'm quite a fan of your exploits. I've read all about you."

Her husband nudged Mrs Boateng gently on one hip with his hand, attempting I think to convince her to calm down a little.

I wasn't too sure how to respond. I haven't really met fans before, and the concept was a little strange to me.

I scrambled for an appropriate response. "Um ... thank you." Gathering my thoughts, I started again, conscious that I had lost the thread of what I was saying and now questioning whether that had been a deliberate tactic on her part. "I'm afraid I need to ask you a few questions, Mr and Mrs Boateng."

They both nodded their heads and followed my hand as I indicated a pair of chairs to my right. The cabin was too small for more chairs than that, so I was going to have to stand.

Mrs Boateng didn't move immediately, so when her husband did, he bumped against her shoulder. Mrs Boateng hadn't yet moved because she was cautiously peering around the doorframe into their bedroom.

"He's not still in there, is he?" she inquired.

Lieutenant Schneider answered, "No, Mrs Boateng, the deceased has been removed."

I indicated again toward the two chairs, but started firing off my questions before they could get there.

"Had you met the man before?"

They responded unanimously: they did not know who he was and had most definitely never seen him before. Their response might have been genuine, but could just as easily have been practised in advance for it was a very obvious question for me to ask them.

"What caused him to target your cabin specifically?" I pressed them, holding them in place with my eyes.

The couple glanced inward at each other, each questioning the other what they thought the right response to my question might be. They both replied that they had no idea what might have caused the man to enter their cabin. In their opinion they had nothing worth stealing.

Mrs Boateng had a few items of jewellery, but in her opinion anything of worth, such as engagement and wedding rings, was on her body already and not left in the cabin. She raised her hand to show me the rings. Both pieces were very nice, but they were not worth a great deal.

I quizzed them further, questioning their movements since they came on board, who they had met and where they had been. I also challenged them to explain what it was that made them so special - a man or men broke into their cabin, and one had been killed by his partner or partners.

I was close to the limit with that particular line of questioning because it was borderline accusatory. It was my final play, if you like, a checker to make sure their body language matched up to the story I was seeing.

When I was confident they were telling me the truth, and they had nothing they were knowingly hiding from me, I apologised.

"I'm sorry for that, Mr and Mrs Boateng. I did not for one moment truly believe that you were involved, but I needed to be sure. We all want to be sure that I get the right person and do so as quickly as possible. I hope you understand."

Mrs Boateng responded before her husband had a chance to voice his opinion.

"It's perfectly all right, Mrs Fisher. I actually rather enjoyed it. And now I will get to tell my friends that I was grilled by the famous Patricia Fisher on board the Aurelia and was involved in a murder inquiry. Can I get a selfie with you?"

The lady looked genuinely pleased at this point to have found a dead man in her cabin this morning. Somewhat taken aback by her request, I wasn't fast enough to say yes or no. Mrs Boateng had her phone out and was positioned next to me before I could react. The picture was taken though goodness knows what face I was pulling in it.

Having established my belief in their innocence, I handed over to Lieutenant Schneider and my assistant, Ensign Sam Chalk. They would take the Boatengs through their belongings as a duo of stewards packed them. Everything they owned would be moved to their new accommodation and that presented the best chance for the owners to confirm nothing was missing.

While they did that I stopped in one corner, staying out of the way and drinking some tap water to keep myself hydrated. My brain was working fast, examining little bits of detail here and there. Kind of like doing a jigsaw, when you pick up a piece and try to fit it in a dozen different places, I looked at each small clue and tried to figure out if it linked to any of the other pieces. The investigation had just begun, so it was no shock – just a disappointment – when nothing fit at all. Sticking with my jigsaw analogy, each piece went back into the box. I would find new pieces to try and slowly, over time, I would build up enough of a picture to know what it was I was looking at.

It took just a little more than ten minutes for the pair of stewards to pack all the Boatengs' belongings, that slow only because Schneider was continuously questioning the couple as each drawer was opened and each item was removed. His diligence did not, however, produce a result. So far as Mr and Mrs Boateng were concerned, nothing had been stolen.

It was just as the Stewards were reaching into the closet for Mrs Boateng's two elegant ball gowns - which would be carried rather than folded and creased - when something surprising happened.

6

A DARK AND MYSTERIOUS HOLE

The second ball gown, the final item to be removed from the closet, caught on a catch inside the door. The steward hadn't noticed and was turning to walk away with both ball gowns hanging from their hangers on an extended index finger.

Sam saw what was about to happen, and worried the gown might tear, darted forward to grab it. The steward saw his sudden movement and jumped backwards, yanking the gown which refused to release its grip on the hook inside the door. The air filled with the awful noise of material tearing, but that wasn't all we heard.

The closet had moved.

Mrs Boateng and her husband were in the passageway outside with the other steward and their bags all loaded onto a trolley. They thus missed both the sound of Mrs Boateng's ball gown being ruined and the small clonking sound as the closet rocked against the wall.

Inside the bedroom we were all staring at the offending item of furniture. We are on a ship, and even though the Aurelia is a big lady designed to roll very gently in anything short of a hurricane, it is common practise to bolt everything down that can be bolted down.

A flash of memory zipped into the front of my brain, driving my eyes down to the spot on the carpet where I had spotted the tiny flakes of sawdust. Suddenly I knew what they were from.

The steward, a guilty expression etched on his face, retraced a step and gently unhooked the gown. I watched as he touched the small tear in the bottom hem. It could be fixed, or it could be replaced, but I was vastly more interested in why the closet was loose.

The only question in my head was whether the Boatengs knew anything about it or not. I called to them.

"Mr and Mrs Boateng, could you come back into your bedroom, please?"

With the steward out of the way, Schneider nodded to Sam to grip one side of the closet. Schneider closed the doors and gripped the top. It was fitted quite snugly into a gap between bulkheads. The cabin on the other side would have a matching closet fitted into a gap next to it, or so I assumed.

Mr and Mrs Boateng reappeared in the doorway to their bedroom, questioning looks upon their faces as they wondered why they might have been recalled. Their looks turned to curiosity as they watched Sam and Schneider wrestle the closet forward an inch.

It was hard going to get it moving, but once he had shifted it that first small distance, Schneider was able to reach over the top to grip the back edge with one of his ridiculously long arms.

Tensing his muscles, the Austrian turned around to face his audience, saying, "You might all want to back up a little."

As we scurried out of the way, he gave the whole thing a hard yank. It tipped, reaching a balance point and then falling forward. Schneider was ready and caught it with two meaty mitts. He wanted to lower it safely to the deck, but there wasn't enough space in the bedroom to achieve that. It came to rest three quarters of the way down when the doors met with the mattress of the bed.

None of us were looking at that though I can assure you. We were all looking at the hole in the bulkhead behind the closet. A panel, presumably there for access when the ship was being built, had been removed and was now resting against the bulkhead beneath the hole.

Like we had perhaps discovered a new porthole to Narnia, beyond where the bulkhead should be was pure blackness. Sam was first to fumble for his phone and get the torch working.

With a beam of light shining into the darkness, we discovered a conduit roughly a yard deep and two yards across through which two thick pipes descended. Gawping at it as I was, there came a sudden sound of rushing water. It shot through the pipes, drawn by gravity to descend through the ship.

There are huge water tanks down in the lower decks of the ship, there to supply hot and cold running water to the many cabins and passengers on board the ship. Swimming pools, laundry facilities, kitchens ... all these things required a constant supply of water that went up and went back down. Each time we came into port, the grey water - what I knew to be the correct term for water that was no longer potable - would be pumped out and fresh water pumped in to recharge the tanks.

So I had a rough idea for what the pipes were and where they went, but more importantly, I now knew why Vincent Pompeo had been dressed in climbing gear. The sawdust on the floor had been from the screws used to bolt the closet in place. He had removed them and then cut a chunk of the bulkhead away to gain access to a hidden tunnel.

Schneider balanced himself and scrambled over the top of the closet, sliding down to land next to the rough hole.

I said, "Be careful!" as the tall Austrian gripped the bulkhead with one hand and leaned into the dark hole. Using the flashlight function on his own phone, he cast a beam downwards.

We all saw him swinging it to the left and right and then reversing its trajectory to look upwards as well.

When he brought his head back into the room, he turned to face us.

"It goes so far that I cannot see how far it goes," he remarked. "My guess would be that it goes all the way down to the bottom of the ship."

I was content that the bewildered expressions the Boatengs bore on their faces were yet another indication of their innocence. It was that or they were particularly good actors. I told them they were free to go and wished them a less eventful remainder of their time on board. Delivered as a jest, I got a nervous laugh from them in response.

They departed along with the stewards, leaving Sam and me with Lieutenant Schneider.

"What do we do now, Mrs Fisher?" Sam asked, his eyes never leaving the hole behind the closet.

I puffed out my cheeks and thought. My head was still reeling from this latest bizarre discovery and trying to figure out and list all the things I needed to do now. For a start, I needed to get back to the gym on the sixteenth deck because we had another dead body there. Nicole's killer might already be off the ship, but that wouldn't stop me from finding out who it was and making sure they paid.

Barbie was in the brig, and that was something I wanted to resolve quickly. I could not imagine what secret she might think was so important she would go to jail to protect it. She and I were going to have words when I found out what it was.

Baker and Bhukari had seen the groupchat messages Nicole had been sending and receiving – the one in which Barbie threatened to kill her with a dumbbell – but I had not, and it was something I needed to correct very soon.

However, at the top of my list right now was the need to find out where the hole went.

Of Lieutenant Schneider, I asked, "Do we have any climbing gear on the ship?"

Schneider's eyes rolled up and left as he consulted his memory.

"I don't think so," he replied. "However, we're in dock, so it will be simple enough to hire or buy something."

I nodded my head, my own eyes also glued on the mysterious hole.

"I think that's what we need to do. I shall be most interested to find out where Mr Pompeo was trying to go. Or rather I suppose, where it was that he went. I'm sure we must have some expert climbers somewhere among the crew who can operate the gear. Sam and I will head to engineering. I'm sure there are schematics that will help us to determine where that conduit goes."

Sam raised his hand when I included him, and I turned to see what question he wanted to raise.

"I can stay here to guard the cabin if you like, Mrs Fisher," Sam volunteered. "I think perhaps Molly might like a break from standing outside in the passageway."

Hearing us, Molly called through, "I really would, if it's not an inconvenience."

That was decision made so far as I was concerned. It was not something that required any input on my part.

Turning toward the door, I shot Molly a smile since she was peering through from outside with a hopeful expression. Schneider and Sam were both following me out of the cabin, which for now I was mentally labelling as the cavern of wonders. Where on earth did that conduit go?

Lieutenant Kashmir had it right at the start. This case really did register high on the mystery meter.

7

COMMANDER PHILIPS

Commander Philips made me wait. Whether he genuinely had things that required his attention or if he was just being unnecessarily awkward, I could not determine. He was not in his office, but to be found on deck four where he was supervising a maintenance task of some description.

One of his engineers attempted to explain it to me, giving up when he saw my eyes glazing over. Engineering is all rather fascinating, I'm sure, but I suspected I required an advanced degree in a related subject to even understand most of the words the man before me was attempting to employ.

I waited patiently with Molly, filling in the time we had by catching up all that had happened in her life. Since I last saw her, she had attended the cruise line's training school in America and graduated successfully. She clearly saw it all as a positive experience because she spoke about her time there with such gusto.

"My gosh, it was wonderful!" Molly gushed the moment I led her into the subject. For a young lady from rural England with blue collar parents and a choice of jobs that ranged between working in a fast-food outlet, a supermarket, or as it turned out, performing menial tasks and cleaning in my grand house, life as a security officer on board a cruise ship was a significant culture shock.

Thrown together with dozens of other recruits for her training, Molly had made a number of friends from around the world. Purple Star Cruise Lines specialises in employing multi-nationally because they want passengers from all nations to feel at home when on their ships.

Initial training was over, but she had many more months of subsequent testing and learning to go as she demonstrated her ability to perform the role. On top of that, she was required to learn two new languages. My former housemaid chose French, because she had a reasonable level of understanding from her studies at school, plus Arabic. Molly laughed at herself when she admitted the choice came about because there was a really fit Iraqi boy in her tranche of recruits.

I was left with the impression that she was possibly regretting her second choice, but it was far too late now.

Upon my encouragement, she tried a couple of sentences on me. Not speaking a word of Arabic myself, I had no idea if what she had said even made any sense, but it sounded convincing enough to my ears.

I was saved from finding a new topic of conversation by the young engineering officer reappearing.

"Commander Philips is available to see you now, Mrs Fisher," he announced. "I'm afraid to say he also remarked that he has very little time to spare regardless of how important you think your visit might be." The man then held up his hands in surrender before adding, "His words not mine, Mrs Fisher."

Molly screwed up her face. "Doesn't he know who Mrs Fisher is?"

"Don't bother," I sighed as I started walking. 'He knows exactly who I am. That's half the problem."

Commander Philips didn't like me, but it wasn't something that was going to keep me awake at night. I avoided him wherever possible and when it was not possible, I was annoyingly polite and engaging. If he chose to dislike me based on our first meeting, I was going to make him look petty and small.

Molly and I followed the engineering officer along a steel-mesh catwalk. We were on deck four above the ship's mighty engines (at least I think that's what I was looking down on). Things were noisy and kind of oily smelling and there were lots of pipes and hoses and things that were vibrating.

He led us through a bulkhead, reversed direction and closed it behind us. That shut out ninety percent of the noise. Around another corner, following blindly for I had no idea where we were, I spotted Commander Philips ahead of us. He had a large electronic tablet resting along his left forearm and was consulting it, pointing his right finger at another engineering officer, this one wearing over-alls smudged with grease.

When we approached our escort attempted to announce us.

"Com …"

Commander Philips shook his head, a small motion that did not interrupt the flow of speech coming from his mouth as he instructed the officers around him in their tasks. Our escort stopped speaking instantly, clearly used to being treated so ignorantly.

Once again, we were being made to wait, Commander Philips doing his petty upmost to demonstrate his power. I found it rather tiresome. When he finished what he was doing a few moments later and the men around him darted away in various directions, he continued fiddling with the tablet for a further thirty seconds before finally turning his attention my way.

Except, he didn't look at me, he looked at Molly who visibly shrunk beneath the senior man's gaze.

"Name?" he barked.

"Molly," she blurted. "Sorry, sir. I mean Ensign Lawrie."

"Well! Where's my salute, young lady?"

Turning crimson, Molly's right arm flashed out and up. "Sorry, Sir!"

"I take it you're one of the new bunch who arrived last night." He sniffed deeply, eyeing her in a manner that suggested great scru-tiny, and I realised what he was doing - he was looking for a fault that he could latch onto and then belittle or berate her for. I had no time for that.

Just as he found something and was beginning to open his mouth, I stepped forward and got right in front of his face.

"Commander Philips, I'm sure that your time is highly important, so we're not going to waste any of it on the young officer who was kind enough to escort me down here, are we? I have a very serious problem to report to you. Specifically you, that is, because I fear someone may have accessed the ship's engineering areas with the sole intention of messing with it. You can listen to me, or you can listen to the captain later. Which is it to be? I have no need to have my time wasted either."

Commander Philips reacted as if I had slapped his face, but only for a moment. I couldn't tell whether he forced his expression to change or if it was genuine, but a smile broke out and then a deep booming laugh as if he found me particularly amusing.

Choosing to ignore him, I delivered my news.

"A short while ago, a body was discovered in a cabin on deck twelve. Our investigation revealed that one of the closets in the bedroom had been removed from the wall to expose a bulkhead. That bulkhead was then breached - cut through so that a person or persons with climbing gear could access a conduit leading down through the ship."

The smile on Commander Philips' face froze and then fell. His mirth, fake or otherwise, leaving his eyes.

"What?"

I felt that his response summed him up rather nicely and demonstrated his level of intelligence quite neatly.

"Exactly what I just said, Commander Philips. A passenger who faked his departure from the ship was found murdered in cabin 1215. He was wearing climbing gear and there is a hole through the wall in the cabin. It accesses a conduit with pipes carrying water. That he knew precisely which cabin he needed and what was behind the closet suggests a precisely constructed plan. My concern, as one might imagine, is that because at this time we do not know his motive or his destination, he may have been attempting to reach the engineering decks to damage the ship. I'm sure you are aware that a former crew member snuck back onboard and attempted to scupper the ship not so very long ago."

I was referring of course to a former deputy captain, a man called Robert Schooner, who had plotted and murdered as he sought revenge on me, Alistair, and the ship in general. He killed people and ended up dead himself, lost forever to the icy Northern Atlantic. It wasn't public knowledge, but the crew knew the tale, and how close we had come to riding the ship to the bottom of the ocean.

Commander Philips, as if jolted by an electric shock, started walking away from me at speed. Suddenly in motion, I was about to call after him when he twisted from the waist and gestured urgently with his right hand, his eyes wide as he indicated for us to follow.

"Come along, Mrs Fisher. I need you to show me precisely where this conduit is."

Well, this was better than I expected. At least the stubborn, haughty man hadn't chosen to argue and deny it could happen as I worried he might. Hurrying after him, I had Molly by my right elbow and the young engineering officer coming along behind us.

Commander Philips moved fast enough that I almost had to jog to keep him in sight. The engineering levels are a maze of passage-ways. Intersecting and crisscrossing, there were walkways leading over giant machines that plunged down through two or three of the ship's decks.

I called out, "Where are you taking us?" but got no answer. I found out why a few moments later when I turned another corner and discovered that he had stopped. Wherever it was that he wanted to go, we had already got there.

We were in a hub of some kind with banks of monitors and gauges watched over by what must have been ten or more engineers performing functions I would never understand. Most of them glanced our way as we came into the room though it was not so much a room as a space between other places.

Like I said: a hub.

In the centre of the space, reminding me of the bit in the

middle of Doctor Who's Tardis, was an octagonal central console with yet more screens, gauges, and thingamabobs.

Commander Philips had gone directly to it, and by the time I caught up to him he had a large digital schematic of the entire ship displayed on a screen at eye level. His eye level, not mine. I had to look up because he's most of a foot taller than me.

Molly was looking around with an expression caught somewhere between bewildered and impressed and I saw her mouth "Wow" as she gazed around at all the technology.

"Deck twelve you said?" Commander Philips wanted to confirm.

I replied, "Cabin 1215 to be precise. The conduit ran behind the forward bulkhead." I had to consult a mental map in my head, jiggling my fingers in the air to orientate myself so I was certain I had that right. After a couple of seconds, I confirmed my claim. "Yes, definitely the forward bulkhead."

Commander Philips was doing something with the mouse and keyboard that was zooming in and manoeuvring around on the rendered 3D digital image of the ship on the screen above. Demonstrating how clever the technology was, within just a few moments he knew precisely which bulkhead and conduit I was referring to.

As if struggling to believe it, he was shaking his head.

"How on earth did they even know it was there?" he murmured. I suspected it was a rhetorical question, but I wasn't going to offer him an answer either way. Tearing his eyes away from the screen to look down at me, he asked, "Was there any equipment with the victim? Did you have a sniffer dog check the cabin for explosives?"

His question instantly filled me with doubt. Had I missed something vital? Should I have immediately assumed that the ship was in great peril and ordered for the dogs to check? Then my brain caught up with me.

"We don't actually have any sniffer dogs, Commander Philips. However, if you feel the presence of explosives is a possibility we need to confirm or deny, I am quite sure we can get some from the Port Authority. Can you tell me where that conduit leads?"

Commander Philips was grinding his teeth together, the back of his jaw going from side to side. His eyes had not moved away from my face since he looked down at me to ask the question about the sniffer dogs. Whatever he was thinking remained private though as he chose to answer my question.

Pointing up to the screen, he said, "If you track it upwards," he did something on the mouse to move the screen up and down, "it just goes to the other decks, all the way to the top. It's the central pipe carrying effluent from the toilets down to a tank on deck two. They could do a fair bit of damage to the ship just by putting a hole in that pipe. However, if you follow it down, obviously it terminates at deck two, but after I asked you the question about the sniffer dogs, I suddenly realised what is next to the effluent tank."

He made me wait, delivering that line and then not giving me the answer. It was as if he expected me to dance like some kind of trained monkey and ask the question he so obviously wanted me to pose. I felt like kicking him in the shin, but I had no time to waste and far too much to do.

So as he expected, I asked, "So what is it that is next to the effluent tank, Commander Philips?"

A tight smile drew his lips into a thin line before he said, "Why, Mrs Fisher, I'm surprised you do not already know. Right next to that tank, is the ship's vault."

8

RELATIONSHIP WOES

What happened next could accurately be described as a flurry of frantic motion. Commander Philips alerted Alistair to the hole in the bulkhead, making me feel as if it was the first thing I should have done.

I let his barbed comments wash over me without acknowledgement. I doubted Vincent Pompeo's intentions were sabotage or terrorism and Commander Philips was good enough to not argue with me. However, he was right that we needed to be certain, so I had Lieutenant Commander Baker and the others abandon Nicole Tibbett's crime scene to focus on the task of getting sniffer dogs from the Port Authority onto the ship. Pippin was sent to assist Sam in making sure that cabin 1215 was secure - the task had just increased significantly in its importance.

Schneider was already ashore at a local indoor climbing club. He would have found one easily enough with an internet search and was doubtless planning to bring equipment and probably one or two members of staff back to the ship.

I had to be speedy in coordinating my team because I intended to accompany Commander Philips. He was already leading a gaggle of his engineers directly to the terminus of the conduit. While I was on my radio, doing my best to coordinate my team, I could overhear the head of engineering saying that it would come out above the effluent tank as the pipes continued downwards into it. They were all heading there right now.

Dragging Molly along with me, not that she didn't want to come, I tagged on behind the group of engineers as they set off.

Led by Commander Philips himself, he demonstrated the urgency he felt by setting off at a run. It wasn't a fast run, but let me tell you this, the cute shoes with the inch and half heel I picked because they went so well with my outfit today were not designed for running in. You might think I could just take them off, but the next thing I have to tell you is that the steel mesh flooring, which dominates in the engineering areas, is not something one can run on barefoot.

So I hobbled.

What I really needed to be wearing was a pair of running shoes, but though nothing had ever been said about what I should wear when employed in my role as the ship's detective, I felt it necessary to dress smartly.

I prayed we didn't have far to go, but even though I managed to keep up, our destination proved to be a deck down and about eight hundred yards from where we started out. That might not sound like very far, but half a mile is a long way to run in shoes designed to be walked in. To be fair, the exact distance was really rather hard to judge, because as I said before, the engineering areas are like being in a maze. So much so in fact, that my determination to keep up was partly due to my belief that I might never find my way out again if I were to lose the chaps I was attempting to follow.

I could tell from the shouts ahead of me that we had neared our destination before I could see anything, and as I came through another bulkhead, I found myself in a space the size of a cathedral. The ceiling was more than double height to accommodate some of the machinery and fittings I was now passing.

Looking up, and expecting to find the two pipes I'd seen through the hole in the bulkhead in cabin 1215, what I found instead was multiple pipes. They were everywhere. Quite how anyone could discern one pipe from another I had no idea.

Just as I found in many areas below the passenger decks, it was noisy. Water gurgling through pipes, pumps pumping water and goodness knows what else, plus a hundred other unidentifiable machine noises that combined to create a cacophony of background sound. It wasn't loud, but it was constant.

There were blisters on my heels from running awkwardly, so I was rather glad to find that we had finally arrived at our destination. Molly and I coasted to a stop behind the engineering team who were fanning out ahead of us.

Commander Philips was barking orders as usual, directing his crew port or starboard or forward and aft, sending them off to find any trace that something had been tampered with.

As they all spread out, leaving Commander Philips by himself, I went straight to him.

"Where is the vault?" I asked him, looking around as I tried to spot it for myself.

He started backing away, crooking a finger in my direction before spinning around to lead me yet deeper into the ship.

Whatever else I thought about Commander Philips, I had to acknowledge that he knew his way around the ship. With a fist, he wrapped his knuckles on what I thought was a bulkhead, but according to him was the ship's giant effluent tank.

He led us around it, where on the other side he stopped and used both arms, flamboyantly like a game show host, to indicate a pair of doors set into a wall.

"Your vault, Mrs Fisher," he declared. "A foolish man would claim it to be impenetrable. I, as an engineer, know that there is no such thing. However, it does not look like anyone has been tampering with it."

He was correct in that the doors looked intact, and I could not see any sign that anyone had been attempting to mess with them.

"What is in there?" I asked, testing his knowledge since he seemed to know everything so far.

"All of the money that the ship holds, less those amounts held in the currency exchange offices and other places. Also, we get quite a number of seriously rich passengers who wish to travel with price-less belongings. I believe we once had three Picassos from a single collection stored in here. You can only imagine their worth."

When Commander Philips revealed that the conduit came out close to the ship's vault, Vincent Pompeo's climbing gear, his faked departure from the ship, and his subsequent murder all made sense. He had been on board the ship to carry out a clever heist, intending to break into the vault, steal something of incredible value, or perhaps just a whole lot of cash, and then disappear from the ship without a trace.

His death suggested that his partner or partners double crossed him. Perhaps he was the one who knew how to get to the vault, or maybe he was the safecracker who was going to open it. Now that we knew who he was, we could find out so much more about him. I would have answers soon instead of guesses.

However, Vincent's murder was also confusing because at this moment I could not see that they had made it into the vault. Had their attempt to pull off this robbery failed, a fit of disappointed rage on the part of his partners culminating in his death?

Whatever else happened, the contents of the vault would need to be checked and that would require the bursar.

When I voiced my thoughts aloud, Molly grabbed her radio and offered to handle the task of making contact, demonstrating how much she had grown in the short time she had been away. When working as my maid she had been pleasant enough, but hardly what one would call proactive. If anything, at the time I had thought her to be a little lazy, yet here she was volunteering and making herself invaluable.

Around me, their voices echoing off the steel bulkheads, the team of engineers were shouting backwards and forwards to each other. They were checking machines and things, reporting back each time that nothing untoward had been found. I was adding no value to their efforts, but in this part of the ship for the first time, I chose to explore a little.

The giant door of the vault did not look like the image I held in my head. Admittedly the image came from watching TV shows, not from having ever seen one in the flesh. I was expecting a big spinney handle thing next to a tumbler with lots of numbers on it and could picture Vincent Pompeo as a safecracker wearing a stethoscope to listen as he fiddled with the dial. Instead, the door to the vault had what appeared to be palm and retina scanners plus a small keypad where a digital code could be entered.

I was curious to see if perhaps Vincent Pompeo and his accomplices might in fact have cut their way in around the side or at the back, but after several minutes of exploration I concluded that the front door was indeed the only way into the vault.

When I returned to Molly's location, she was able to tell me the bursar himself was on his way. I wasn't going to wait for him, which I might have done had I not so many other pressing tasks that required my attention. Using my radio, I contacted Lieutenant Commander Baker.

"Mrs Fisher?" his voice sounded far away as it echoed inside the confines of the ship's hull.

I wasted no time with chatter. "Martin, anything on Barbie? Has she stopped messing around yet?"

Martin Baker's reply disappointed me greatly.

"I'm afraid not Mrs Fisher. Barbie is remaining tight lipped at this time."

I tutted, annoyed. One of my most reliable friends was adding to my workload.

"She's in the brig, right?" I sought to confirm. Martin let me know that she'd been handed off more than twenty minutes ago so would already be confined to a cell and getting bored. It was not the place for one of my friends to spend any amount of time and it distracted me to know that she was there when she could not be guilty of the crime that had caused her incarceration. No power on earth could convince me she had murdered Nicole Tibbett.

"I'm going to head there on my way back up," I let Baker know. "I'll see if I can talk some sense into her. Has there been any development with Nicole?" I asked. Barbie was hiding something that she felt necessary to keep private. If she didn't want to tell me what was going on, but we could find sufficient evidence to exonerate her, then perhaps that would be the speediest method to get her out of the brig.

In an apologetic voice Lieutenant Commander Baker replied, "We are just getting started, Mrs Fisher."

Of course they were. The discovery of Nicole's body was less than an hour ago; unless we got very lucky, it was going to take time and effort to figure out who killed her and why.

I ended the conversation with Baker, leaving him to get on with his work. Goodness knows there was enough of it today.

Giving myself a few seconds to consider what I needed to do next, my thoughts were interrupted by my phone ringing. Scooping it from my handbag, I was rather pleased to discover the name displayed on the screen was that of my boyfriend, Alistair Huntley, otherwise known as the captain of the ship.

"Hello, darling," I purred as I answered the phone. He was probably calling for an update. He was ashore, I assumed, leaving the ship to attend his meeting. We were not going to get to spend much time together today - the two investigations I had ongoing made that patently clear. However, there was no good reason for the two of us to speak to each other in anything other than kind tones. So you can imagine my surprise when my attitude was not reflected by his.

I heard a tut and a sigh before he spoke.

"Where are you, Patricia? I need to see you straight away." There was no pleasantness in his demand, no real sense that he felt any affection towards me at all, in fact.

"Whatever is it?" I asked. "What has happened?"

He sighed again, a sort of harrumphing sound of displeasure and disappointment. It was not only most out of character, but also the first time I had ever heard him aim such negative emotions in my direction.

"I am genuinely surprised that you cannot figure that out for yourself, Mrs Fisher."

He called me Mrs Fisher. He had not done that, except in a playful manner, for so long I could not remember the last time. I was Patricia or darling or some other pet name he chose to employ. I needed to know what had brought about the sudden change.

"Darling, I have no idea what it is that might have upset you so, but I can assure you that if I am somehow responsible then I am sorry." Remembering that he said he needed to see me straight away, because now I needed to see him too, I said, "I am at your disposal. Where do you wish to meet me?"

"I asked you where you are, Patricia," he repeated in a tired voice, making it sound as if he believed I had deliberately chosen to avoid giving him that piece of information.

Gabbling my words now, because I felt as if I were truly on the backfoot, I said, "I'm on deck two right next to the vault. Do you want to come to me?"

"No, Mrs Fisher." Alistair all but snapped his reply. "I am the captain of the ship. People come to me, not the other way around. I am on the bridge"

I was beginning to get annoyed. His attitude was unjustified though he clearly felt otherwise. He had never spoken to me in such a manner at any point in the past, yet felt it was acceptable now. I had to bite my tongue when I replied.

"Very well, captain, I shall make my way directly to you." Unable to stop myself, I then thumbed the red button to end the call before he could say anything else, or possibly before I could tell him what I was thinking at that precise moment.

Stuffing my phone back into my handbag I could feel that my heart rate was elevated, and when I spotted Molly doing her best to pretend that she hadn't heard the exchange, I felt my cheeks redden too. I was going to do precisely as I said and go directly to the bridge - this situation needed to be resolved immediately. Alistair felt that he could talk to me as if I were a subordinate. I know that from a technical standpoint that's exactly what I am, but that was never part of my deal. Were my relationship with Alistair to end, I doubted I would remain on board the ship.

Setting off to find the nearest elevator, I found an engineering officer to carry a message to Commander Philips – I was heading to the bridge and would not want people trying to find me because

49

they didn't know where I had gone. Molly was going to return to the mysterious cabin on deck twelve and I hoped to find her there later.

Worrying thoughts filled my head as I questioned what could possibly have upset Alistair so deeply. However, the truth of it was beyond my scope to conceive and quite unbelievably, it wasn't going to be the worst discovery I would make in the next few minutes.

9

LEAKED NEWS

U pon arriving at the bridge level, I was escorted by Lieutenant Jafar, the only member of the crew from Zangrabar, to a small room not far from the captain's quarters. There was no one waiting for me in the room, which left me alone to fret when I really didn't want to be. The room had a window looking aft over the ship, so I got to see the sundecks and the helipad stretching back towards the stern of the enormous ocean cruiser.

Mercifully, I was not made to wait very long, the door opening just a minute or so later when Alistair strode in. Under any other circumstances, I would have closed the distance between us and expected to be greeted with an embrace since we were in private. Entirely unsure where I now stood, I remained where I was with my back to the window.

"What is happening, Alistair?" I asked, surprised by the timidity I heard in my voice. If he was acting out of character, then so was I in response. With anyone else I suspected I would be staring them down and challenging them - with Alistair it felt like the wrong tactic to employ.

He did not answer my question. Nor did he cross the room to

pull me into a hug as I had hoped he might. Instead, he paused just inside the door to deliver a question of his own.

"Patricia, please tell me why it is that I have two dozen treasure hunters on the quayside trying to get on board my ship."

I blinked in confusion as I tried to figure out what he was asking me. Alistair was looking at me in a manner that suggested he was expecting me to have an answer to his question, yet I was drawing a total blank

The response I settled on was, "How should I have any idea, Alistair?" I didn't like it, but I was facing off against my boyfriend and could feel myself falling into analytical detective mode. I watched him for facial cues and small mannerisms, and guarded my words so I would give nothing away. I was deliberately silent too, leaving a void in the conversation for him to fill.

Alistair shrunk a little, some of the anger leaving his face as if (I hoped) he could not maintain it when it was aimed at me.

"Oh, Patricia." He strolled across the room to look out the window over the ship, walking right by me to get there. "If you had just warned me, I might be able to prepare myself to answer Purple Star's questions. This is a real problem this time. Far worse than those complaints."

I was out of the loop on whatever it was Alistair was referring to and getting bored.

"Alistair Huntley," I said his name as if I was stamping my foot. "Tell me what is going on right now! What is it that I don't know? What is it that you are talking about? Better yet, why is it you think I would know anything about treasure hunters outside the ship?" He turned to look at me, his beautiful eyes meeting mine beneath a deep frown.

He was about to say something when my eyes locked onto his jacket, and I gasped in shock. My eyes were flaring about as wide as they could, and I was closing the distance between us whether he wanted me in his personal space or not.

"What is this?" I demanded to know, snatching up a lustrous, long strand of red hair from the shoulder of his uniform. It was a rhetorical question, of course, because we could both see what it was. Really I was asking how it got there and what it represented.

Alistair adjusted his gaze, staring down at the hair I was holding too close to his face.

"Whose hair is this?" I raged, anger boiling in my blood as I waited for him to respond. A day ago, a drop-dead gorgeous redhead woman had approached me to claim she was Alistair's lover. It disturbed me, but I saw no reason to believe she was telling the truth. I hadn't exactly put her words out of my mind, but since that one encounter, I hadn't seen her again. Until now there had been no sign that she even knew Alistair.

"It's a hair, Patricia," Alistair replied dismissively. "I brush past passengers sometimes. Can we get back to the matter in hand?"

"What is the matter in hand?" I snapped at him. I let him change the subject to stop myself from levelling an accusation. I didn't want to point the finger at him - not until I had something more tangible than a single piece of hair. Nevertheless, my brain was spinning at a million miles per hour and threatening to shoot off on a terrible tangent.

Was Alistair cheating on me? The thought was too abhorrent to be permitted residence in my head. I banished it quickly, but only so I wouldn't dissolve in front of him. I needed time to gather my thoughts … and gather evidence.

The redhead would be hard for most men to resist, but that isn't the same thing as saying Alistair was pretending to be true to me when he wasn't. I felt certain that were he to choose someone over me, he would do so honestly and openly, letting me down in the most humane manner possible.

The pain of rejection would sting no differently, but might be easier to accept in the long run.

Dragging my thoughts back to reality, Alistair said, "The report you sent to more than three dozen online newspapers, Patricia. That is the matter in hand." His tone was matter-of-fact now, his features unreadable, but far from kindly.

I blinked, waiting for him to say something else. I was still holding the red hair in my hands, absentmindedly fiddling with it as his words sunk in.

"You think I sent a report to some journalists? What was it about?"

Alistair sighed, frowning and pursing his lips as he looked down at me.

"Patricia, they name you as their source. All of them do. The bosses at Purple Star are going nuts." I was about to repeat my last question because he was yet to explain, but he produced his phone, thrusting it into my hands so I was forced to drop the hair. "Here, Patricia. This is everywhere."

I dragged my eyes down to the screen, absorbing what was written there as quickly as I could. I needed only a couple of seconds to recognise what I was reading: it was my notes from my computer.

It read like a news report, which was exactly the way I had written it and it was all about a mysterious albino stowaway and the uncut gems we found in his gut just a few days ago. The article, which was posted in English on a site called 'World News' even had a picture of me in the top right corner where it listed me as the author.

I was still reeling from the shock of it when Alistair demanded I answer a new question.

"Did you write this, Patricia?"

I was horrified. I was embarrassed. However, far more than either of those, I was angry. Turning my face up from the screen to look at Alistair I spoke as calmly as I could manage.

"Yes, Alistair, I did write these words. However, do you really believe that I sent them to anyone? I am not a complete idiot, Alistair. What possible advantage could I gain in sending this to a newspaper?"

"If you didn't send it, Patricia, then who did? Who else has access to your computer?" Alistair at least looked pained by his need to question me. It was a small comfort, but now I was going to have to tell him some of the things I had been keeping secret.

"Someone cloned my email account," I explained.

Alistair screwed up his face in disbelief. "When did that take place? Why wouldn't you have told me this before now?"

It was a perfectly reasonable question, but it had an even better answer.

"Because I really didn't have anything to tell you yet, dear. We discovered this yesterday. Someone got into my emails and sent Barbie a message that she believed was from me. Whoever sent it intended to split the two of us apart." Alistair was listening, but whether he believed what I was telling him I was yet to determine. "Someone … someone who is probably on this ship, is trying to create problems for me. I suspect it is the same person behind the malicious complaints, all of which are lies as you well know. That same person must be behind this leaked document."

"Why, Patricia? Why would anybody wish to target you in such a manner and why would they go to such extreme lengths?"

A sad chuckle escaped my lips. "Really, Alistair? You find this genuinely surprising, do you? How about … oh, I don't know, the Godmother? Admittedly, I think it's more likely she would just have me killed if she were coming after me. However, someone hacked their way into my computer, cloned my emails, sent malicious messages, and I think we can now assume they also found the notes I wrote about the uncut gems." Seeing the doubt in his eyes, I added, "You don't have to take my word for it, *darling*. Lieutenant Commander Baker and his team, plus Barbie and Jermaine are all in the loop. I didn't tell you, *darling*, because you're the captain of this ship, as you felt it so necessary to remind me earlier, and do not need to be bothered with trivia. I would have told you about it when there was time or perhaps when I had discovered who was behind the attack."

Alistair was looking a little embarrassed now, a trace of colour rising in his cheeks. I got that he was under a fair bit of pressure just from the daily demands of his job and he absolutely did not need Purple Star on his back bothering him with nonsense about his girl-friend. Yes, in theory one could say I was to blame because it is I who attract these crazy people. However, I genuinely felt he should have my back.

"This really wasn't you, was it?" Alistair remarked. Seeing the truth of it, Alistair was backing down. I was not, however, going to let him off that easily – it was time to go on the offensive.

Before he could say another word, or perhaps apologise, I snapped, "Of course it wasn't me! Now how about if you explain where that red hair came from?" He was on the back foot for once and I was pressing home my advantage.

I watched his face, believing he might suddenly look guilty or haunted or ... something. Instead, he offered me a confused expression.

"What red hair?" he asked.

I thrust the phone I was still holding back into his hands; it was his after all. He took it, but I wasn't paying any attention, I was staring down at the carpet where I hoped to once again spot the lone strand I had plucked from his tunic. I could not see it, of course, and was not going to get on my hands and knees to look for it. Deciding I did not need the physical evidence in my hands, I looked back up at him with fierce eyes.

"The one I just took from your uniform, Alistair. It comes from the skull of a redhead I met yesterday. Why don't you tell me who she is, darling?"

Alistair looked utterly bewildered. Though I could not help but feel a little relieved to see him floundering to make sense of my questions, I pushed him a little further.

"Tall, statuesque, blazing green eyes beneath flowing auburn hair and a figure most women would kill for," I described her in detail as if attempting to jog his memory and right then I saw a spark of doubt cross his face.

A knock at the door interrupted what I was going to say next. I was about to start interrogating him and perhaps he sensed that for he cut me off by responding to whoever was outside.

"Come in," he barked, the door opening less than a second later to reveal Commander Philips. The head of engineering paused in the doorway to deliver a salute which his captain immediately returned. Commander Philips' eyes never once strayed in my direction, and he was beginning to speak before his right hand had returned to his side.

"Sir you requested a report the moment I had completed my checks on deck two. I am yet to determine what they were after when they accessed that conduit, but we were unable to find anything on deck two that suggests their intent was sabotage. It is of course possible once they accessed the second deck that they found a way out of the immediate area and went somewhere else. I'm afraid to report that it may take several days to be absolutely certain they have not sabotaged the ship in a manner that will not become apparent until after we set sail."

Alistair accepted the engineering officer's report with a weary nod.

"The ship is indeed vast, Greg. You suspect they may have breached other areas?" Alistair was rightly concerned. If someone wished to sink the Aurelia or perhaps just cause a lot of damage, getting into any of the lower deck areas would give them all the opportunity they needed.

Rather than answer the captain's question straight away, Commander Philips turned his attention to me.

"Have you successfully arranged for sniffer dogs yet, Mrs Fisher?"

I felt my jaw clenching. I suspected he was asking the question in front of Alistair, in the hope that he could catch me out. If it was still on my to do list, he could embarrass me and comment on my lack of progress. Well, he was going to have to work a lot harder than that to catch me out.

"I delegated that task, Commander Philips," I replied dismissively and moved on. "Have you considered that deck two was never their intended destination?" I threw a question back at him. "The conduit goes up *and* down, does it not?"

Commander Philips saw fit to smile at me, as one might a simple person or a child. "What is it that you're suggesting, Mrs Fisher?" he asked with a grin. "You think perhaps we had our first cat burglars on board? The trick of removing a wardrobe to get to the bulkhead and access the conduit could not be repeated in the same manner to get back into someone's suite or cabin, Mrs Fisher. Were they to somehow accurately estimate where to cut, they would find themselves cutting through a bulkhead and into a closet. It would make too much noise and the cutting gear required would set fire to the closet long before they were able to gain access."

I did not bother to respond. I rather liked that he chose to explain things in such a simple manner, for he attuned my thoughts to consider what else Vincent Pompeo and his accomplices might have been attempting to achieve.

Alistair said, "Very good, Greg. Please continue your search with all haste. I will deliver the news of this breach to Purple Star and advise them that we may not be able to leave port on schedule."

Surprised by his words, I asked, "You will delay the ship's departure?"

Both men looked my way and Alistair said, "Until we are sure that the ship has not been sabotaged in some subtle way, and can confirm no explosives are present, I cannot risk the ship, the crew, and all the passengers. Purple Star may even insist that we evacuate all but essential personnel from the ship."

I had not thought the problem through fully. That much was clear. I dearly wanted to continue my conversation with Alistair, most especially the part about the redhead, but there was a fresh urgency to my steps now as my feet twitched toward the door.

"Can we consider the business of my news report on hold for now?" I pressed Alistair. "We can pick it up again later, when I will demonstrate what has been happening."

Alistair gave me a curt nod. It demonstrated how tense things were between us today. On any other occasion, he would have at least kissed my cheek before I departed his presence. He wasn't even looking my way when I went out the door.

Heading for the elevator that would take me back down from the bridge to the upper deck, I fished around in my handbag until I located my radio and pressed the send button.

"Lieutenant Schneider, are you back on board yet?"

10

PROPER VEXED

I arrived back at cabin 1215 to find Sam standing outside the door. I checked he was doing okay and went inside where I found Molly. Her back was to the door until she heard me coming through it.

"Mrs Fisher's here," she announced to whoever was in the bedroom.

Schneider's voice echoed back out to greet me a moment before he appeared in the bedroom doorway.

"We have two members of the local climbing club with us, Mrs Fisher. This is Andreas and Marco," he introduced me to two young men in their late twenties. They were both tanned and athletically built in a wiry, lean way.

I shook their hands and introduced myself as Patricia.

On the bed were several neatly tied sheaths of climbing rope, the multi coloured lengths looking brand new. Both men were wearing climbing harnesses over tee shirts and shorts, plus fingerless gloves and climbing boots. Their safety helmets were on the bed waiting to be donned before they went into the dark hole.

The hole itself was now fully exposed, indicating that someone from maintenance had been in to dismantle the closet more completely. The component parts of it were stacked in one corner against the wall by the small dressing table.

Explaining what I needed them to do, I started with, "This conduit goes all the way down to deck two at the bottom of the boat, gentlemen. There it terminates in an engineering area, but a search has been conducted and it does not look like that is where whoever made this hole was trying to reach. They may have gone up or down, so please be on the lookout for anything that suggests someone accessed one of the decks between the top floor and deck two."

"Are there access points on each deck?" Marco enquired.

I shook my head, saying, "I really don't know, but I suspect the answer is a firm negative. Hopefully, that will mean if the people who made this hole got off somewhere, it will be patently obvious."

I didn't go into how important it was that we worked out what Vincent Pompeo and his accomplices were up to - Andreas and Marco did not need to know that. I waited, hanging around for a couple of minutes until the two volunteer climbers found an anchor point to which they could secure their ropes and were getting ready to climb into the hole.

They played rock, paper, scissors to determine who would stay and who would go. The conduit being a small space, they determined it would be better for only one of them to descend or ascend. The other would belay a safety line just in case.

Marco won, collecting his helmet from the bed before attaching the rope to his harness and clambering feet first through the hole in the bulkhead. We got one last cheesy grin before his face vanished from sight.

Upon my advice they tried going down first. It was nothing more than a hunch, but it seemed so much easier to go down than to go up. Coupled with Commander Philips' claim that this was not a good way to access another cabin, I was willing to believe they had been aiming for the bowels of the ship.

"I'm going to leave you here," I let Molly and Schneider know. Though I was anxious to see if my hunch played out, there were many other things I needed to do. I got three paces before a question occurred to me. Pausing in the doorway, I turned to face Lieutenant Schneider. "Schneider did you spot anyone who looked like they might be a treasure hunter when you left the ship?"

He chuckled. "Yeah, I sure did. There's a whole pack of them. They seem to think we have the first clue to the whereabouts of a famous treasure."

I groaned and closed my eyes – Alistair had not been exaggerating then. Remembering the words in my notes, I recalled speculating about what the uncut gems might represent. The albino man we found murdered in the hold was nothing short of an enigma. He'd swallowed the gems – a mix of diamonds, rubies and other priceless stones – presumably to keep them from whoever killed him. I'd written all this down in my personal notes about a day before we realised someone had hacked into my computer and cloned my email account.

It was obvious now they had also copied my files and found one they could use to cause me embarrassment. The reporters who had then published the report probably hadn't even had to embellish it much. I'd had a couple of gins if my memory served, and was in a romantic mood, speculating about whether the stones might be part of an undiscovered pirate horde.

Hearing me huff a frustrated sigh, Sam poked his head through the door. "Is everything all right, Mrs Fisher?"

"Yeah, you look proper vexed," agreed Molly.

11

DANGEROUSLY DERANGED

"What's next?" The question was posed by Jordan, a young man of mixed descent whose mother moved from Taiwan to England with her parents when she was six. She married an Englishman, but was left widowed within a year just as the bump in her belly was starting to show.

Jordan grew up just outside Croydon in a tenement apartment where hunger and boredom were constant companions throughout his school years. Determined to throw off the mantle of poverty, he studied hard and stole harder. Never once caught by the police – because he was smarter than them in his opinion – Jordan tried to earn an honest living when he graduated university with a first in computer science. Having a boss did not suit him, especially when he was significantly smarter than anyone who wanted to employ him. Worse yet, he was expected to repay his student loans and that left him with too little on which to survive unless he stayed with his mum in her rundown apartment forever.

Finding illegal ways to use his computer skills took almost no effort, returning to a life of perpetual criminality as easily as taking his next breath. It was lucrative too, and all under the radar so he paid no tax, and his student loans would remain forever as a debt on a ledger somewhere.

When the posh, middle-aged woman advertised for a role on the dark web, he snapped it up – travel and work? Yes, please.

What she wanted him to do was simple enough. Hack a few computers, clone an email account … simple. He was, however, becoming increasingly concerned about his employer's level of sanity. She smiled too much, and there was nothing nice about the smile. Ever.

Jordan imagined she would happily watch someone being tortured in much the same way that he might grab some popcorn and put on a movie. Someone meant Patricia Fisher, of course. Not that Jordan had the faintest idea who that was.

His employer wanted to ruin Mrs Fisher's life, and when he asked her why, the reply was as simple as it was instant.

"Because she deserves it!" She didn't say it though, she screamed it, the memory of Patricia Fisher's past transgressions sufficient to make Jordan's employer instantly apoplectic with rage.

Jordan hadn't asked again.

"What's next?" Jordan's employer repeated the question. "Hennessy needs to confirm that she was successful this morning. If she was, then that element of the plan will begin to gather its own speed. Her role is pivotal – I am too old to achieve what I need her to do."

Jordan waited to confirm his employer had finished speaking – she did not like being interrupted.

Speaking tentatively, he asked, "I, um … I meant what do you need me to do next?"

His employer paused, looked down at where he sat in front of the laptop.

"You have hacked into all the accounts on my list?"

"Every one of them."

"Then perhaps it is time I had a little fun." She giggled, though Jordan had no idea what was funny. "Hennessy is supposed to be obtaining a key to her suite … her royal suite," Jordan's employer growled the words out, the smile she held a moment ago banished by the next thought. "What is she doing in a royal suite?" she demanded to know, making it sound like it was a personal affront. "We shall see how she feels about her royal suite when I have finished with it. Perhaps I will find something nice for her dogs to eat."

The last sentence drew another happy giggle from the deranged woman, scaring Jordan just a little more than before. Was he even safe to be in her company? Maybe he ought to look at carrying a weapon. Just in case.

The door to the cabin opened, Hennessy entering with the key card brandished for all to see.

Jordan turned back to his computer, wondering what she might have done to obtain it, but absolutely unwilling to ask.

12

FLEEING THE SCENE

I made my way back to the deck sixteen fitness centre to begin in earnest my investigation into Nicole's death. Lieutenant Commander Baker was there to greet me, but he was without Pippin and Bhukari now. They had been dispatched to liaise with the team of sniffer dogs coming onboard.

Right or wrong, I was doing all I could to stay on top and be in charge. Commander Philips, to name just one of my detractors, would find a way to undermine me if he could, so I was relieved to have wasted no time in having Baker contact the port authority for their help.

If Vincent Pompeo had been anywhere near any explosives, we would know about it soon enough. They would check the body and then cabin 1215. If necessary, they would then search elsewhere, but I believed they would either find traces on the victim or not at all.

While that was happening, I wanted to uncover what had befallen Nicole. Since it could not have been Barbie who crushed her skull, there was a killer at large and people were expecting me to figure out who it was.

Baker knew about the hole in the bulkhead on deck twelve, of course. "Schneider said he has climbers in the hole already."

I nodded. "That's right. I just hope they find something. Otherwise, the Aurelia might be stuck here until we can be sure it's safe to put to sea. What have you found here?"

We were back in the main room of the fitness suite. Nicole's body had been removed; taken to the morgue where Dr Nakamura or Dr Davis would perform an autopsy to confirm the precise cause of death. Arranged around the floor were little flags to indicate what had been found where and I knew there would be hundreds of photographs taken to show her body from every angle.

It was a macabre subject, but one I was stuck with.

I asked, "Who inspected the body?"

"Dr Nakamura."

"Was he able to hazard a guess at the cause of death?"

Baker pulled his lips into a tight line. "He wouldn't commit, but he commented that the only wound on her body was the one to her skull. He didn't sound like he expected to find anything else."

"Okay," I moved the conversation on. "Has someone been to her cabin to take a look yet?"

"I went myself. There was nothing out of the ordinary … well, except for one thing. It's probably nothing." Baker knew I liked to be given all the information which was why he was telling me about something he considered to be either trivial or a red herring.

"What?"

"She had a schematic of the ship on her wall. It's not that strange," he defended her. "But I'm more used to seeing that sort of thing in the Engineer's cabins. It was probably left there by the previous occupant."

I thought about it for a second, filing it away in case it had some relevance later, but had to admit it sounded like nothing.

Moving on, I asked, "What about the other persons involved in the discussion about fitness? How many have you rounded up?"

Baker's reply was instant and confident. "All bar two." I waited for him to supply the names. "Annabelle Grimm and Andrea Bassinet-Blatch. The latter has the day off. We haven't found her yet, but her comments on the group were probably the most supportive of Nicole's. We'll catch up to her at some point. Miss

Grimm is more interesting. She's the ballet choreographer and quite the Rottweiler if public opinion is to be believed. She had some cutting remarks for Nicole when she attempted to defend her stance on yoga."

"Miss Grimm is not onboard?" I questioned. I'd heard of the former ballerina, but we were not acquainted. I could not comment on her general demeanour.

Baker shook his head. "She went ashore early this morning. Actually, she was one of the first crewmembers to leave."

"Fleeing the scene," I remarked to myself.

"Possibly," Baker commented. "Or she might have been keen to go shopping or meet someone. Either way, she is off the ship and isn't answering her phone. That's not a crime …"

"But it is suspicious when we add it to her interaction with the victim. Okay," I focused my thoughts, "we need to make sure security knows to look out for her upon her return and we may need to speak with her colleagues. Who is interviewing the other names on the list? How many are there?" I added the second question when it occurred to me. Were we looking at three people or thirty?

"Deepa and Pippin would have started already, but the thing on deck twelve had to take priority."

I nodded my understanding, the danger – minimal or otherwise – that someone might be trying to sabotage the ship, took priority over almost everything else.

"I'll handle the interviews myself," Baker continued. "Including Miss Grimm there are six people I want to talk to – all ladies who were throwing unpleasant comments about. That's including Barbie unless …"

"I'm going to the brig right now if you don't need me for anything else."

Lieutenant Commander Baker shook his head. "No, Mrs Fisher. Good luck." He turned away to speak with another security officer – a junior lieutenant who had a question about the crime scene.

Good luck. His words resounded in my head. Was luck what I needed? Which bit of my life was it that needed luck the most?

Pushing the redhead from my mind as the memory of her

surfaced yet again, I left the fitness suite to head to the brig in the bowels of the ship.

    I didn't get there.

13

TREASURE

"Lieutenant Schneider for Mrs Fisher," the Austrian's voice echoed by my hip as if it was my handbag talking to me. I fished around with my right hand until I found the radio stuffed in a dark corner.

He repeated his message twice before I was able to get the radio out and up the right way so I could press the send button.

"Mrs Fisher here."

"Can you come back to 1215, Mrs Fisher?" Schneider wanted to know. "The climbers have found something."

He didn't elaborate and I didn't ask him to - the less said over the airwaves the better. Anyone could overhear us if they had a radio tuned to the right channel. Barbie was just going to have to stew in the brig for a little longer. It bothered me, but only because she is my friend, and I knew she was innocent. She had to be.

There would be a good reason why she wouldn't admit the truth earlier – I had no idea what it could be, but she would have to 'fess up' sooner or later. Whatever it was, it couldn't be as bad as killing Nicole.

A new thought occurred to me – was she trying to keep the

secret while hoping I would solve the case? If I did that she would be released by default.

Speculating was wasting vital brain power and achieving nothing. I put Barbie's predicament from my mind and quickened my pace. The climbers had found something, but while my mind filled with all manner of scenarios, the truth of it turned out to be far beyond anything I could have imagined.

"They did what?" Now back in cabin 1215, I needed Schneider to repeat his previous statement.

Andreas was no longer doing anything with the safety line which had initially confused me. I thought perhaps Marco had descended all the way down to arrive on deck two, but that was not the case. What Lieutenant Schneider had just told me was that a ventilation grill was missing roughly one hundred and twenty feet below the hole in the bulkhead and Marco was now on what Schneider believed to be deck six.

Schneider was guessing to some extent, yet his knowledge of the ship was such that from Marco's description of what he could see, the Austrian was confident we would find him in the depths of the enormous ship without taking too many wrong turns.

"Then I guess that's where we're going next," I remarked.

Marco's shouts were echoing back up the wide conduit, but I was struggling to hear what he was saying. Liquid, and whatever else it was, ran through the pipes in the conduit every few seconds making it hard to hear if the echo itself wasn't bad enough. Marco could have ascended once more, but the decision was made to leave him where he was – finding him would confirm we were in the right place.

I could have spoken with Commander Philips and requested he identify precisely where the climber had emerged - my level of confidence that he would pinpoint the exact location was high. However, I had already had my fill of the ship's chief engineer for one day.

The radios crackled, Lieutenant Bhukari's voice coming through crystal clear when she said, "Lieutenant Bhukari for Lieutenant Commander Baker, over."

"Baker here, over."

We got to listen as she informed him that the port authorities' sniffer dog team had scoured sufficient parts of the ship for them to feel confident there were no explosives to find. It was a big relief. Deepa was seeking authority to stand the team of sniffer dogs down, a request that was relayed to the captain, intercepted by the deputy captain, and authorised just a few moments later.

I was beginning to see some advantage to carrying a radio. It was an annoying device to me, though less so to the security officers, who had a lightweight version that pinned to their uniform. Mine was in my handbag most of the time, though I had a tendency to forget to pick it up, or to charge it. Thus, quite often when I needed it, it turned out to be dead or back in my suite. On this occasion it was keeping me in the loop.

I left the cabin on deck twelve, leaving Molly behind with Andreas and taking Sam and Lieutenant Schneider with me as I made my way to the nearest elevator.

No one spoke in the confines of the steel car as it descended, each keeping their own thoughts. Mine kept returning to Alistair and to the mysterious redhead. I knew no good could come from dwelling on the subject - goodness knows I had other things I ought to be thinking about, but the horrific scenario that Alistair might be cheating would not leave me alone.

It was a mercy then, when the elevator stopped on deck six and my train of thoughts were interrupted by Schneider speaking.

"I believe Marco is in one of the passenger storage areas. There are several of them, but if I have my orientation right, I believe I've narrowed it down to perhaps a choice of two."

I hoped he was right, and we would not spend an age looking for our intrepid climber.

The term *passenger storage area* failed to provide my feeble imagination with a sufficiently colourful picture. Schneider used a security pass code to gain access to a door beyond which I expected to find some shelves and perhaps a few boxes. However, when the automatic lights flicked on above our heads, I found myself in a room that looked not dissimilar to the one in Hogwarts. I had to rack my brain for a moment to come up with its name – *the room of requirements*.

There *were* shelves, but the kind you find in warehouses stacked to the ceiling with boxes of all shapes and sizes. There were cars, or at least what I took to be cars, beneath shrouds to keep them free of dust. The floor was covered with wooden crates and paraphernalia too numerous and diverse to list.

I was so busy gawping at the vastness of the storage room that it startled me when Lieutenant Schneider shouted.

"Marco! Marco are you in here?"

Sam joined in, bellowing for the climber to identify himself. No answer came back so we moved onto the next storage room, a hundred yards and two passageways over. We had struck out on Schneider's first guess, but the moment we stepped into the second storage area it was clear we had found Marco's location.

The lights were already on for a start, and he called out to us while we were still coming through the door.

"We found him!" Sam beamed. He set off, following the sound of the climber's voice as he took a side passage between crates.

I was going to follow when a sound stopped me.

"What was that?" I wanted to know. In truth, I knew precisely what it was that I had just heard, it was the chattering sound of a monkey. Or, more precisely, it was Buddy.

Schneider recognised the noise for what it was too.

"I guess this is where they put him," he remarked while looking around for the offensive ape. "They are planning to ship him back to Gibraltar tomorrow, that much I know. I suppose this was as good a place as any to secure him until then."

Moving away from the door, I spotted a cage - the same cage we had put Buddy in just a short while ago. The door to it was hanging open and of the ape there was no sign.

An exasperated gasp escaped my lips.

"He got out." The statement was as unnecessary as it was obvious. I was looking around for him, hoping I would spot the small brown primate before he threw anything unpleasant in my direction.

"Mrs Fisher!" Schneider and I both heard Sam calling. "Marco's over here and I've found treasure."

I was more interested in recapturing Buddy than I was in whatever it was that Sam had found. In Sam's language treasure could mean anything. Thinking he probably meant jewellery or possibly a treasure trove of Xbox games, my response was a little dismissive.

"We'll get to you in a minute, Sam."

A flash of brown fur zipping between one stack of crates and another caught my eye. I flashed out an arm, pointing at what I had seen and darting toward it.

"There he goes!"

Schneider called after me, "What is it that you are going to do, Mrs Fisher?"

I hadn't thought that far. I also hadn't looked where I was going, stepping in the something unspeakable I was so fervently hoping to avoid. Whether Buddy had left it there as a deliberate booby trap I could only guess.

Whatever the case, I slipped, cartwheeled my arms and managed to grab the first thing my hands found. It turned out to be a large glass tank. It ought to have acted as an excellent anchor point but had been mounted on a slide out rail.

Instead of arresting my fall as I hoped, the tank followed me, whooshing outward.

What I ought to have done was let go, but panicked as I was I clung to the tank, pulling it to the edge of the sliding shelf and into free air.

Had it not been for Schneider, the tank might have done me some serious damage. Mercifully, he was not only strong and fast, but he was close enough to grab one end as it angled toward my body.

It stopped moving, my hands losing their grip as I continued my path toward the cold, steel deck. With a yelp and a bump, I landed gracelessly on my rump.

"Everything okay?" Marco's voice drifted out from the depths of the storage room. "Shall I come to you?" Undoubtedly, he was wondering what all the noise was about.

I wanted to say something flippant about this being completely normal. It would have been the truth after all. Patricia Fisher creating a disaster accompanied by a backdrop of noise akin to launching a one-man-band from a circus cannon was nothing unusual.

Schneider deftly placed the large glass tank back on the shelf and offered me a hand up.

"Are you all right, Mrs Fisher?"

Dusting myself off, I eyed my soiled shoe with the contempt it deserved and looked around for something I could use to scrape off the offending muck that clung to it.

"I guess this is to make getting heavy things on and off the shelf easier," Schneider remarked as he slid the glass tank out and back in again to make sure Patricia the super klutz hadn't damaged anything. "I wonder what was supposed to be in the tank?" he tapped the glass with a fingernail.

I looked at it properly for the first time. It looked like a large fish tank, but keeping piscine creatures was not its purpose. There was a lid for it lying to one side fitted with a complicated temperature management system. In the base of the tank lay an inch of sand and there were a few plants and rocks. They had shifted from their original positions and the sand was gathered at one end where I had almost thrown the whole thing on the deck.

"It looks like something you would keep a reptile in," I observed, thinking it looked like the tanks one would see in the reptile house of a zoo. I couldn't remember what the correct name for such a habitat was until Schneider supplied it – a vivarium. The name for it was entirely secondary though to the more interesting question: what was once in it, and where was it now?

The lid was already off when I grabbed it which to my mind meant Mr Snakey, or whoever was previously residing inside the vivarium was now enjoying the full run of the ship. He would need to be found, for though I had no love of snakes and other reptiles, I didn't like to think of the poor chap trying to find food in such a steel environment.

To steer me back to our reason for being in the storage room, Sam appeared.

"Everything all right?" he asked, a curious edge to his usual smile. Marco was with him. "Ooh look, it's Buddy!" he cackled and pointed back in the direction of the door.

I shot my head and eyes around just in time to see the ape scamper out through the storage room entrance.

I said a rude word.

To my great surprise, Buddy's head reappeared around the edge of the door. I'm not going to claim I can read primate expressions, but he looked mad to me. To further convince me, he flipped me the finger again, showing me his teeth in an angry leer before vanishing from sight. I guess he was holding a grudge about being captured earlier.

We raced to the door, but by the time we got into the passageway outside he was long gone.

I said another rude word.

Schneider used his radio to alert the crew to the presence of an animal on deck six. Whether Buddy would stay on deck six was another thing entirely. While Schneider was doing that, I wandered back to the glass tank for another look.

Now that I was looking for it, I found what I assumed to be owner's marks on the exterior. It did not list the contents, but provided a name we could easily look up in order to contact the shipper. Purple Star made money where they can, my assumption being that whatever was inside the crate was being shipped to a zoo or a private collector or something. Then a new thought occurred to me that perhaps they were the pets of a person staying on board.

"Schneider, can you use your doodad thingy to look up Reece Mefford, please?" I requested of the tall Austrian standing beside me. In seconds I had my answer: he was indeed a passenger. Schneider also checked his current status to confirm the man in question had not left the ship today.

I would break the news to him later and at the same time discover what had been in the glass tank. It was probably something I could look up – someone would have it listed on a manifest somewhere, but there appeared to be no immediate need to do so. I felt sure it would be a reptile of some kind, but continuing to look around, more from concern that it might find me first, I could see no sign of it. The radio crackled as a report came in from someone in engineering - Buddy had just been spotted. We were going to have to go through the process of catching him all over again.

Dreading to imagine what mischief he might get up to this time, I turned my attention back to the task of working out why Vincent Pompeo had gone to such lengths to get into this storage room.

"I had a look around," Marco reported, "but I couldn't find anything that looked like it had been messed with."

I gazed at my surroundings and encouraged my skull to itch. There was something going on. Something that scored high on the mystery meter though so far I had no idea what it could be.

Schneider leaned his face toward the radio pinned to his lapel. "We should get the sniffer dogs down here … just to be sure."

While he did that, I took Sam by the arm.

"We need to do a sweep of the storage room, Sam. As thoroughly as we can." Marco came too, happily chipping in to help us search. I think he found it quite exciting to be part of a criminal investigation, even if we were just poking around inside a dusty storage room below decks.

We searched high and low, scouring the shelves and the items placed on pallets on the floor looking for any sign that something was missing or that something had been opened or tampered with. I started off feeling thoroughly positive, but fifteen minutes into the search I was beginning to lose hope. If there was something here which lured the criminals to employ such desperate lengths as were needed to obtain it, then we were failing to spot it.

Had I got it completely wrong? It was a missing ventilation grill that led us here, but how long ago had that grill been removed?

I called out to my fellow searchers, getting three responses to confirm that no one had found any dust-free patches to indicate that something was missing or any other sign that we were looking in the right place.

Frustratingly, this put me back at square one and I would need to start afresh. Had Vincent been aiming for the vault after all? Had it simply proven too difficult for him to crack and that was why we could find nothing stolen?

I was standing motionless in the middle of an aisle, roughly in the centre of the storage room and attempting to force my brain into coming up with a new theory when Schneider's voice drew my attention.

"Mrs Fisher?"

"Yes?" I rotated on the balls of my feet to face in the direction his voice had come from. Using the door to orientate myself, I estimated that he was somewhere over near where the conduit would pass, and Marco had been able to gain access.

Schneider's voice rang out again.

"You really need to see this, Mrs Fisher." I was already making my way toward him when he added, "Sam was not joking when he said he found treasure."

My heart gave a sudden double thump and the image of the scrawny albino man we found just a few days ago swam into my consciousness. He had been murdered … three decks beneath us, but not so very far from here, I realised. Found with uncut precious stones in his gut, the man had met a gruesome end and my detective's brain was certain it came about because he was attempting to hide or defend the treasure he'd found.

Rounding the corner of some shelves toward the rear of the storage room, I discovered Schneider, Sam, and Marco looking down at something the three of them were gathered around.

They parted as I neared to reveal what I instantly believed to be the location where the albino man had been residing. Or hiding might be a better word. A sleeping bag - thin, grubby, and torn in places - lay on a steel floor against a bulkhead. I could see nothing beneath it to soften the cold hard surface. It was the resting place of a desperate man.

At the open end of the sleeping bag a small knapsack appeared to have been used as a pillow. There was a greasy stain where a head might have rested on multiple occasions. In an untidy pile just about a yard from the sleeping bag were discarded food cans. I could not guess how long the stowaway had been hiding in the storage area, but there were enough cans to have sustained a person for more than a week. The one clue we had so far was the body of a small insect which Hideki plucked from the albino's hair. He was native to only one island, but we had not stopped there, and it really wasn't a lot to go on.

The cans and the sleeping bag would be taken away and examined with the hope they would yield more clues. If we were really lucky, we might find his passport or some other document that might identify him. Certainly, this was more than we had when I got up this morning.

It was, however, the pile of gold coins and items of jewellery which held everyone's attention. They were spilling from the open neck of the knapsack. Like a dragon's horde, there were so many gold coins that the mound they formed was heavy enough for gravity to pluck at them.

I crouched to pick a coin from the deck, holding it up as the three men closed in tight to see it.

"Any idea what it is?" I enquired.

No one did, but it was old, it was solid gold if the weight was any indication, and there were a lot of them.

"Is this part of the treasure I was reading about online?" asked Marco, reminding me of my earlier, unpleasant conversation with Alistair. Had it not been for that, I would have no idea what the climber was talking about. Unfortunately, he stood as further proof that Alistair's claims were not exaggerated. I needed to put a lid on this and fast.

Turning to Lieutenant Schneider, I said, "We need to secure this area. No one gets in or out of here without my express permission."

There was no need for me to say anything else, and by the time I swung my gaze back to Marco - still waiting for an answer to his question - Schneider was already on the radio drumming up additional personnel.

"What should I do, Mrs Fisher?" Sam enquired.

I made Marco wait a moment longer, placing a hand on Sam's

shoulder to impart, I hoped, the importance of the task I was going to give him.

"Sam, we need to catalogue everything that is in here. Can you please go to Lieutenant Commander Baker and bring the forensic kit here?"

Looking thoroughly pleased to have been given something important to do all by himself, Sam hurried away. He made his way around the ship well enough that he would not get lost and would return with others, so would have no trouble finding his way back.

Having waited so patiently, Marco deserved an answer, however I was not going to give him one. Lieutenant Schneider was finished with his radio messages just in time to be given a fresh task.

I was facing the helpful climber and offering him an apologetic smile when I said, "Lieutenant Schneider please escort Marco back to the cabin on deck twelve." To Marco I said, "I want to thank you so much for your efforts today. However, I'm afraid I must restrict access to this area and beg that you repeat nothing of what you have seen here." He opened his mouth to argue, unsurprising because this would make for a good tale to tell over a drink later, but I cut him off with a warning. "People will kill for the information you have, Marco. The only safe play is to forget you were ever here. You did not see the knapsack and the sleeping bag. You did not see gold coins and jewellery. If you read about the treasure, then you must know the owner of the knapsack was already murdered."

Marco looked disappointed, but nodded his understanding and went with Lieutenant Schneider.

Left alone as their footsteps receded towards the door, I felt an eerie chill pass over me.

Lieutenant Kashmir's mystery meter was proving to be even more accurate than I could have imagined. Did Vincent Pompeo somehow know about the treasure? Was that his purpose for coming down here and all the effort it took to do so?

I didn't think it could be and based that belief on the randomness of the albino's location. I was convinced this was where he had been sleeping and that it would not prove to be the possessions of a different stowaway. Surely, no one could have known to look here? We found this location by chance.

Not for the first time, I questioned what it was that I had uncovered. A dead man with a fortune in uncut gems in his belly, and an even greater fortune stuffed into his knapsack. In death the man had looked like a homeless person without a penny to his name, yet in his possession were millions. Where had it come from?

14

A PASSENGER ARMED WITH KNOWLEDGE

Boarding the ship at almost precisely the same time that Patricia was staring down at the albino's possessions, was a man who believed he knew the answer to that question. Xavier Silvestre had changed his plans most swiftly upon learning an artefact from the San José had been found. He killed three men in under a single day to ensure no one else found out, so was most disappointed to discover that news of the treasure had been leaked.

Silvestre did not think of himself as a treasure hunter – he was a business entrepreneur, even if most of his business dealings were illegal. However, he had grown obsessed with one story when he was still a boy and the fire it started in his belly had never died. If anything, it burned hotter over the years as his research revealed small clues.

The San José, a Spanish galleon loaded with gold, silver, and jewels from the mines of Peru was making its annual voyage back to Spain when it vanished. Supposedly sunk by the British, Silvestre had long believed they sunk a different ship - the similar but ultimately worthless by comparison, San Juan de Ulua. There were many clues if one looked hard enough and over the years Silvestre followed the work of others as he tried to piece together what really did happen to the San José and the priceless treasure in its hold.

It was more than four-hundred years ago, so any reports he found in historic journals had to be considered carefully and only in conjunction with other information that could correlate or throw into doubt what he already knew. Nevertheless, after reading hundreds of theories by historians and treasure hunters alike – goodness knows there had been many a salvage team attempting to find the wreck – he settled on a theory of his own: the captain stole it.

Fleet Commander Admiral José Fernandez de Santillan chose to leave without his military escort, attempting the treacherous journey home without them. To Silvestre it felt like a deliberate move – anyone else would have waited. But what became of the San José? The captain would have needed the support of at least one of his officers, though the crew and those officers not trusted to be involved were most likely murdered once the treasure was safely delivered to wherever they took it.

Something else then had to have happened because the billions in precious metals and jewels had never resurfaced. Just two pieces had been found, both in England. A dagger and a cup, both displaying the emblem of the House of Asturias, a family known to have been sailing home from Peru on the San José, came to life in the late nineteenth century. Their discovery in a small church in a village in Surrey led to much speculation at the time and since, though ultimately nothing came of the find.

Leading theories to explain their presence and their location surrounded the likelihood that they were never on board the San José and had been stolen before the ship sailed. The thief must have later found himself in England and in need of funds.

Xavier Silvestre pondered all this and more as he waited in line with the common folk to board the giant cruise ship through the main entrance on deck seven. He saw the line of treasure hunters attempting to gain access to the ship and marvelled that anyone could be so dumb as to reveal what they knew. Of course, he was glad too, because now he had a name – Patricia Fisher.

The woman was named as a source for the information published online in dozens of journals and news reports. There was something incongruous in it though – he looked up the name because it sounded familiar, discovering a woman he knew from other news stories. Patricia Fisher was the woman credited with toppling the world's largest organised crime syndicate. Clearly, she was no fool, so how was it that she was foolish enough to attract attention to the murder of a man on board the ship on which she served, and alert the world to the presence of the mysterious gems found inside his body?

Regardless of how it happened, Silvestre was thankful for it. More than thankful. Combined with the cross he now possessed – taken from a museum in Brazil - the news article revealing the uncut gems confirmed what he already believed - that the treasure in the hold of the San José had been found. More than anything, he wanted to interrogate the man who found it. Since that was not possible – finding his body was the event that triggered everything – Silvestre came to the Aurelia to find whatever information was available.

To him, Patricia Fisher's foolish revelations were almost a trea- sure trove in themselves.

Unlike Patricia, Silvestre knew the albino's name. He also knew who had murdered him. The albino, an Irishman called Finn Murphy, was killed by a man called Carlos Ramirez. According to Ramirez who only surrendered the information when given suffi- cient pain-related motivation by Silvestre, the Irishman had only one piece of the treasure about his person when he died. Murphy went to his grave without revealing where he found the treasure, and Silvestre had only been able to get Ramirez to reveal a country where they met – Morocco.

Murphy's tale would never be told, but Silvestre had never expected such a magnificent treasure to surrender itself without a fight. He would find Patricia Fisher and wring from her whatever information she possessed.

The line shuffled forward, the ship's crew operating with slick efficiency despite the vast number of new passengers waiting to board. It was a deliberate choice to book passage as a humble person of limited means, as was the decision to wear a disguise. No one was to know his real identity – he expected to have to kill whoever he spoke to about the treasure, so disguises and pretence were necessary steps.

The family to his front had two small boys: spoilt brats really. They bumped into his suitcase for perhaps the tenth time as they wrestled with each other and ran riot without their parents bothering to rein them in. Silvestre focussed his mind elsewhere, retreating inside his imagination as the queue moved forward again and he continued to wait.

He would find Patricia Fisher soon enough.

15

BENEFACTORS AND BUTLERS

rmed with a cabin number for Reece Mefford, I elected to go via my suite on my way to him. I could have delegated the task of informing the passenger that his vivarium had been opened, but everyone I worked with was already thoroughly busy dealing with today's incidents.

It was one of the busiest days I could ever remember having, though there were a number of contenders on the list. Two separate murders on a single day - unrelated as I felt convinced they were – was unusual, but not unheard of. I would get to the bottom of both cases, of that I felt entirely certain. I could do, however, without the additional drama of my notes being leaked.

That the person behind it would turn out to be the same one who hacked into my emails I considered to be a foregone conclusion. I had not the slightest idea who that was which made the mystery just one more item on my list of things to figure out.

My pair of miniature dachshunds leapt from the couch on which they were sleeping to rush at me when I pushed open the door to the Windsor Suite. I enjoyed the luxury of the ship's finest accommodation at the pleasure of the Maharaja of Zangrabar. The cost to him, given that he was the third richest man on the planet, was likely akin to finding some pocket change down the back of the sofa to anyone else.

I had been uncomfortable with the concept of a benefactor to begin with, but over time had settled into my new way of living.

"Your jacket, madam," Jermaine remarked. I turned my back to him so he could slip the outer layer off my shoulders. If I failed to mention it earlier, you might find it pertinent to know that I have a butler. He comes with the suite, but is also permanently employed by the Maharajah to be my butler. Should I ever leave the Aurelia, I believe he will come with me. Willingly so, for he and I have what many might call a rather special relationship.

Entirely platonic, and evermore shall be so, for if the almost twenty-five-year age gap between us was not sufficient to banish any romantic inclinations, Jermaine's sexual preferences would be. He is my protector when such a task is necessary, and when not, he is my anything else I should need him to be.

"Thank you, Jermaine, dear. Have you had a busy morning?" I posed my enquiry as I bent to scoop the two dogs currently scratching at my ankles. I had been out for several hours, and they wanted some affection. They were probably about ready for a walk too.

"Not so busy as yours I'll wager, madam." He spoke with a voice that was a little guarded, my ears picking up on it before my brain connected the dots. He was best friends with Barbie, their relationship deeper than the one I held with her, and he must have heard about her incarceration.

I turned to face him, gently placing my dogs back onto the carpet before I replied.

Catching myself in the habit of biting my lip, something I do when I am not sure what to say, I went with, "I am getting her out of the brig just as soon as I possibly can. I hope you will believe me when I say that I have not the slightest belief that she is in any way involved in what happened to Nicole Tibbett."

Jermaine inclined his head. "Of course, madam. Perish the thought. Coffee?"

Coffee sounded delightful, but I wasn't done with the subject of our mutual friend yet.

"Barbie is hiding something. It might help me immensely if someone were to tell me what it is. She clearly didn't want to tell me ... you know how stubborn she can be."

A smile twitched at the corner of Jermaine's mouth. He knew full well how fiery and independent the Californian blonde bombshell chose to be on a regular basis.

"I am afraid, madam, that on this occasion I am entirely in the dark." His expression turned thoughtful, and I waited because it was clear he had a question to pose. "Madam I heard rumour of a newspaper article you submitted." seeing my expression, he came to the correct conclusion. "These were notes that were stolen from you, yes?"

I nodded, annoyed but trying not to let negative emotions rule my day.

"Yes, I only skim read the article myself, but it would seem that they took my case notes on the stowaway we found in the hold and rewrote them to look like a newspaper column. The issue requires scrutiny, but I do not have time for it right now. Suffice to say that it is yet another attempt to tarnish my reputation and ruin my good name."

A frown creased Jermaine's brow; he did not like to see me upset. To head him off before we got onto the subject of what he could do to help me, I asked, "Could I have that coffee now please, dear?"

I drank it on my sun terrace. Facing out over the ocean in the lee of the ship, I was in shade and sitting outside was pleasantly warm. In direct sunlight I would have been too hot. Even though it is late in the year, we are close to the equator, and the temperature is high.

The few minutes of respite from running between storage rooms, engineering areas, the cabin on deck twelve, and the fitness suite on deck sixteen, allowed my brain to cool slightly and attempt to sift through the facts I had seen so far. It didn't help much, and my list of things to do seemed to be getting longer. Worse yet, I needed to do each one of them right now.

Trying to decipher which of the tasks was most important, another one popped onto the list. I had been meaning to phone Felicity Philips, a wedding planner for the rich and famous, for more than a day now. It wasn't something I was going to tackle right now, but I had promised John Oswald, a billionaire in his eighties, and his twenty-something fiancée, Betty Ross, that I would see if she was available.

Her number was in my phone, and it would have been easy to pick it up and make the call. I chose not to though – it just wasn't pressing enough.

Instead, I focused on the murders and the awful hate campaign being conducted against me. I had to discern between the personal and professional elements. Someone was trying to ruin my professional career and I had only been in the job of ship's detective for a few weeks. Figuring out who was behind it needed to feature high on my list, but that was a personal need. So too the worrying presence of the beautiful redhead. My heart ached from the idea that Alistair might be involved with her, though my brain argued that I was being ridiculous. He was too good of a man to do that to me.

Then again, I had been completely blindsided by my ex-husband's cheating.

I also needed to get Barbie out of the brig. The driver for this was also personal, though there was a professional element to it because I needed to eliminate her from the list of suspects. In my head, she had never made it onto the list, yet she was locked in a cage with no alibi and damning evidence against her.

Draining the last of my deliciously satisfying espresso, and subliminally feeling a burst of energy from the caffeine now charging through my body, I picked up Georgie and Anna, my two dachshunds who had contentedly gone to sleep on my lap, and placed them back on the couch in my suite.

Even though it would be easy to argue there were more pressing tasks, I was going to deal with Barbie first. She was going to tell me what it was that she didn't want to tell me. Once that was out of the way, I felt certain I could beg of her help in figuring out my quandary with the redhead and identifying whoever had hacked into my computer.

On my way to do that, I was going to deliver my news to Mr Reece Mefford.

"May I accompany you, madam?" asked Jermaine. He was coming back into my suite through the door to his adjoining cabin. No longer dressed in his butler's livery, his strong muscular body was now clad in a fine woollen suit in a pale cream colour. The waistcoat beneath it clashed violently in a blood-red crimson shade matched by a pocket square and a cravat around his neck. Upon his feet were a pair of spats, polished to such a shine on the toe cap that any drill sergeant on the planet would be proud to display them.

Conscious that the dear fellow spent far too much of his time tending to my needs in the suite, I was only too happy to have the flamboyantly dressed Jamaican at my side.

"That would be lovely, dear. Let's take the dogs with us too."

Just a few moments later, with my left hand hooked into the crook of his right elbow, and a dog leash in each of our free hands, we set off from my suite as if promenading. With Jermaine accompanying me I felt more confident in my hope to persuade Barbie to confess her secret. Even if that meant sending Jermaine in alone.

Wouldn't you know it? We didn't even get ten yards before my plans were changed for me.

16

SIGHTS ONE REMEMBERS FOREVER

From the recesses of my handbag a muffled voice echoed, "Secretary, secretary, secretary." My heart performed another double thump. How many times was that already today? It seemed like cardiac dysrhythmia wanted to be the flavour of the day.

The radio message continued. "This is Lieutenant Jessop. Crew cabin 652 deck six, out."

The message was like ice through my veins. I had no idea who stayed in cabin 652, but it was a member of the crew and that meant it could be someone I knew. Unable to articulate my thoughts, I looked up at Jermaine.

We had come to a halt in the middle of a passageway, the pair of us pausing to gather our thoughts.

In a quiet voice, I asked, "Do you know whose cabin that is?"

Jermaine's deep, rumbling bass replied, "No, madam."

It meant it was unlikely to be one of his close friends, but though there were enough crew that one could work on board for years and never meet some of them, they were still a tight-knit community. The loss would be felt by enough people that crew morale would be affected.

Jermaine did not need to confirm that our plans had changed, and we were no longer on our way to speak with Barbie. He knew well enough that I was going directly to cabin 652. I would not be the first one there, but my presence was absolutely necessary.

"Come along, sweetie," I remarked, giving Jermaine's arm a little tug. I didn't say much else because my brain was still reeling. How could it be that there was a third dead body? It wasn't even noon yet and the morgue was running out of space.

I was getting better at figuring out different locations on the ship, but it was such a vast thing, with so many cabins, and the numbering was not arranged in a sequence that would lend itself to tell a person whether a particular cabin was forward or aft, or port or starboard. Thankfully, unlike me, Jermaine had been forced to study and pass a test when he was taken on as crew - crew members were expected to not get lost and to be able to assist those passengers on board who happened to find themselves geographically embarrassed.

With his help I was able to find the cabin in question without a single wrong turn. As before, I knew that we were in the correct passageway when I saw a guard in white uniform standing like a sentry outside an open door.

The guard was Lieutenant Jessop, the man who raised the alarm. He saw us approaching, turning his head to say something to whoever was inside the cabin while we were still out of earshot.

In response, Lieutenant Pippin's head appeared around the doorframe.

"Mrs Fisher." He gave me a lopsided smile that I took to mean 'Not another one' or words to that effect.

When I removed my hand from Jermaine's elbow, he held it out to take Anna's lead from me. The dachshunds would need to wait in the passageway when I went inside, but they were acting strange as we grew close to the open door.

"Come along, ladies," chided Jermaine, his bass baritone voice accompanying his actions as he tugged the tiny dogs back to his feet.

They were persistent though, their tails ramrod straight and their hackles up as they strained against their collars to sniff the air. Both were pointing at the cabin, desperate to get inside.

"Is there food in there?" I asked Pippin, curious to know what might be getting the dogs so excited.

Pippin, half in and half out of the door, ducked his head back inside to check before reporting, "Not that I can see. There might be something discarded in the trash, but I don't smell anything."

They were curious little dogs sometimes.

"Patricia will not be long, sweeties," I cooed at them, bending to pat each on the head as they continued to stretch their noses toward the cabin. It would be nice if they could speak, but I suspected being able to hear my pets' voices would freak me out.

Since I had no way of getting them to let me know what they could smell ... I realised that perhaps I could, but to do so would require taking one or both into the cabin and we were not ready for that yet.

Leaving them behind, I took a pair of plastic gloves from a pouch in my handbag and followed Pippin through the door.

"What do we have?" I asked, my fists clenching as I prepared myself to see whatever terrible sight awaited me.

Lieutenant Commander Baker blocked my view momentarily, shifting to one side when he saw me coming. His movement revealed a pair of bare feet sticking out from the bedroom door.

"Well," he reached up to remove his hat and scratch his skull. "You might not believe this, but it's another dead member of the fitness team. His name is Sanjeev Bhaskar, aged twenty-eight. He's British according to his passport, but of Indian descent."

"He didn't turn up for work today," added Pippin. "Someone came looking for him."

"Murdered?" I assumed that was the case, but needed to have it confirmed. I was leaning to my left to peer around Baker. Not that I wanted to see the body, but ... morbid curiosity is just that.

Baker finished scratching his head and put his hat back on, adjusting it so it sat right before answering.

"Not sure, Mrs Fisher." To my raised eyebrows, he stepped out of the way and encouraged me to look for myself. My trepidation was diminishing; not obviously murdered had to mean the body was just a body, right? He wouldn't be missing his head or had multiple bloody knife wounds where someone had gone full psycho.

Wrong.

Expecting to see a man lying on the deck of the cabin, I was not prepared for the contorted, agonised mess I found. Feeling giddy, I backed away and turned around, finding a bulkhead to grasp as dancing lights threatened to shut off my consciousness.

Telling myself not to faint in front of the security officers, I did my best to straighten up again.

"What the heck happened to him?" I blurted.

Baker shrugged. "No clue."

Composing myself, I tried again, pushing off the wall to point my feet back toward the bedroom. This time, better prepared for what I had to look at, I was able to view the victim analytically.

His face was red, and his terrible bloodshot eyes were bulging from his skull. His tongue too as if it was attempting to escape his mouth.

"Was he poisoned?" I asked, leaning against the bulkhead with my head bowed until the sparkly lights went away.

Baker said, "Unknown, Mrs Fisher. There is no obvious sign of injury and nothing to indicate he was involved in a struggle. We moved him just enough to see if there was a wound on his back, but whatever killed him, it wasn't a gun or a knife. He wasn't strangled. So ... maybe poison."

"What else did you find?" I enquired.

Baker answered, "You got here less than a minute after we did, Mrs Fisher. We are yet to look around."

No further words needed to be exchanged. We were all wearing gloves, the three of us each turning to face a new direction as we split up to search the small cabin.

I was closest to the bedroom, but there was no chance I was going to step over the body. What if it moved? I knew escaping gasses inside a body could cause twitching and sometimes even what sounded like a dead person exhaling. If Sanjeev did that, I would probably have a cardiac event on the spot plus wet my knickers.

Seeing me perform a fast reverse and head to the smallest room, Baker accepted his fate. We spent the next few minutes going through the recently deceased man's belongings. Working methodically, checking all the drawers and hidey holes was a quick task for three people, but we found nothing untoward.

That is until the sound of approaching footsteps in the passageway outside drew me to glance that way.

"Has anyone looked in that suitcase yet?"

Pippin and Baker paused what they were doing to see what I was referring to.

By the door, a small suitcase, the kind you can use as carry-on baggage on flights, was positioned right next to the door. It was what you would do if you were planning to pick it up on your way out and that was odd.

I posed the question in my head, "Why would a member of crew be taking a suitcase anywhere?" If Sanjeev was going ashore today, which he might have been when he finished his shift, he would want his wallet, phone and ID.

"On the bed?" asked Pippin, crossing the room to pick up the luggage.

Lieutenant Schneider appeared in the doorway, filling it in both directions – it was his feet I could hear approaching.

"The sniffer dogs went around the storage room, but there was nothing for them to find," he reported. That was a relief, but curiously he added, "They went nuts over something though, really got the handlers pumped up because they thought they had found a bomb."

"But it wasn't a bomb?" Pippin checked, worry in his voice.

Schneider smiled at his young colleague. "No, Pippin, apparently the ship will not explode today. The dogs give signals to indicate when they have found different substances like drugs or cash or explosives and this was none of them."

"What was it?" asked Baker.

Schneider shrugged. "They couldn't find anything. The dogs were picking up the scent of something in the air. An animal was their best guess. The handlers' best guess, I mean, not the dogs."

"An animal?" I echoed Schneider's words. "Did they have any idea what it could have been. No, forget I asked," I countered my foolish question when I remembered Buddy had been running around inside the storeroom leaving his scent all over it no doubt.

Pippin picked up the suitcase, instantly announcing, "This thing is empty." He took it to the bedroom to check, nevertheless, tiptoeing around the body where it lay. Lieutenant Commander Baker instructed him to wait a moment before he put the case down, reaching for the sheets so that he could cover poor Sanjeev.

The bed was unmade or the covers had been pulled off when whatever happened to Sanjeev took place. From a bundle of untidy linen on the floor, Baker selected the one on top. I grabbed the other end to help Baker stretch it out, discovering that we had hold of the duvet cover which was more than sufficient to form a shroud over the lifeless form at our feet.

With a nod from his boss, Pippin placed the suitcase on the bed. Secured only by a zip, he had it open two seconds later, flipping the lid through one hundred and eighty degrees to prove his claim.

It was empty, but it meant nothing. The suitcase could have been by the door for any one of a thousand reasons.

Sanjeev had met with a terrible end, but if he had been murdered, the method of dispatch was not one with which I was familiar. I was going to have to wait for an autopsy report to learn what might have happened to him.

Upon thinking that very thought, a voice in the passageway speaking with Lieutenant Jessop turned out to be Dr David Davis the ship's senior physician.

"Mrs Fisher," he nodded his head in my direction as he breezed into the cabin. "Chaps." He gave the security officers a brief acknowledgement too.

Dr Davis had Baker and Pippin remove the duvet cover and knelt next to Sanjeev to do what needed to be done.

His arrival caused a pause in our activities, but I wasn't sure what else there was we could do anyway, not until the cause of death was determined. Given a moment of peace to think, I realised what was missing.

"Where's Deepa?" I asked. The other three officers were with me. "Where's Sam, for that matter?" I had sent him to find Lieutenant Commander Baker an hour ago. He was to fetch the crime scene kit so we could investigate the stowaway's belongings and perform a better inspection of the storage room. There might be fingerprints around the missing ventilation cover or even on the cover if we could find that.

Baker answered, "Deepa said she had something personal to which she needed to attend. I did not enquire what it was. She would not have mentioned it if it was not important. And Sam is still in the storage room to the best of my knowledge." Baker aimed his eyes at Schneider.

"He was there when I left," Schneider confirmed.

Baker said, "We were just getting started with the task of documenting what is in that storage room." By which he meant the treasure in the stowaway's knapsack and his other belongings. "I left Sam there to make sure nobody else messed with it." He wasn't going to ask if I agreed with his actions, but I could see in his eyes that he was seeking out confirmation that leaving Sam alone met with my approval.

"Jolly good," I replied. "Best if we don't leave him there for too long, eh?" Getting back to the task at hand, I looked down at Dr Davis.

I could not see the doctor's face, but it sounded as if he were sucking on the inside of his cheek.

"Most unusual," he remarked to himself. Falling silent again, he continued to inspect the body, checking his watch and taking poor Sanjeev's temperature. We watched, respectfully quiet until he rocked back onto his haunches and stood up. Catching his eye, I delivered his next line for him.

"You'll know more once you've performed an autopsy."

My comment got a smile from the good doctor who nodded his head in acknowledgement and said, "Precisely. I will get to it just as soon as I can, but I'm sure you're quite aware that I have a queue forming." He chuckled like he had delivered the punchline to a joke, sniggering until he saw our faces. "Yes, well. I'll be in the morgue."

I held up a hand to stop him exiting. I was blocking the doorway anyhow.

"Can you at least estimate time of death?"

Dr Davis fielded the answer easily. "Yes, Mrs Fisher. The current body temperature would indicate he died between nine and ten this morning."

It was several hours after Nicole and Vincent, who had died within an hour of each other. Did that mean anything? I filed it away for later examination.

With the doctor ready to leave, Lieutenant Commander Baker flipped the suitcase closed and zipped it secure.

"I'll have the body taken to the morgue once we've taken pictures and such," he stated. The team's forensic kit was getting a workout today and I made a mental note that we needed to scare up some budget for another one. Evidence from all three locations – Sanjeev's cabin, 1215, and the fitness centre on deck twelve – would all be taken to our operations room on deck ten. It was our dedicated space for collating and sifting evidence and thoughts.

I could see the room becoming quite full of evidence as we had three lives to inspect at an intimate level already. If the death rate continued at its current speed, we would need a bigger room.

Partially blocking the bedroom doorway and knowing that I was stopping the gentlemen inside the room from leaving, I gave myself a moment to think and to look around the cabin one last time. Three bodies discovered all within a few hours of one another. The deaths, too, had to all have occurred within a small window of time. If there was anything tangible I could use to link the three deaths, I would be harbouring the term 'murder spree' and wondering whether to use it publicly.

As it was, while Sanjeev's death was odd, I wasn't certain that it was a murder and there was nothing to connect Nicole or Vincent to him. Yes, Sanjeev was another member of the fitness community, and that required some exploration, but he wasn't involved in the heated fitness discussion that may or may not have been the cause of Nicole's murder.

Potentially, I had three separate murderers on the ship. Or they had committed their crimes and immediately disembarked, hoping to evade justice through the medium of distance. Were they crew members who would come back before the ship sailed? Were they stowaways like Vincent? If that were the case, even identifying them might prove impossible. We had some forensic evidence to go through, but truthfully, I was not feeling buoyed by hope.

Before Dr Davis, or anyone else felt it necessary to politely clear their throat, I accepted that there simply wasn't anything to be gained by lingering in Sanjeev's cabin. His body would be removed once sufficient photographs had been taken and the cabin would be dusted for prints and such. Otherwise, for the time being and since our resources were already stretched to maximum, the door would be locked, and the contents would remain untouched. If I needed to come back for a second look at something, I would find it just as it was now.

Leaving the cabin to find Jermaine patiently waiting for me, I accepted Anna's dog lead, hooked my left hand into his offered right elbow, and set off once more on our journey to the brig.

17

WHAT WAS IN THE GLASS TANK?

"**W**hat do you mean she isn't here?" I demanded, the volume and pitch of my voice rising as I stared at the door to the brig.

For rather obvious security purposes, the brig is kept completely secured much the same as any prison one might find anywhere in the world. We arrived at the outer door where I expected to announce my presence and be permitted entry.

Instead, the officer inside saw no reason to let me in because he had no prisoners.

"Miss Berkeley was released half an hour ago, Mrs Fisher. You should be more aware of your team's activities."

"What? What does that mean? Who let her out?" I almost yelled at the intercom, jabbing the annoyingly inhuman device with my index finger.

His answer came back instantly. "Lieutenant Bhukari."

I abandoned attempting to gain access to the brig, savagely yanking out my radio instead.

"Mrs Fisher for Lieutenant Bhukari," I spoke calmly and clearly, just like I was supposed to on the radio. Until I had to repeat myself for the third time that is. By then, having received no response, and probably due to the stress of Alistair, the redhead, whoever was hacking my computer, and all the other things chipping away at my sanity, I snapped. "Deepa, this is Patricia! Answer your radio!"

Baker answered. "Mrs Fisher, can you meet us at the operations room?"

He got a, "Roger. Out," voiced in a manner that was entirely unfair given that he had done nothing wrong. Trying hard to control my frustration, I took a deep breath and closed my eyes. The face of the gorgeous red head swam unbidden into my brain. She laughed in my face and put her arm around Alistair. Pain in my fingers caused my eyes to flutter open – I was strangling the radio, squeezing it so hard all my knuckles had turned white. My jaw hurt too from clenching.

"Is everything all right, madam?"

I had my back to Jermaine so he couldn't see the angry grimace ruling my features, but he hadn't missed my attempt to kill the communications device. The radio got dumped unceremoniously back into my handbag and I turned to face him.

Ignoring his question, I asked, "What is going on, Jermaine?" Not that I expected him to have an answer, but it felt good to voice my thoughts anyway.

Barbie was being ridiculously secretive about something, but it appeared that she felt content to share whatever it was with her good friend Deepa. Wasn't I her good friend too? Why wasn't I allowed to know the secret that was so important she was prepared to spend the day in a jail cell to protect it?

It was possible that Deepa was in a part of the ship where radio transmissions did not work, however every single deck was fitted with relay transmitters (not that I actually knew what one of them was) to ensure radio signals were bounced to all parts of the ship. Did that mean that Deepa was in on Barbie's secret? My paranoia assured me she was, but I still had no idea what it was they felt such a desperate need to keep from me.

Jermaine allowed me to remain silent, honestly it's one of his greatest skills. On this occasion, it wasn't really helping me, but just like Baker, he was not to blame for my mood.

We rode the elevator in silence to deck seven where we needed to switch over to one of the passenger elevators. Then we rode to deck ten. Jermaine reached for the button, however in an act of childish defiance, I pushed his hand to one side and pressed the number fifteen.

To answer Jermaine's unspoken question, and to apologise, I said, "Sorry, sweetie, I need to deliver some news to a gentleman in cabin 1589. If I don't do it now, I might forget to do it at all." I had said I would deliver the news to Mr Mefford, and I had not told Baker how long I would be in getting to him in the operations room. This would be a small detour, nothing more. Naturally, by the time the elevator spat me out on deck fifteen, the head of steam powering my decisions had diminished sufficiently for me to think straight again.

Employing my phone this time, though it was not the approved method of crew-to-crew communication, I phoned Lieutenant Baker. Over the radio waves, even though we were tuned to the security channel, there were plenty of crew who could hear our conversation and who would have heard my earlier, embarrassing outburst.

"Mrs Fisher?"

"Martin, was there something specific you need me to come to the operations room for? I remembered that I volunteered to deliver the news of the empty vivarium to the owner. I'm doing it now so I don't forget, but I will be with you momentarily."

"We have the interviewees from Nicole Tibbett's *discussion group*," he chose his words carefully, "to speak with, Mrs Fisher. Should I go ahead and get started?"

Of course, there were so many tasks for the team to perform. We would be busy in the wake of a single murder. With two and a probable third yet to be proven, we were three times as busy, and here I was holding things up.

"Please, yes, Martin." I used his first name as a sort of apology for my earlier terseness. "I will join you very soon," I promised yet again.

We were already in the passageway that would lead us to Mr

Mefford's cabin. I rapped my knuckles smartly twice on his door and stepped back to wait. The sound of a television being muted reached our ears. I hadn't realised I was even hearing it until it stopped. Moments later the door opened.

The man looking out at me was tall and thin, with a pasty white complexion beneath a prematurely thinning head of almost black hair. Reece Mefford was not a handsome man, yet all his features were in the right places and the correct proportions.

"Can I help you?" he inquired, getting the question in before I had a chance to introduce myself.

"Mr Mefford, my name is Patricia Fisher. I am the ship's detective." I had to raise my hand to quell his visible rising worry to say, "I am not here because you have done anything wrong," I assured him.

"So why are you here?" he begged to know, glancing back inside his cabin before choosing to step outside into the passageway. He pulled the door to behind him, making sure it didn't close but shutting off any view I might have to the inside.

"Mr Mefford, I apologise for the intrusion. During a routine inspection this morning," I lied because no one onboard needed to know about Vincent Pompeo, his death, or whatever he was up to, "your glass tank in storage room four was discovered to be …" my words trailed off because I was watching the colour drain from his face, "… empty." I concluded.

"Empty!" he blurted, shocked by my statement. He looked about ready to faint.

"Yes. I'm terribly sorry, sir. Can you tell me what was in it, please?"

His head, which had been bowed slightly, snapped up to meet my eyes. The look on his face could only be described as haunted.

"In it?" he stuttered.

"Yes," I nodded. "It looked like a vivarium," I proudly remembered the correct name for the habitat, "so if there are reptiles of some kind loose on the ship, we need to know about them."

"Especially if they are dangerous, sir," Jermaine added helpfully.

102

"Oh, um, they are my pet snakes, um ... Bertie and um ... Brian," Reece Mefford replied.

He had given me an answer and it was one which gave me the heebie jeebies. I would never wish ill on any of God's creatures, but why did he ever think to make snakes? I hated their little forked tongues, and their beady eyes, but most of all I hated that they had no limbs. How was a person supposed to grapple with a creature who cheated by having nothing to grab? It was the big ones that really freaked me out and keeping my mouth closed so I could be sure I wouldn't stutter, stammer, or just plain scream my next words, a memory surfaced of an article I once read about a man being eaten by an anaconda.

I had grabbed the glass tank earlier and almost pulled it on top of myself. What if I had succeeded? What if the snakes had landed on me? Okay, they had already escaped by that point, but what if they had been mere feet away from where I was standing?

"What species of snake are they, sir?" Jermaine enquired, while I ran around screaming in terror inside my head.

"Boa Constrictors," he replied, this time sounding more certain of the answer he gave.

"That's a big one, isn't it?" I gibbered, terror handing the steering wheel over to my mouth for a half second before snatching it back again when he nodded.

"Yes, very big. These are both adults. It's really quite important that I find them. My wife will be ever so upset if I return home without them."

Now that I knew what kind of snake it was, the horror of being squeezed to death filled my head and made my legs weak. When I said nothing, my brain now in freefall as I pictured the giant snakes landing on me, their heads inches from mine as their little forked tongues poked out, Jermaine took over.

"Sir, the crew will be tasked with looking out for the missing reptiles, but as I am sure you can understand, the vastness of the structure will make them difficult to find. Do you have something you could use to lure them out? Will they gravitate towards a source of warmth?"

Reece was muttering his horror at our news on loop. "I can't believe this. I can't believe this. This cannot be happening. What am I going to do?"

I was no lover of snakes … okay they completely freak me out, but I got the attachment a person forms with a pet. If someone threatened Anna or Georgie, I could not be sure how I would react. His concern drew me from my personal nightmare and back to reality.

"Can you hazard a guess at how they got free, sir?" I could guess, my question was just to fill in a blank space while I got my brain up to speed. The snakes had almost certainly got free when Vincent Pompeo or one of his fellow criminals disturbed them. I remembered the lid for the tank was set to the side; it must have been knocked off when Vincent took whatever it was he broke into the storage room to get.

Going through the manifest for the storage room was yet another task on my team's list of many things to do, though I felt certain it would actually fall to someone else. Whose job was it to manage what went into and came out of the stores? The bursar? I didn't know, but Baker would.

"Get free?" Reece questioned. "They can't do it by themselves. The lid has locks on it. They ate before we set sail and would happily travel all the way home without needing anything other than a little water which is already in their habitat. It's a temperature and humidity-controlled environment. I'm not sure how long they will survive outside of it."

He was sagging against the wall and not only pale, but also looking a little sick.

"Perhaps we should get you back inside your cabin, sir," Jermaine suggested, reaching around Mr Mefford to push the door inward.

"I'm fine," Reece insisted. "It was just a shock is all. I must get them back. At any cost. Is there anyone I can talk to about helping me to look for them?" Reece asked.

The wobble had left my legs, the blotchy vision receding with it.

Regaining my composure, I felt able to re-engage in the conversation.

"Mr Mefford I will see to it that the crew are all looking for your … pets and any sightings are reported to me. You will be notified as soon as there is any development, and I will personally ensure you get a report each day whether there have been any sightings or not. Where is your final destination?" I asked.

"Miami," he supplied before posing a question he wanted to ask. "I won't be able to look for them myself?" His desire to be involved in the round up came as no surprise.

"The area they went missing in isn't one where it would be safe to have passengers wandering." Seeing his crestfallen face, I had to offer him a ray of hope. "What I will do is enquire about getting an escorted visit. The captain will want them found almost as much as you, I am sure."

He looked a little relieved, but the colour had not returned to his face. Would I look the same if one of my girls went missing? I glanced down at Anna and Georgie, getting a tail wag from each of them when they noticed me looking their way.

Reece begged, "Please don't delay. I really must find them."

I promised once again to do my utmost and left him to worry as we withdrew. By the time we reached the bank of elevators, Mr Mefford and his snakes were already out of my mind – I had too many other things to consider. I felt sorry for him, but my effort to find the snakes would be all about the safety of the ship and the crew, rather than concern about what his wife might say.

My skull itched and I froze to the spot.

"Madam?"

I didn't respond to Jermaine other than to raise an index finger to beg that he give me a moment. There had been something in my head, a fleeting thought that was gone the moment I tried to focus on it. Had I missed something? Was it to do with Reece Mefford?

I tried to focus my brain, but the answer wouldn't come. After ten seconds of staring into nothingness, I gave up and started moving again.

We needed to get to the operations room.

18

DISGUISE

Xavier Silvestre settled into his cabin without a second thought for the cramped nature of the lower deck accommodation he insisted his valet book. He could easily have afforded the finest suite on the ship, but that was not the role he was choosing to play. Anonymity was what he sought most of all.

For his disguise, he had chosen an outfit that would fit in with the brash nature of those around him – loud board shorts and a gaudy t-shirt. A blonde wig and moustache distorted his features enough that no one would ever recognise him, but he knew well enough to add something that people would remember. In the past it had been a hook in place of his hand or a patch over his eye. Today it was a jagged, red scar that cut across his left cheek. He'd already seen several people look away suddenly when he glanced their way – a sure sign they had been staring at it.

It would be all they remembered and were they to ever be in his presence again, they would have no idea it was not the first time because the scar would be gone. A man with a weak ego might have congratulated himself on his brilliance, but for Silvestre the thought never crossed his mind. His thoughts were singular in purpose –

finding the treasure horde from the San José's hold. Nothing else mattered.

The restricted nature of his accommodation was just another part of the disguise. People might notice the rich man staying in the expensive suite, but no one would see the little man travelling alone in a low-level cabin.

How long he would have to be onboard and what he would have to do was going to come down entirely to what information he could extract from Patricia Fisher. Whatever she knew he would soon know and if he thought the information too sensitive, he would remove her from the playing board.

Leaving his cabin, his disguise firmly in place, he set off to find her.

19

ELEPHANT IN THE ROOM

Coming through the door to the operations room, I was surprised to find that none of the fitness ladies or dancers were inside being interviewed. More surprising though was the presence of Lieutenant Bhukari and Barbie.

Forcibly quelling my desire to jump straight into the subject of what the heckity heck was going on with my blonde friend, I asked about the suspects in the Nicole Tibbett murder case.

"They appear to all be innocent," Lieutenant Commander Baker replied. "Of the twelve - Barbie is already being discounted," I flicked my eyes in her direction, but did not comment, "eleven have alibis and were shocked by the news that their banter might have resulted in Nicole's death."

I needed to ask him which one didn't have an alibi and get him to talk me through their statements. Honestly though, I was finding it hard to concentrate because there was a massive elephant in the room and all eyes were looking at me. Martin had stopped speaking and no one else was saying anything. Wondering what was going on, I looked at Barbie, raising my eyebrows to encourage her to say something.

She obliged, but expecting her to start confessing to why she felt the need to keep a secret from me, what she said threw me for a loop.

"We want you to know that we are all here for you, Patty."

I blinked a couple of times and glanced around at the people in the room. Every set of eyes offered me sympathy.

"What's going on?" I frowned as I posed the question.

Barbie looked at Deepa, who said, "You have to tell her, Barbie."

"Tell me what?" I demanded to know, getting impatient and feeling my annoyance level rising because I was in the dark about whatever it was that everyone else knew.

When I flared my eyes at her, Barbie started talking. I immediately wished she hadn't.

"I didn't give you an alibi for where I was last night because I was following the captain."

I got that heart double thump thing again.

"Following him where?" I posed the obvious question and looked around for a chair. My feet felt disconnected from my body and the thought of sitting down now sounded like a jolly good idea. Jermaine saw what I was doing, moving faster than me to manoeuvre one of the office chairs in behind me. He remained close by my side for what I assumed was going to be news I wouldn't like.

Barbie waited until I was in the chair before continuing.

"I finally figured out who the redhead is. It took me a while because her hair is dyed black for her passport photograph and I had to go through hundreds of pictures, cross referencing each one and digging into their social media profiles and such. Her name is Hennessey Gates."

"And?" I begged her to get to whatever it was she had so desperately kept secret. A feeling of weakness was gripping me, making me feel sick as worry crept through my body.

"Look, Patty, I don't know anything yet, okay? Nothing is proven."

"Just spit it out, Barbie. Please." I couldn't keep my head up, the impending news making my ears ring as blood hammered through my head. Why was my heart beating so fast? "Where did you follow him to?"

I heard Barbie shift her feet, the task of delivering bad news making her uncomfortable too.

"He went to a cabin on deck eight, Patty. It's the redhead's cabin."

I gasped a breath, fighting against a crushing sense of dread, and managed to murmur one question.

"Did he go inside?"

Barbie made a huffing noise, crossing the room to kneel on the deck by my feet a moment later. She took my hands in hers.

"He was inside for thirty-two minutes, Patty. It doesn't mean he is sleeping with her."

I felt my head nodding and some words left my mouth.

"Yes, it does."

Silence ruled for a moment, no one in the room able to find a thing to say. Any second now they were all going to start talking about how sorry they were and condemning Alistair for how he had treated me. I didn't need to hear it. Part of me felt like I had just skipped back in time to the day I caught my ex-husband, Charlie, in bed with my best friend. The sense of betrayal, the confusion and uncontrollable rush of emotions that went with it were what caused me to run away.

I ran away to sea. All the way to Aurelia. On reflection, Charlie cheating on me had been the best thing that could have ever happened. Stuck in a humdrum day-to-day existence that gave me no purpose and brought me no satisfaction, I might have gone to my grave without ever discovering the bigger world waiting for me outside of my unfulfilling marriage.

With a snap of fresh attitude, I stood up. It startled Barbie who had to jump back to get out of my way. Baker, Schneider and all the others were looking at me with surprised expressions – this was not the reaction they expected.

My heart felt like a piece of lead hanging heavy in my chest, but I wasn't going to cry over a man. There would be a conversation between Alistair and me later. It would be at a time and place of my choosing, and when it was done, I would move on. I was not to blame for his infidelity – I repeated that in my head a few times and knew I would have to repeat it many more even though I believed it to be true.

In the desirability stakes, the redhead had me beaten hands down, but Alistair and I were not children, and he had no right nor reason to act as he had. Sneaking out to meet his needs in the middle of the night? He deserved nothing more than my contempt and he was going to get it.

Fixing my eyes on the far wall beyond the faces watching me, I read from a white board covered in notes.

"You said none of the fitness suspects from Nicole's group chat looked good for her murder," I reminded the people in the room of Baker's words. "Tell me more about them, please."

Barbie had dropped her grip on my hands when I stood up, but was still blocking my route to the white board. She started talking again when I ducked around her to get a better look at what was written.

"Patty, are you okay? Don't you want to …"

"No," I stated firmly. "I do not. Let's focus on the case." I had crossed the room, passing between my friends to reach the white-board. Now they were all behind me, I turned around to look at them. "We have killers to catch and cases to solve. Everyone has failed relationships," I tried a smile that had nothing but my will behind it. "I see no reason to waste time talking about mine and nothing to be gained from doing so." I clapped my hands together, acting enthusiastic even if I didn't feel it. "Come on, people."

The security officers, Barbie, and Jermaine exchanged glances and I thought someone was going to feel it necessary to raise an argument. They didn't though; they bit their tongues and shuffled across the operations room to join me.

Even Anna and Georgie came to see why all the humans were gathered in one place. At any other time, I probably would have scooped them or bent to give them a pat, hugging them to my chest for comfort. However, despite my determination, I was on the cusp of dissolving and needed to avoid anything that might tip me over the edge.

There were four names on the whiteboard.

"Run me through these," I requested, pointing to the bottom one because it was written in different handwriting. "Someone mentioned Andrea Bassinet-Blatch earlier, didn't they?"

Martin Baker answered first. "Yes, but I only interviewed her because she was involved in the conversation. We would have interviewed Barbie too for the same reason."

Barbie added her opinion. "I put her name up there because she's not very nice." We all looked her way. "Well, she's not," Barbie defended herself. "In most circles, she would be referred to as a word beginning with a 'B'."

We all knew what she meant.

"She has an alibi for the time though, yes?" asked Schneider, going on to say, "Sorry, I missed all this. I was dealing with the storage room."

"Is Sam still down there?" I asked, my tone making it obvious that anyone saying 'yes' was giving me the wrong answer.

Martin's cheeks coloured, so too Schneider's when I looked his way.

"I'll go," Schneider volunteered.

I touched his arm to stop him before he could turn to leave.

"We'll all go in a moment. He's waited this long; he'll be fine to wait a few more minutes." Turning back to the whiteboard, I prompted an answer. "Her alibi."

"She was in bed with someone."

"She has a boyfriend. I know that much," Barbie supplied helpfully

Baker continued, "We just need to follow that up to confirm his account of events correlates with hers, but she was on Nicole's side in the discussion. Andrea supported Nicole's statements."

"Really?" Barbie made it clear that didn't sound right to her.

Martin twisted to get a sheaf of paper from his desk. "Here, read for yourself."

Now confused, I said, "I thought you were involved in the argument?"

With her eyes never leaving the page, Barbie continued to scan the words when she replied, "I was, but I left to visit Hideki before Andrea joined in." She was frowning enough that I had to press her for more information. "This isn't the Andrea I know. Most of the crew call her Andrea Bassinet-Bitch."

"That's true," agreed Deepa. "She has her little circle of friends and anyone outside of that clique knows to stay away."

Martin sat back onto the corner of a desk. "Anyway, I was convinced enough to let her go. She's confined to the ship along with all the others until I say otherwise."

"How did that go down?" asked Barbie.

"Not well. Miss Grimm went nuts when I broke the news to her."

I knew enough about the ballet troop leader to be unsurprised by the news. French, fiery, and in her fifties though she told everyone she was thirty-nine, Miss Grimm was well known for her persistent need to screech her opinion at people. She was right (regardless of the subject), and everyone was entitled to know it.

I asked, "Does she have an alibi too?"

It turned out that she did not, but Baker and the others could find no plausible motive for her to kill Nicole. The Frenchwoman voiced her opinion in her usual brusque manner, dismissing the other women out of hand because they could not possibly be right. She and all her dancers were the epitome of female form and elegance, not overly muscular as she claimed most of the fitness girls were, and twice as supple and flexible as those practicing any other discipline.

Apart from Barbie's, there were no direct threats to Nicole's life though reading through the printed pages of email when Barbie handed them to me, there was no question Andrea had been on Nicole's side.

"Were they friends?" I asked Barbie.

"Not that I know of." She looked at Deepa, frowning. "Didn't they have …"

Deepa didn't know what Barbie was trying to say.

Barbie's frown was threatening to put permanent creases in her forehead. "There's something. I'm sure of it. Might have been a boy they both wanted, or both slept with. I'll have to ask someone."

My request that she do that as soon as possible, but quietly so Andrea wouldn't know we were snooping, acted as a catalyst for our meeting to break up. Sam was still down in the storage room with the albino's belongings and had been alone for an hour now. I felt sure he was fine, but that didn't mean I wanted to leave him down there any longer than he already had been.

Was Andrea a good fit for the crime? I was getting no feel for it either way, but would seek her out myself shortly. Later today there would be a bucket of gin to numb my senses. Until then, I was going to distract myself by solving the strange cases. Heading for the door, with everyone moving in the same direction, Martin continued to outline what information he'd gotten from interviewing the fitness ladies. I had to agree that none of them looked like a good fit for Nicole's death, yet someone had killed her.

Stepping through the door, I asked, "Anything back from the bursary yet?"

THE CONTENTS OF STORAGE
ROOM FOUR

The news was both good and bad. The bursar himself had gone through the vault – presumably with a team of helpers - and had confirmed nothing was missing. Either Vincent and friends were never heading there, or they were unable to get inside. I suspected the former over the latter.

However, the disappointing news was that there was no report about storage room four. Just like with the vault, they were tasked with determining if anything was missing, a task that was going to take several hours if it was to be done properly. Vincent Pompeo had to have a good reason to break in there, if indeed I was right about it being his destination.

Using my radio, I attempted to raise Commander Philips while Lieutenant Commander Baker contacted the Bursary.

"Mrs Fisher," the head of engineering addressed me in a dry tone, which to my mind made it clear how disappointed he was to hear from me.

I did not rise to his bait. "Commander Philips we are continuing with our investigation. Following up on the break in to the effluent conduit, has your extended search revealed anything to indicate where they were going?" Alistair had been clear the search needed to continue.

I got a bored sigh from the man.

"I reported to the captain on this matter, Mrs Fisher."

"I'm sure you did, Commander Philips. However, I am the one heading up the investigation and I'm quite certain you do not want me bothering the captain with trivia when you can give me a direct answer now." The need to constantly spar with each other frustrated me and I made a mental note there and then to see if he and I could find some middle ground where we were able to operate harmoniously.

"No, Mrs Fisher, there is no sign that anyone has been tampering with anything, anywhere in the engineering areas. Is there anything else or can I get back to my job now?"

Goodness me, he could be most tiresome when he wanted to.

Engaging my most effervescent tone, I thanked him for being a dear and ended the conversation. I did so just as Baker finished his.

"The bursar sent representatives down to the storage room to conduct the inventory check but apparently Sam isn't letting them in. It would seem we were seconds from the bursar calling us to complain."

A small chuckle shook my shoulders. I didn't feel like laughing, but the image of Sam denying entry to anyone who wasn't a part of his team tickled me.

With a fast pace, we set off toward the nearest bank of elevators. Jermaine was returning to my suite with the dachshunds and Barbie was going in search of answers. We would take the first car, heading down as they waited for the next one to take them up.

Forming a gaggle in the passageway, we had to move to the sides to let a passenger pass between us. He was looking my way, his eyes, framed by blonde hair and a blonde moustache burning deeply into mine for a second. I opened my mouth to say hello, intending to check that he wasn't in need of assistance with anything, but he looked away before I could speak.

The elevator pinged its arrival and when I looked again, the man was gone.

The two members of crew from the bursary were looking bored and annoyed when we found them standing in the passageway outside the storage room.

The door was shut, Sam having locked them out.

"Ensign Chalk," Baker called out, rapping his knuckles on the door before opening it using his universal keycard.

"Sir," Sam saluted proudly. "Sir, there were intruders attempting to infiltrate the crime scene."

"Well done, Ensign Chalk." Baker took him to one side to explain what was happening.

Behind us, muttering under their breath, the two crew members, both ladies in their thirties, made their way into the storage room.

"Patricia Fisher," I introduced myself, offering my hand. "Thank you for this. If you've not already been informed, there was a murder earlier today."

"Yes, Mrs Fisher, the bursar had us all stop work earlier so he could tell us about Nicole Tibbett. I'm Sangita Parvati, by the way. This is Heike Dietrich," she indicated her colleague who dipped her head in my direction.

I gave a slight shake of my head and tried again.

"No, I'm sorry to have to inform you that there was another murder. This time it was a passenger and I believe he was on board to commit a crime. I'm fairly sure he broke into this storage room." I twisted to indicate the hole in the back wall where the ventilation cover was still missing. "However, I do not know why. That is why you've been sent to conduct an audit of everything in this room." I looked about, taking in the size of the room and the diversity of everything that was in it. I wanted to put a positive spin on the task they'd been given, but I could not see a way to do so honestly. "Sorry, I guess that's going to take a while."

Sangita and Heike were also looking around the storage room, their eyes flaring at the enormity of the task.

"We might need reinforcements," muttered Heike. "Are there any obvious spaces on any of the shelves? Someone taking something might have left a patch behind where there is no dust."

She was thinking clearly, but we had already conducted our own search. I told her that and wished them luck. Sam, Baker, and everyone else were gathered at the portside bulkhead where I knew we would find the albino's possessions including his knapsack full of treasure.

The process of cataloguing everything in it was high on our list of tasks and had been started and then abandoned when today's third body was discovered. About to join my team, I spotted the glass tank which had once contained the pair of adult boa constrictors. I hadn't noticed it earlier, but marked on the shelf where the tank had been placed was an alphanumeric code: H7.

I glanced along the shelf. A few feet away, the next location was marked as H8, and I realised what I was looking at.

"Are the contents of the room listed by location?" I posed the question to Sangita and Heike, pointing my index finger at the shelf.

"Yes, those are to make it easy to find things," Heike explained. "Otherwise, things would go in here and might never be found again."

I got why passengers would need such a service. Most of the cabins were small – big enough to live in comfortably for a few weeks or even months, but if they were travelling from A to B rather than A back to A, and were taking something with them that they intended to use or drop off at B, then they would not want it cluttering up their already cramped accommodation. Reece Mefford was a prime example. If the large glass tank were to be placed inside his cabin, not that it would fit through the door, he would have no space left to live.

Tapping the glass tank with a knuckle so it made a dong, dong, dong noise, I told them. "This is supposed to contain two Boa Constrictors."

Heike's eyes widened at the news, her gaze flicking to the lid which was still sitting on the shelf next to the tank and then to the empty tank itself.

She did not like that the snakes were on the loose. "Where are they now?"

"Not in it," I replied, hoping we might skip the conversation forward. "It was empty when we came in and I wondered if that was because the person who broke in here knocked the lid off in getting whatever he was after."

"Maybe he took the snakes?" suggested Sangita brightly, thinking she had an answer to my quandary.

Heike screwed up her face. "Why would anyone take a pair of snakes?" She faced her friend. "What's the street value of a snake, 'Gita? Is that something thieves steal regularly?"

"Well, someone might have," Sangita argued weakly. "Maybe they really like snakes."

Breaking it up before they could go down a rabbit hole, I said, "The thief was after something of value. We just need to figure out what it is." Flashes were popping to my left, Pippin wielding the camera as the team started to examine the albino's possessions. I wanted to get involved in that, not drag out my day with the ladies from the bursary.

They had caught the short straw this time and had an unfortunate and laborious task to perform. My only reason to still be talking to them was because I wondered if we might be able to shortcut the problem and find an answer quickly.

"So, ladies, the table of belongings lists what is in this storage room and where they are all placed. Can you tell me what was in the immediate vicinity of the glass tank in location H7?"

Neither said anything as they consulted the tablets they each held. Heike crossed to stand in front of the shelves, eyeing the area suspiciously in case one of the snakes chose to pop out to say hello.

There were spaces above and below, left and right at various intervals on the shelf. My belief was that Vincent climbed up to get to what he wanted, probably taking something from one of the shelves above the vivarium and then knocked the lid off climbing back down.

Too interested in what he held, he might not even have noticed that the two snakes were now free, but I had my mental fingers crossed that serendipity was on our side. If I were not so clumsy, I would not have fallen and grabbed the tank, and we might have no starting point for our search. Was one of the ladies about to shout, "Eureka!"?

"Here's something?" announced Sangita, getting my hopes up only to dash them a moment later when she said, "No, sorry. It was a box of Rolex watches, some vintage, but the passenger checked them out this morning when he disembarked the ship."

To my left, my team of security officers were deep in conversation about the treasure Sam found and I was missing whatever it was they were saying.

Another minute dragged by before Sangita and Heike agreed there was nothing obviously missing from the shelf locations around the glass tank.

I blew out a hard breath. "Then sorry, ladies. It looks like the long haul to figure out what they stole. Can you give it your best shot? Someone went to a lot of trouble to break in here and then their partner or partners killed them so they wouldn't have to share it. Figuring out what it was that they took might go a long way to catching the people behind it."

They didn't look enthralled at the prospect, but they promised to do their best and let me know if they found anything missing.

Finally joining my team, I discovered they were finished and packing up.

"We've dusted the area and lifted some prints," said Baker as Schneider and Pippin began loading the knapsack and sleeping bag into plastic bags, "and taken a stack of photographs. There's nothing more we can achieve here."

I asked, "Where are you going to examine all this?"

"In the operations room, unless you have another suggestion."

There was more room in my suite and going there would allow us to spread it all out. Did I really want a dead man's things and all that treasure in my accommodation though? I decided it didn't have to be for very long and I did have empty bedrooms in the suite that never got used.

Baker and everyone else loved my suggestion so that was where the treasure was heading. The last few items – the albino's empty food cans and litter - were being carefully placed into yet another plastic sack. I didn't think that one needed to come to my suite – it could be examined more closely in the operations room if anyone thought it necessary. The rest of it was divided up between the team, all six of us wishing Sangita and Heike good luck as we headed for the door.

It was just after noon and my stomach was starting to rumble. Eating something appealed as did taking my foot off the gas for half an hour as I felt like I had been running since I had breakfast this morning.

There were phone calls to make, though I needed to check if the next of kin had already been informed in the case of all three victims. The captain bore that task and would never consider delegating it. I suspected he would have made the calls within an hour of Sanjeev and Nicole's deaths being discovered, but I wasn't going to call him to find out.

A wave of nausea passed through me again when I thought of Alistair. I pushed it down, refocusing my thoughts on the terrible images of the victims instead. The tactic worked, my sense of balance returning. I would have to address the Alistair issue at some point, but now was not the time.

I could sense that Barbie wanted to talk to me about it, to be there for me much as I would if her relationship with Hideki went abruptly sideways. Maybe I would force myself to face the horror of it tonight when things were quiet, but for now, I was just going to pretend it wasn't happening.

That didn't mean I was going to call Alistair to ask about the next of kin though.

Two dead crew members and one man who was essentially a stowaway having faked his departure from the ship so he could stay on board to rob something. My skull itched.

Vincent's accomplice had to be a member of the crew, right? I ran the idea through my head. It made sense from all angles. Did that mean he was connected to Sanjeev or to Nicole? I couldn't see how he would be – there was nothing to indicate Vincent had ever met the other two and they were vastly different ages. Apart from the tenuous link that Sanjeev and Nicole were both in the fitness industry, there was nothing to connect them at all.

Why was I even thinking about Sanjeev anyway? He was dead,

and his death was mysterious, but there was no obvious sign of foul play. Something about it was sticking in my head though. Maybe it was just the timing of it … so soon after we found Nicole and Vincent. What was the likelihood of three deaths occurring on the same day in such a small population?

My radio squawked.

"Engineering to the ship's detective. Engineering to the ship's detective. We have a Buddy sighting on deck three near the portside generator bank. How do you want us to proceed?"

I was still fumbling for my radio when Commander Philips answered.

"If you get the chance, kill it before it eats through something vital or widdles into a circuit board."

The elevator pinged and the doors swished open, spilling six of us onto the top deck. I got the radio to my mouth, growling out my words.

"Belay that order. No one is to attempt to harm the primate. If you are able to, please corral him into a safe area like a room with only one door and then shut it."

"This is Commander Philips. Pay no attention to what *that* woman has to say. She holds no rank and cannot give orders. Do as I command, or I will make you personally responsible for the repairs."

My cheeks were burning, and my rage, fuelled by the Alistair situation, took me directly from melancholy to murderous in a heartbeat. I was going to tell Commander Philips exactly what I thought of him and everyone with a radio was going to hear it.

Except they didn't.

The one voice that could stay my hand echoed over the airwaves to cut through my soul and steal my voice away like a thief in the night.

"This is the captain speaking. Commander Philips report to the bridge." It was all he needed to say. On me, the effect of hearing his voice was sufficient to make me wilt. Instantly I yearned to know the truth. Had he really cheated on me? On Commander Philips, the effect was a little different.

He said, "Roger. Out." The two words were delivered in such a tone that they left no doubt the two men were heading for a battle that was long overdue. I was the cause of the fight, that much I knew, but Alistair held the trump card, and the head of engineering must have known he was throwing himself on the sword.

He would be left with two choices: admit his wrongdoing and apologise, or stick to his principles and resign from his post. I expected it to be the latter and I hated that it was all to do with me. Right now, I also hated that Alistair was rising to defend me. He could have let Commander Philips and me duke it out, but he chose to step in. Did he feel some responsibility toward me still?

Catching myself in the act of wishing for things that couldn't happen, I could no more undo Alistair's infidelity than I could Charlie's, I lifted the radio to my mouth once more.

"Mrs Fisher to Engineering. If you are able to secure Buddy, please do. Please contact me whatever happens."

We were almost at my suite when I spotted something. It was the man with the blonde hair and moustache – the one who was by the elevators downstairs earlier. I had caught only a fleeting glance this time, but I felt sure it was the same man.

He was gone already and paused in the passageway outside of my suite, I questioned whether I was jumping at shadows. Seeing the same person twice in a short space of time onboard a cruise ship was not a big deal. It was one of those coincidence things. With ten thousand people on the ship, a person could search forever and not find the one person they wanted, but would run into someone else two dozen times.

"Mrs Fisher?"

"Hmmm?" I twitched my eyes toward the voice to find my team queuing at the door to my suite - they were waiting for me to let them in.

I didn't have to, of course, because Jermaine got there first. They hustled through the door, weighed down with plastic sacks filled with the final possessions of a dead man. Would they yield a clue as to his identity?

I was about to find out.

21

NECESSARY MURDERS

Though he felt like slamming the cabin door, Xavier Silvestre closed it gently and leaned against it. Taking a breath and holding it, he centred himself, focusing on calm thoughts and positivity.

His best-case scenario had been to find Patricia Fisher and strike up a congenial conversation. One idea in his head was to act like a starstruck fan. Her name had been in the paper enough that the appearance of an admirer ought not to shock her. She was the one who leaked the news of her discovery – seeking more fame and notoriety, Silvestre assumed, and thus was inviting people to pay attention.

He would ask her about it, carefully asking where it had come from and what had become of the man they found in the hold? He was an albino, wasn't he? There were questions he could ask and if that tactic didn't yield the result he wanted, he would lure her somewhere private. Once out of sight, he would knock her out and when she came around to find herself incapacitated, he would cut off a couple of toes or fingers just to get her attention. He knew from experience she would tell him everything he wanted to know.

The latter alternative was less desirable simply because it would attract attention. Even if he made her vanish, tossing her body over-board if he could, questions would be asked.

It was all moot so far though because the woman moved with a phalanx of guards around her. Five security officers, four of which were armed, who needs that much protection?

He had no desire to sail with the ship when it left tonight though he was quite prepared to do so. The Aurelia was to be at sea for the next two days, setting off across the Atlantic with only a stop off at the British Union Isles, a small collection of islands fifty miles due south of the Ascension Islands, planned before they found land again in Rio de Janeiro.

Rio had been Finn Murphy's destination, that was how Carlos Ramirez had known to seek out Professor Noriega. Murphy clearly knew what he had found and was bright enough to tell no one. Only in death had he revealed where he was going – to one of the world's leading experts on maritime disasters and a San José fanatic.

Silvestre regretted that the professor's death was necessary; there just wasn't any way to convince the man to keep the discovery secret. Ramirez knew enough to take the one artefact he recovered from Murphy to Noriega, hoping it would have worth beyond the value of the gold it was made from. It did, but Ramirez would never have seen it – finding treasure doesn't work like that. Had he just melted it down, he would still be alive and walking around with a fat wallet to boot. Instead, he left the ship, flew to Brazil and in so doing got three men killed.

Silvestre had no time for remorse – it was a child's emotion. The deaths were necessary to secure the secret as he pursued the trail. Now he had to figure out how to get Patricia Fisher alone. Being careful was necessary, however, he'd found her suite and planned to return later when she was asleep.

It meant he was going to have to sail with the ship and that would trap him on board until they reached the British Union Isles. It was less than ideal, but if the uncut gems were still onboard, he needed to recover them. It wasn't greed driving him to snatch the uncut gems Patricia Fisher's news article talked about, it was the desire for confirmation.

A geologist would be able to determine where on the planet the gems had come from, down to within a few miles probably. Rubies and diamonds were only found in certain places, their atomic composition sufficient to tell a geologist from which place they had come. For Silvestre, this was to be further confirmation that the San José had been found. The cross Carlos Ramirez took to the museum in Rio de Janeiro might have been enough for most people, but he needed to be certain.

The gems were still on the ship, he felt certain of that, and suspected Finn Murphy's body might be too. Not that he had any purpose for the dead Irishman - he was way past revealing any of the secrets he held, but a copy of the autopsy report might yield something and for that he was going to need to get into the crew area.

Patricia Fisher could wait – she wasn't going anywhere. If he couldn't get into her suite tonight, he would study her movements and pick a better time to approach her. Today's attempts had been clumsy, but he had not anticipated how many members of security she would have with her. He would do better next time.

She had seen him, he felt certain of that and given what she had achieved in taking down the Alliance of Families, he had to consider that she was smart and aware. He had other disguises with him, but changing his outfit now ran the risk of someone questioning the starkly different appearance.

He resolved to remain as he was, rethinking his strategy to include the assumption that she would spot him more easily now because she had seen him before.

Patricia Fisher was for later. Right now, he was going to see how difficult it might be to get below the passenger decks and into the crew area. What he really needed was a uniform his size.

22

FINN AND HIS FORTUNE

Jermaine prepared a lunch for us all, whipping up fillets of Argentinian seabass served with a passionfruit salad while my team laid out the albino's possessions in one of my spare bedrooms. We took the shortest of short breaks to devour the wonderful dish – the scent of it cooking made us all ravenous – then hurried back to the task that consumed our interest.

The knapsack, into which the spilled gold coins and bejewelled trinkets had been restuffed, was carefully emptied.

"I have a passport," announced Lieutenant Schneider, holding aloft a document that was as tatty-looking as its owner had been. "It was buried in a pocket. Hmm, Irish," he remarked, flicking the pages to find the piece of information we all needed. "Finn Murphy, no middle name."

Finally, we had a name for the stowaway. I was going to ask someone to look him up, but Baker was already on it.

"He was never a passenger. Unless he boarded using a different passport, which seems unlikely, he was able to sneak onto the ship somewhere. Goodness knows how long he was onboard for."

"We have a name," I remarked. "That means we can notify his

next of kin and maybe track his movements backwards. It's more than we had a minute ago."

"Keep looking?" asked Schneider.

Without comment, we all went back to what we were doing. Though I had looked at one of the coins earlier, I had not memorised the markings on it. I crouched, placing my right knee on the carpet to select one.

Deepa was counting them and making piles. Schneider was going through the knapsack to check all the little pockets and cubby holes while Pippin filmed the whole thing on his phone. They felt it was important to document as much of what we were doing as possible.

So far, no one but the six of us plus Marco the climber, knew about the treasure. I wanted to keep it that way and no one was arguing. Baker and the rest of them were well aware of the trouble their colleagues manning the quayside were having today with treasure hunters trying to get onto the ship.

Tossing the coin into the air and catching it again, I announced my intention to investigate the coin, its origins, and worth.

It looked a lot like a modern coin in that it was stamped on both sides, had a minting clearly displayed – 1708 – and when compared to the other coins in the pile was fairly uniform in shape, weight, and thickness. Where it differed was that the coin in my hand was undeniably made from pure gold.

I copied the markings into the search bar on my computer, getting a hit in the time it took to blink my eyes. I was looking at a Felipe VI Segovia Spanish Gold Eight Escudos. That single piece of information was useful, but my brain all but shut down when my eyes caught sight of the next line of text.

The single coin I held in my hand had an estimated value of five thousand dollars. At auction it could attract less, but the most one had ever been sold for was over forty thousand dollars. I felt my mouth go dry.

Unable to take my eyes off the screen, I called out to Lieutenant Bhukari.

"Hey, Deepa?"

"Yeah?"

"How many of those coins do you have in there?"

"I'm still counting."

I was about to prompt her to give me the current number when she supplied it anyway.

"I have eight hundred so far, and there're still another couple of hundred in the pile to count."

I tried to do the math in my head, gave up and used my phone. The number was staggering. Finn Murphy had a lifetime's worth of money in a tatty backpack and was sleeping in a threadbare sleeping bag on a steel floor in the bottom of a cruise ship.

If he could have exchanged just one coin for half of its value, he could have lived like a king instead of a pauper. I had not the slightest idea who he was or how he came by the treasure in his possession, but my heart went out to him.

The person who killed him must have known the Irishman had found a horde of treasure, but unless there had been even more of it, then the killer left empty handed. Certainly, Finn hadn't revealed the whereabouts of his knapsack and must have believed he would be able to escape to return to it.

Deepa wandered out of the bedroom, dusting off her hands so fine pieces of something fell to the carpet.

"Hey, what's that?" I asked.

"Oops, sorry," she blushed. "I'll get something to clean that up. I was just coming to get a drink of water."

I jumped out of my chair, holding a palm out to stop her advance.

"I'm not worried about the carpet, Deepa. I'm wondering if that was a clue."

Blushing deeper, because she hadn't thought of it herself, Deepa danced back a few paces and held out her hands.

"It's sand," she showed me her palms.

"What's going on?" asked Baker, following his wife from the bedroom and twisting his hips around to unkink his back.

"I need ..." Stopping mid-sentence – it was easier to just find what I needed than it was to explain it, I rooted around in the desk drawers to find a small white envelope. "Here," I encouraged Deepa to brush the remaining particles of sand into the folded paper.

Sensing something was occurring, Jermaine left the kitchen and Pippin followed Sam and Schneider out of the bedroom.

"This is a geology thing, right?" asked Pippin. "Someone can use that sand to pinpoint where it came from?"

I shrugged. "Maybe. I think scientists can do that."

Deepa indicated back into the bedroom with her head. "There's more in the knapsack."

I thought for a second, then made a bold statement. "I think this is treasure from an old ship." Okay, so that wasn't much of a giant leap, but my team was listening when I continued. "The coins are dated 1708 and there are a lot of them all in one place. Each coin is worth a fortune and when I searched for them a moment ago, it came back that there were none for sale anywhere in the world. To me that means they are super rare."

"So this stuff hadn't been touched in more than four hundred years," concluded Deepa.

My phone started ringing, interrupting our discussion in an unwelcome manner. I stepped a pace to my left to look down at where it sat on the desk.

The screen displayed Alistair's name.

I rejected the call, switched the phone to silent, and turned it face down. When I stepped back into the hole I left three seconds earlier, everyone was looking at me expectantly.

"Wrong number," I lied though I felt sure they all knew it. "Where were we?"

Pippin said, "Rare coins."

"Yes, right. Deepa's right, I think Finn Murphy found the hiding place of a treasure not seen in four hundred years. Someone else found out and they killed him for it."

Martin's voice was quiet, and a little ominous when he said, "Others will want to do the same. The contents of that knapsack have to be worth millions."

"Add that to the diamonds and other gems Dr Nakamura found

in Finn Murphy's gut," commented Schneider, adding his thoughts, but it was Sam who delivered the question that silenced the room.

"What if there is more?" We all turned to look at my assistant. He grinned back at us. "I mean, did he get all of it, or if this is treasure from a ship or something, did he only take what he could carry?"

No one spoke for several seconds, each of us holding our own thoughts as we pictured what it was that we might have inadvertently stumbled across.

It was the senior officer, Lieutenant Commander Martin Baker who broke the silence.

"So what's next, Mrs Fisher?"

I sucked in a deep breath through my nose, filling my lungs and giving myself a second to think before I spoke.

"I need to track down Finn Murphy's next of kin or contact the Irish consulate here. His body needs to be repatriated and his family have to be informed." Had he been a passenger, the task of contacting the next of kin would have fallen to the captain of the ship. Since the dead man was a stowaway, I wasn't sure there was even a precedent to follow, and I wasn't about to contact Alistair to get his advice.

I would deal with it in my own way.

"And the rest of us?" Martin prompted since I had only stated what I was going to do.

"We need to finish cataloguing everything in the knapsack and then secure it somewhere." I glanced across the room to an oil painting behind which a safe could be found. I remembered the trouble it caused when the former deputy captain, Robert Schooner, wanted to see inside it and I didn't have the key. "We can use my safe."

Everyone frowned.

"You're not going to declare the find to the captain?" questioned Martin, getting an elbow from Deepa for his lack of tact.

It was my turn to frown now. "No, I am jolly well not." Relaxing the muscles in my face lest they cause more wrinkles to form, I also softened my voice when I added, "I don't think we should tell anyone. Someone already leaked the information about Finn Murphy although mercifully we didn't know his name then. The world knows there was a stowaway onboard who got murdered and who had a fortune in uncut gems in his belly. That little snippet of information created havoc this morning with treasure hunters lining the dock. Imagine what would happen if it got out that we have a bag full to the brim with gold coins and pieces of jewellery." I didn't have to colour the picture in for them; they all understood.

"But we can't just keep it," worried Deepa, questioning what my plan might be.

I chuckled. "That was never my intention. What I propose we do is find out as much as we can and contact the appropriate authorities. The coins are Spanish so that is where I will be aiming my initial research. We don't have time for this right now though. There are three dead bodies in the morgue, two of whom are crew and that has to be our priority."

Martin clapped his hands together to get everyone moving. "Right, let's finish up going through Mr Murphy's belongings, identify any clues that might help us figure out what he found and get it locked away like Mrs Fisher says."

They split up, enthusiastic noises echoing around as they scurried back to the task. I was heading back to the chair at the desk and thinking an early afternoon gin and tonic sounding like a good idea when the door to my suite suddenly opened.

23

LIES AND ALIBIS

"I was right!" declared Barbie, bursting through my door.

The dachshunds exploded from the couch, the suddenness of her arrival disturbing their slumber. Their barking drowned out what she said next, and I had to ask her to repeat it.

She had fallen into a crouch to pet the dopey sausages who were now on their backs to get tummy tickles. She dealt with them first, cooing and praising them before she finally delivered the news she felt warranted her rushed entrance.

"Andrea and Nicole had a big falling out about a boy more than a year ago. I knew there was something screwy about her supporting Nicole's argument. I don't think they were friends at all, and Andrea isn't the forgiving kind."

"Did it come to blows, or were they just throwing insults?" I wanted more details than I was getting and was reaching for my handbag to get my notebook when another question occurred to me. "Wait, who ended up with the man in question? Or was it neither of them?" Who stole whose man could play a big part in whether Andrea thought vengeance was due.

Thankfully, Barbie had all the answers. "Oh, um, Andrea took Nicole's boyfriend. I think he was seeing them both for a while before he ended up with Andrea. It's not really my circle of friends and I only know about it from gossip – this happened before I came on board. I guess he picked right though because he is still with Andrea now."

"So that's who she was with last night then," I murmured mostly to myself as my pen hovered above a blank page. Andrea gave an alibi that covered her for the time of Nicole's death, but that didn't mean she hadn't lied. Perhaps they were both guilty and there was a reason they targeted Nicole. I raised my voice, "Martin?"

The sound of someone getting to their feet from a crouch – the grunt of effort to overcome gravity was followed by footsteps and then the form of Lieutenant Commander Baker as he left the bedroom with the treasure in it to see what I wanted.

"It looks like Andrea might have lied." I told him.

"She has history with Nicole," Barbie revealed.

"It might be nothing, but I'm going to follow it up right now. Can you come with me?" I wanted Martin because he was the one who interviewed her earlier. If her answers now failed to correlate with what she said previously, he would know it.

"Are we going to speak with Luis Velasquez first?" He looked around for his hat. It wasn't where he had left it, but that was because Jermaine insisted upon keeping my suite spick and span. It had been placed neatly on a shelf in the lobby five seconds after Martin left it where it didn't belong.

Barbie's face screwed into a confused expression. "Luis? The paramedic? Why are you speaking with him?"

I had been about to say something, but her question changed my own.

"That's her boyfriend. Isn't it?"

Barbie looked like she couldn't figure out what was going on. "No. Why would you think that?"

Baker had been halfway to the door to collect his hat but stopped mid-stride. "Because she gave his name as the man she spent last night with."

Barbie's jaw dropped open, and she employed a rude word to describe Andrea's promiscuity.

Baker and I were looking at each other and then back at Barbie, our confusion obvious to anyone with eyes. I still had to prompt her to tell us what we didn't know.

"Barbie! Who is Andrea's boyfriend?"

She could have said almost any name and I would not have known him. Or I might know the name but be unable to connect a face to it. However, when she next spoke, my blood ran cold.

Looking at me like I ought to be better informed, she said, "Sanjeev Bhaskar."

My skull itched and I let my backside drop back into the desk chair. Baker made a choking sound of disbelief. I was yet to meet Andrea Bassinet-Blatch, and right now that bothered me immensely. She had lied, given a false alibi - probably by pulling a name out of the air – and had strolled away from her interview knowing we were onto her.

If she had killed Nicole, then she also killed Sanjeev, and that meant the first thing she would have done after Baker let her go was grab her things and leave the ship. She was on the run, and it was down to us that she had escaped.

Baker's first thought was no different to mine, but he was faster on the draw and was already barking orders and questions into his radio. As Deepa, Sam, and the others spilled into the suite's main living area to see what was occurring, their boss was ordering the guards at the ship's entrances to be on alert. If they saw Andrea, she would be apprehended, but they were also checking the log to see if she had already left.

We all got to listen with bated breath until Lieutenant Cabrera confirmed she had not passed through any of the gates. There were other ways off the ship for a determined person, but in all likelihood, she was still on the ship somewhere.

While he was coordinating with ship's security, sending a general message to them to be on the lookout for our new suspect, Barbie explained to the others about the recent development.

Deepa smacked herself in the forehead.

"I should have seen that," she berated herself.

Baker ended his call in time to say, "Babe, you were dealing with sniffer dogs and other things. You were not in the interview room. Besides, we still have to check out her alibi. Maybe she was telling the truth about Luis Velasquez. Maybe she did spend the night with him. We'll find out soon enough."

"She's been going steady with Sanjeev for more than a year," argued Barbie.

No one had a response to give, and none was needed. This was no time for speculation. We were going to ask hard questions and get honest answers. Sensing that we might be closing in on our prey, a welcome feeling of imminent success filled our bodies.

Pippin said, "We're almost finished with the treasure." It was clear his comment was meant to show that if we waited we could all go, but I was not of a mind to delay, and this really didn't need all of us.

Leaving Sam, Pippin, and Schneider behind, Baker, Deepa and I set off to find the two people we needed to talk to.

24

GUILTY OF SOMETHING

We were still going out of the door when Lieutenant Kashmir radioed to confirm Andrea was not in her cabin and not in her place of work. That changed our intended destination. If we assumed she was still on the ship, it left far too much territory to search so we had to hope one of the security officers would spot her.

If it came to it, we would use the public address system to ask her to come forward, but that would be a last straw tactic – if she was already hiding or looking for a way to escape, inviting her to hand herself over was unlikely to work.

That she wasn't anywhere we might realistically expect to find her gave further rise to believe she was our killer. When I say 'our killer' I mean for Nicole and Sanjeev. She was the link between the two and the only tangible one so far at that.

Catching Andrea did nothing to solve the Vincent Pompeo case, the very nature of which still defied explanation. What was it that lured him into the conduit and down into the bottom of the ship? Was it something in storage room four? Or had he left the storage room to go somewhere else? Knowing that speculation would do me no favours, I pushed the more mysterious case from my mind to focus on the one I hoped to solve in swift order.

Luis Velasquez's role on board is that of paramedic. We have aid stations on every deck, there to cater to passengers' ailments whatever they may be. Too much champagne in the sun, a stubbed toe … these were things any fool could treat, but when someone has a heart attack in the middle of the ocean, it pays to have a trained medical professional close to hand.

We found him on deck seventeen and his behaviour looked shifty the moment he spotted us. Even more so when he murmured something to his colleague, and she walked away. He did that before we were close enough to hear their exchange and he faced us as we approached, making it look like we were expected.

I copied Luis' example and whispered to Martin and Deepa just before we got within range for him to be able to hear us. He saw me speak though and got to watch my colleagues nod their acknowledgement. That I never once took my eyes from his was not missed by Andrea's guilty looking alibi who swallowed hard just before we stopped in the doorway of his medic's room.

No one spoke.

Luis' eyes flicked from mine to Deepa's to Martin's and then back to mine. He was beginning to look quite haunted, and I could feel his panic mounting. It was my whispered suggestion to say nothing and see how he reacted that was freaking the poor fellow out. He caved after five seconds.

"What?" he begged. "What is it that you want?"

"Where did your colleague go?" asked Martin.

Luis' worry-filled eyes flicked from face to face again, this time settling on Martin's.

"To get coffee," Luis stuttered. "We are due a cup of joe."

He was probably telling the truth, but it was a mask to get rid of her so she wouldn't hear our conversation.

"What is it that you have to tell us?" asked Deepa, drawing him out a little further and making it sound like we already knew what he was hiding.

We didn't, but the guilty always want to confess, even if they don't think they do. Provide enough doubt, let them stew in it for a while, and then offer them an easy way to relieve the stress.

Just confess and it will all feel so much better.

Luis blurted, "What? What do you mean? Tell you what?"

"Hey!" I snapped the word to get his attention, making him jump. "How well do you know Sanjeev Bhaskar?"

I was expecting the colour to drain from his face, but instead he tilted his head to one side with a surprised expression. Whatever he had been expecting me to ask, that wasn't it.

"Sanjeev …"

"Bhaskar," I supplied.

Luis shrugged. "I don't even know if that is a guy or a girl. Are we talking about a crewmember or a passenger?"

"He's Andrea Bassinet-Blatch's boyfriend," I supplied, getting a hit this time when his cheeks reddened.

Luis' eyes flared, shock registering. He looked as guilty as could be.

Baker hit him with a question. "Can you account for your movements between midnight and three this morning?"

The paramedic's eyes flared again, his lips flapping open and closed a few times before his brain caught up.

"I was with Andrea in my cabin." The words tumbled out, and he sounded relieved to tell us, not like it was a confession at all.

I hadn't pictured him as part of the two deaths until we saw how he reacted to us. Lovers kill each other, that is something everyone knows – the passion that burns can be a negative force just as easily as it can a positive one. All it needs is the right nudge.

Now wondering if perhaps Andrea had an accomplice rather than an alibi, the medical centre on the seventeenth deck, with its open door and passengers going by just a few feet away, was no longer the right place for us to question Luis. Confirming Andrea's alibi had turned into a need to grill the paramedic - I had no doubt that he was hiding something, and I expected to discover it was murder.

"Please take Mr Velasquez into custody," I requested, my eyes never leaving Luis' face.

He couldn't believe it. "What!" He began to protest, but nothing he said was going to make any difference at this point - we needed to get to the bottom of what he and Andrea had gotten up to last night. Until we caught up with her, our focus would be on him.

Or so I thought for about twelve seconds.

Baker and Bhukari dealt with taking Luis into custody just as his colleague returned from the coffee shop bearing two extra-large travel cups with lids. To my mind it was a little too warm to be knocking back hot drinks – the temperature had gone up ten degrees since noon.

Deepa brought her into the medical aid post and got the woman to arrange for a replacement paramedic. There were to be two on duty at all times and though we were taking Luis into custody so we could question him properly and in private, we also couldn't take him away from his post until a replacement arrived.

I didn't know how long that would take and I didn't get to find out. Unbeknownst to me, two things had just happened elsewhere on the ship. I wouldn't find out about one of them for a little while, though that was my fault. The second one was just as unexpected as the first, but I got to hear about it straight away because everyone had been instructed to alert me in the first instance.

I am referring to a Buddy sighting, of course. My radio squawked, the muffled sound coming from my handbag as usual though the disembodied voice was clear enough for me to tell it was my name being called.

"Mrs Fisher," I said my name and released the send button.

"Mrs Fisher, this is Engineer Second Class Briggs. I have an order to contact you if we see the monkey?" He posed the statement as a question, hoping to hear that he had done the right thing.

It was a relief that someone from Engineering was calling. The last I heard of Commander Philips, he was on his way to see the captain. I knew that probably meant the kill order he placed on Buddy had been rescinded, but since I was still ignoring Alistair, I wasn't sure how their meeting had ended.

"Is he okay?" I enquired, making Lieutenant Commander Baker snigger. He thought it was funny that I was worried about the

Gibraltar Rock Ape. Buddy was very naughty, but I put that down to being alone and afraid in an alien environment. Giving Martin a look that told him to be quiet, I listened for Engineer Briggs to respond.

"Um, I guess so, Mrs Fisher. He just killed a giant snake."

I needed a second to process the news.

Because I hadn't replied, Martin tilted his head to the left, speaking into his own radio mounted on his lapel.

"This is Lieutenant Commander Baker. You said the ape killed the snake?"

"Yes, sir. A couple of the lads spotted the monkey and went after it, but the snake appeared out of nowhere and scared the living sh … scared them senseless," Briggs chose to tailor his language. "Then the monkey picked up a toolbox and slammed it on the snake's head."

"It's definitely dead?" I wanted to be doubly, trebly certain before I went anywhere near it.

Briggs made it sound like he was trying to explain something to a particularly thick person when he said, "Its skull is about half an inch thick now, Mrs Fisher. I'm not sure how to check a snake's pulse … I mean, it's kind of all neck, but I would be prepared to bet my pension on it."

My phone rang, the trill noise coming from my handbag in an insistent fashion.

Using my other hand, I dug it out, saw Alistair's name, and let it drop from my fingers once more. It vanished back into the dark recesses of my handbag where it would remain until I got a call from someone I wanted to speak to.

Pressing the send button on the radio, I asked, "Where are you?"

25

THE REDHEAD

B aker and Bhukari had to stay in the medical aid post until a replacement came to release Luis, but I knew where I was going well enough to find it for myself, and it wasn't as if I needed to arrest the snake.

Briggs believed Buddy had scarpered no sooner than the snake breathed its last, pausing only to perform his party trick of flipping the bird at the engineers before leaping across the steelwork and vanishing from sight.

He was somewhere down in the hold, and I was really going to have to focus on catching him again at some point soon. Food would do it – I doubted he was finding anything to eat in the sterile, steel habitat in which he found himself. Much like getting the rest of his friends and family off the ship before we left Gibraltar, I would prepare him a feast and lure him into a cage that way. Hunger would be his undoing.

I was feeling alert today, on edge because of the Alistair situation and my determination to keep my emotions in check. It also meant I was more aware of my surroundings, my eyes roving back and forth which was probably why I saw the redhead at the same moment she saw me.

A smile pulled at her lips – my pain giving her pleasure. She wasn't blocking my way as she had been last time, but she had to have known where I was and had positioned herself to intercept me. It could have been coincidence that placed her in my path, but I didn't believe that for a second.

"Poor Patricia," she goaded. "I told you I would win. Alistair is mine. He always has been. You were just a temporary fling."

There were passengers around us and a good thing too or I might have thrown myself at her throat. She had several inches on me and looked both fit and strong. I do not consider myself to be a fighter and that's not something I wish to change, but an irrational part of my brain wanted to cover the redhead with jam and leave her staked out in the sun for the ants to find.

"What do you want?" I growled.

She laughed at me. She actually tipped back her head and laughed.

"Only to gloat, Mrs Fisher. You should think yourself lucky he ever showed you any interest. I mean, what is it that you think he would see in you? We've been laughing about it, you know? In bed … afterwards."

Her words were like cruel barbs gouging pieces of my heart and tearing them from my body. I could feel my pulse hammering in my veins again and if ever I needed a lesson on how it was that crimes of passion took place, I was getting it now.

Rage rose through me, boiling my blood until a calm voice I barely recognised posed a question. Inside my head, the rational version of me asked, '*If he is laughing about you in bed with this woman, why did he buy you a stupidly expensive sapphire necklace just a day ago, Patricia?*'

I blinked, time standing still as all around me people went about their day and the redhead continued to smirk down at me. There was something wrong with what I was seeing and hearing – it didn't correlate with what I knew.

I knew Alistair loved me. Didn't I?

Was she lying? I fervently wanted to believe so, but why would she do that? I had no idea and doubted she would furnish me with an answer, so I asked something different, knowing I could catch her out if she was.

"Alistair has a birthmark …"

"The footprint shaped thing on the inside of his right thigh?" she supplied, breaking my heart all over again. Only a mother or a lover would ever be close enough to see the mark and she wasn't the former. Seeing the hurt etched into my face, she clapped her hands together. "Oh, my. You were still hoping, weren't you? Oh, what a darling you are."

I could stay in her presence no longer, and the tears I had fought all day were threatening to burst forth in a torrent. I could shout at her, I could rage and curse and even get violent, but I could not change what was.

Engineer Second Class Briggs was waiting for me on deck six and I needed to be somewhere else. Rushing to escape her cruel gaze, I tried to get by her, only to have her grab my arm. I tensed my body to throw her off, but she anticipated which way I was going to jerk my weight. When I shifted, she went with me, sending me off balance and then adding a little push so I sprawled across the deck to the sound of gasps and shocked cries from the passengers around us.

Everyone froze to the spot, their eyes flitting between the woman on the floor with the terrible expression, and the statuesque redhead now standing over her.

"If you feel too overwhelmed and wish to take your own life … well, it might be for the best, don't you think?" She delivered her final line, then with a swoosh of her silky, shampoo-advert-perfect hair, spun on her heels and strolled away.

People within earshot gasped when they heard what she said, but no one tried to stop her, and she walked confidently down the passageway and out of sight.

"Are you all right?" asked a voice by my head.

I turned to find a woman close to my age looking down at me with concern in her eyes. There were two dozen or more people doing exactly the same – an outpouring of sympathy I just didn't need.

Without a word, I clambered to my feet and pushed my way through the press of those around me to escape. There were mutterings behind my back that barely registered even though I heard them, the voices trailing away to nothing as I fled toward the elevator bank.

I prayed the steel car would be empty, but of course it wasn't. People got on and off to ensure someone rode with me all the way down to deck seven where I had to get off and switch to a crew elevator to take me lower.

By then, my heart had slowed down a little and I was able to think a little more clearly. My relationship with Alistair was over. It had to be, but I still couldn't make sense of his desire to give me the necklace. Not so very long ago, we were planning to move in together, sharing his captain's quarters high up on the bridge. The plan only changed when Barbie sneakily contacted the Maharaja, and he bought my suite on the ship so I could live in it.

There was something else … something about the redhead. I was on deck seven, wandering aimlessly and trying to sort and order the thoughts colliding in my head.

It was her smell.

The memory of a scent I got when she grabbed my arm, chimed like a bell in the back of my head. I knew that scent from somewhere. Where though? After a second of thought, I dismissed the question. It didn't matter what she smelled of because she had clearly been sleeping with Alistair.

Even if it was only the once, a stupid one-night thing he might even regret and wished hadn't happened, it clearly had, and we could never now be what we were.

My phone rang again, my teeth grinding against each other when I reached for it, and again when I saw Alistair's name displayed. I rejected the call yet again, but the interruption served a purpose – it broke my train of thought.

Pushing myself to get moving, I refused to even look at my phone when a text message pinged through. I was heading down to deck six to see the dead snake.

26

CRIME SCENE SERPENT

Finding the location I needed was easy once I arrived on deck six. All I had to do upon exiting the elevator was follow the susurration of conversation which, as I drew nearer changed into more of a hubbub and finally into a din.

I knew the crew had been advised there were two large snakes and an ape on the loose on the crew decks. What I hadn't given any thought to was how the testosterone-fuelled dummies below decks would react. Approaching the rear of the crowd, I could hear them arguing about who had seen what first.

They had been placing bets.

"Excuse me!" I shouted to be heard. "Excuse me! Move aside, please, I need to get through." Even with raising my voice and nudging people, it still took longer than expected to fight my way through the crowd of men. In fact, it was only when I spotted Lieutenant Kashmir and caught his eye that I was able to get to the centre of the gathering. As the crowd parted just a little to let me through, I was rewarded by the sight of the unfortunate boa constrictor and wished I'd sent someone else.

Reece Mefford, the owner of the snakes, described them as large adults. I can tell you first hand that failed to fully capture the enormity of the beasts. I don't know how big they can get, but if asked to guess, I would have said this one had to be getting close to ten yards in length. At the thickest part, the diameter of its body was as wide as one of Jermaine's muscular thighs.

Just as Briggs had claimed, the serpent's head was as flat as a pancake. This did not, however, make it look any friendlier. If anything, it added an evil slant to the snake's appearance.

Coming to my side, Kashmir asked, "Are you alright, Mrs Fisher? You look a little green around the gills."

"I skipped breakfast," I lied, doing my best to cover up how woozy I felt. Forcing myself to stare down at the snake, I began to question why I had even come to view it. The snake wasn't a tangible element in any of the crimes I was supposed to be investigating. Yet I asked the question of myself because I knew the answer already - I was trying my darnedest to stay busy as a defensive mechanism. If I was busy, I wouldn't have to think about Alistair. As if on cue, my phone rang yet again. This time I didn't even bother to look at it.

Coming to see the snake helped me kill time until Baker and Bhukari were ready for me in the brig with Luis. Or perhaps until someone found Andrea - speaking to those two was the highest task on my priority list and would remain so unless there was a sudden development in the Vincent Pompeo case.

The circle around the snake had expanded a little, the sea of faces forming it all looking at me and clearly expecting something clever to come from my mouth.

It was going to get weird if I didn't speak soon, so I said, "Is there a Briggs here somewhere?" Engineer Briggs had led me here, but was yet to identify himself. On the opposite side of the circle a hand raised to waist height.

"That's me," Briggs looked to be about thirty years old and was wearing a boiler suit with a few dirty smudges on it, plus heavy work boots. His hair was straw coloured and a little messy as if he had perhaps tidied it this morning, but then absentmindedly scratched his head with a greasy hand. "What would you like us to do with the snake, Mrs Fisher?" he asked. "Can we just chuck it in one of the bins? Or is it evidence?"

His question drew a chuckle from another man standing at the leading edge of the crowd. He had something clever to say it seemed.

"Anyone got any chalk?" he asked the crowd. "We need to draw an outline around it. Two straight lines ought to do," he finished, descending into a fit of giggles which spread and rumbled through the crowd.

Someone else said, "Should be an easy one to solve. The monkey did it!"

The mirth ceased abruptly when a new voice rang out.

"What is all this?" boomed the easily recognisable sound of Commander Philips. Unlike when I attempted to get through the press of people, it parted before the head of engineering like the Red Sea. He arrived in front of me a second later, an angry expression on his face. He didn't say anything, at least not at first. He just glared down at me. When finally he chose to break his silence, he uttered only a single word, "Explain."

I opened my mouth to do precisely that, only to have the ignorant head of engineering raise a palm outward toward my face.

"Not you," he barked, pointing a finger in the direction of Engineer Third Class Briggs. "I want him to tell me what is going on."

Briggs looked terrified and mortified at the same time. I could only guess at what had been said between Alistair and the head of engineering, but whatever it was had only made Commander Philips meaner.

Before Briggs had a chance to say a word, I started talking.

"Commander Philips you have no jurisdiction here." Muffled gasps rippled around the crowd of people surrounding me. It hadn't gone unnoticed that a fair percentage of them had taken the opportunity to slip away the moment Commander Philips appeared.

Looking at me with an incredulous face, Commander Philips repeated my words. "No jurisdiction? I never credited you with much brain Mrs Fisher, but surely you realise that we are standing in one of the engineering areas and I am the head of engineering." He was good enough to say exactly what I predicted.

If I had a gauge that showed my rage level, it would have burst by now, the glass cracking and the needle flying off. Yet somehow under the gaze of a man I had grown to loathe, I was able to speak and act with calm self-assuredness.

A smile tweaked my mouth when I replied, "Correct, Commander Philips. And I am the ship's detective, appointed by Purple Star Lines themselves if you wish to take it up with them. There have been three murders so far today." I included Sanjeev in the count now because I was convinced Andrea and Luis had killed him. "If you attempt to impede me, I am authorised to have you taken into custody." The gasp this time was far more audible.

I thought for a moment, much like everyone else present, that he was going to raise his voice and begin shouting, goodness knows he was well known for his willingness to bark at people. Perhaps sensing that was expected of him, he chose instead to tip back his head and laugh, reminding me of the cruel redhead. Commander Philips existed to me in the same category of barely human vermin.

I waited patiently while he did his best to make the laughter sound real, not that anyone was fooled into thinking it was. When I failed to react and had a pleasant smile waiting for him when he finally looked my way again, he switched weapons.

"So this is a crime scene, is it, Mrs Fisher? You think the snake had a hand in the recent murders, do you?" He looked around with his smiling face at the engineers and crew members who had been too close to have snuck away when he arrived. Either through fear or loyalty, most of them returned his amused expression, though I watched the smiles drop away again the moment he wasn't looking. Only mine stayed in place as I remained quiet, encouraging him to continue with his insults. "Interesting choice of murder weapon, wouldn't you say? He continued playing for the crowd. "Or are you suggesting that the snake is the mastermind behind it all?"

I was waiting for him to run out of steam, but something he had said caused my skull to itch.

The snake as a murder weapon.

Focusing on that, I missed what the loathsome head of engineering said next. There was something about the snakes that I had missed. I needed to concentrate my mind on this particular conundrum, yet I wouldn't be able to do that with Commander Philips annoying me.

"Finished?" I enquired politely, checking to see if he had anymore nonsense to spout. With a flourish of his hand, he offered me the floor. "I have yet to determine the purpose of the snake and what part it may or may not have played in the events I am investigating. To that end, this *is* a crime scene, and it will remain so until I deem it to be otherwise. As I said at the start of this conversation, you have no jurisdiction here. Do you wish to challenge me?" I raised an eyebrow, inviting him to do precisely that if he did.

I sincerely hoped he didn't call my bluff because there was no way I was going to have him arrested. There was something troubling me about the snakes, but I couldn't justify doing anything about it if Commander Philips ordered the snake be disposed of. I was already on dodgy ground with Purple Star, not because I had done anything wrong, but because in these early days of my appointment someone had been messing with me. For all I knew it was Commander Philips, though I was telling myself he lacked the imagination required to be behind the complaints, the email hacking, and the other problems currently making me look bad.

He had of course already weakened his own position by challenging Alistair. I didn't know how that had gone, but I could not see how the head of engineering could have come out on top. If Alistair deemed it necessary, he could simply remove Commander Philips from his post. So far as I knew, the captain didn't even need a particularly good reason.

All trace of mirth had faded from the Commander's face. He was livid. Clearly so, the barely contained volcano beneath the surface of his skin sufficient to cause more of the people around us to back away. They did so without him noticing, the Commander's focus wholly on me.

Letting my own smile drop because playtime was over, I asked, "What's it to be, Commander Philips?"

I got the fake smile again, the man opposite me wrestling his emotions under control so he could save a little face.

With a smile that didn't reach his eyes, he said, "I shall be there when you run out of luck, Mrs Fisher."

It was an ominous statement that felt very much like a threat. I wanted to demand what his comment meant, but he had already spun around on his heels, pushed Engineer Third Class Briggs roughly to one side, and stormed away. A small fraction of the crowd I found when I arrived now remained, all of them looking rather embarrassed by the interplay they had just witnessed.

I had won this round, but I did not fool myself into believing the commander would let it lie as it was.

Addressing Lieutenant Kashmir, I said "Please be a dear and find something to put the snake in, would you?"

Looking uncertain, he asked, "Where do you want me to take it, Mrs Fisher?" he asked. It was a valid question, but I had an immediate answer.

"To the morgue, dear fellow. To the morgue."

I wasn't going to follow it. I could quite happily never see the snake again. However, I was going to phone Dr Davis and let him know why I was sending a dead animal in his direction. Had it not been for Commander Philips, I probably wouldn't have considered doing anything with the carcass. It would have gone into a bin somewhere and I would have made sure Mr Mefford was alerted to the unfortunate death of his pet.

However, I could now not shift the itchy feeling at the back of my skull. I had definitely missed something. Vincent Pompeo had gone to a lot of trouble to get into that storage room. I still believed Sangita and Heike would uncover something valuable was missing. It would explain the effort Vincent went to, and subsequently why his partner or partners murdered him once it was retrieved.

I didn't think it was possible to employ a snake as a murder weapon, and I'm not suggesting that was what happened to Vincent - the bruising I saw was consistent with being strangled by another person. Nevertheless, once Commander Philips said it, the idea that the snakes escaping might have been something other than an accident lodged itself in my head. I needed to check several things, but if my itchy skull was right, I just caught a glimpse or something that was going to help me solve one of the cases.

While Lieutenant Kashmir rallied the crew persons not swift enough to make good their escape - he needed help with the snake's body - I took out my radio. I was yet to hear from Baker, and it felt like enough time had passed for a replacement paramedic to have arrived. Wouldn't you know it though? Before I could get the radio to my mouth, someone was calling me on it.

It wasn't Baker or Bhukari though. It wasn't anyone from my team. The voice coming over the airwaves was Barbie's and before her words even registered, I was able to hear the heartbreak in her voice.

"This is Special Rating Berkeley for Mrs Fisher. Special Rating Berkeley for Mrs Fisher."

I answered her immediately. "This is Mrs Fisher. What is it?" I held my breath while I waited for her to reply, certain that whatever news she had was going to be something terrible.

"Can you come to your suite?" she asked. "You need to come to your suite right now," she amended her question so that it was a demand. Then added two words that sealed the deal, "It's Jermaine."

27

PERSONAL VENDETTA

In the quiet confines of the elevator, alone for once for no one got on or off at any point, I took out my phone to read Alistair's message. Before my eyes got to it, I knew I would be right – he had been trying to tell me about Jermaine.

He wasn't dead – I knew that from Barbie, but not dead didn't mean all that much. I needed him to be okay. Someone had broken into my suite and had trashed it, hurting Jermaine in the process.

I closed my eyes and raged at myself. Jermaine was hurt and Alistair had been trying to let me know. I still didn't want to see him or speak to him, not now that I knew the awful truth about the redhead, but my rotten luck held because he was in my suite when I got there.

I saw him first. Even before my brain caught up with the devastation all around me. He was standing in the middle of the suite's main living space, holding court as everyone else in the room scurried about. My team was absent, all involved in other tasks I knew, but just when I needed a friendly face to come to my rescue, Barbie appeared.

She touched my arm, placing her fingers on my skin so I would turn to see who it was. Then she folded me into a hug, a sob making her spasm when she tried to talk.

"They took him to the medical centre," she managed to get her words out. "He's all banged up and they say he was hit with a stun gun."

The stun gun explained how anyone was able to get the better of him – Jermaine is a Jamaican ninja. Good with his fists and feet, I have seen him take on multiple attackers in the past, each time emerging victorious with barely a scratch on his skin or a ruffle in his impeccable suit.

Alistair came closer and was about to speak when I got in first.

"Not here," I announced in a tone that could not be questioned or challenged.

He frowned, looking surprised or perhaps unsure about what might be behind my remark. Of course, he didn't know that I knew, so was operating in the blissful ignorance of a man who believed his cheating had gone undetected. I wanted to slap his face, but I wasn't going to undermine him in front of crew members – that would just be tacky.

Sensing my mood and that my words were a warning, he backed away again, busying himself by checking on what three of his security team were doing. It gave me a chance to look around and it was then that the thing that was missing struck me.

"Where are my dogs?" I blurted. It hadn't occurred to me to question it when I strolled through the open door of my suite to find a dozen people inside, but now their absence was stark.

My breathing became ragged, and the world spun around my head.

"They're in your bedroom," Barbie reassured me, but Alistair had seen my reaction and felt the need to offer his support.

He came to my side, and this time he gripped my shoulder in what he intended to a be a tender gesture.

It was the straw. Whether it was the last straw or the straw that broke the camel's back made no difference because it burst into flames before the pyroclastic flow exploding from the crazy woman.

"Don't touch me!" I screamed, spinning around to face him.

Barbie gave me the room I needed to manoeuvre, but remained at my side, shifting her grip to hold my hand in support. "Don't you dare touch me," I repeated, my voice lowering to become a growl.

Alistair, unflappable and always utterly in control, bore a shocked expression. Everyone in the room was silent. You could have heard a pin drop and they were all looking our way until they realised they were watching their captain and his girlfriend going into full lover's tiff right before their eyes.

I wanted to demand he leave my sight – toss him out of my suite for what he had done, for how he made me feel like my insides were being scooped out with a garden fork. I didn't do that though. Still clutching Barbie's hand, I twisted on my heels and walked to my bedroom.

To get there we had to walk past the destruction that was my suite. I didn't know who was behind it or whether this was another part of the same systematic attack I had been suffering all week.

Barbie closed the door behind me, anxiously eyeing me to see what I was going to do, but all my attention was on my dogs. I scooped them both, hugging them to my chest. All around me, my room was a scene of destruction. Clothes were spilled from my wardrobes and drawers, and I could see they had been ripped and sliced. I couldn't tell just by looking, but my guess was that every item I owned was now ruined. Makeup and perfumes had been smashed and trampled, my souvenirs were broken. Someone really had it in for me.

Small mercy then that my dogs were unharmed. They were licking my chin, imparting their affection.

"Oh, Patty," sighed Barbie, coming around the bed to pick up one of my ball gowns. It was a designer item I had paid too much for. It had been slashed with something sharp and was nothing but rags now. She dropped it again, biting her lip as she tentatively used one finger to lever the wardrobe door open. She did not open it fully, shielding me from the view inside.

"It's all just stuff, Barbie. I can replace everything." I knew this to be true, but there was little conviction in my words.

Barbie crossed the room again, heading for my dressing table. I heard a stifled cry and looked up from the dogs to find Barbie's hand at her mouth.

"Tell me," I figured it was easier to hear it all now rather than keep finding a fresh wave of horror to discover for myself.

"It's your jewellery, Patty."

"It's smashed?" I guessed, assuming my rings and things had gone under the hammer quite literally.

"No, Patty, it's gone." She was looking in my jewellery box and I didn't need to get up to know that it was empty.

Like the clothing it was all replaceable. Except it wasn't. The one item that appeared as a mental image was the sapphire necklace Alistair bought for me just a couple of days ago. It was exquisite, but that was secondary to what it represented. It was a token of love from a man who at the time I believed wanted to marry me.

Thinking about it now proved to be too much. I was hiding in my bedroom and that wasn't good enough. I pushed myself off the bed, scooping both dogs as I blinked away the tears threatening to form.

"Come along, Barbie. I need to see Jermaine." The destruction of my personal possessions needed to be addressed, but human life would always take priority. Also, I couldn't deal with Alistair right now, and since he was in my suite, I couldn't deal with that either.

I was heading for the medical centre, and on the way there I got Barbie to fill me in as best she could.

A passing couple had found the door to my suite open and caught a glimpse inside as they passed by. Shocked by the scene inside, they then spotted what they thought to be a body and called for help. The suite had been trashed; things thrown everywhere as if someone was searching for something.

"The treasure!" I blurted the words as my brain linked the dots. "They were after the treasure." It felt like a natural conclusion to draw even though only a handful of us even knew about the knapsack and I trusted each of them with my life.

Should I?

The horrible question echoed inside my head, and I squashed it instantly. Yes, the temptation a fortune in gold and jewels represented could turn man against man in a heartbeat, but if I thought like that … I needed to trust my friends and until I had reason not to, that would remain my policy.

Otherwise, we would be at each other's throats, questioning every little thing and suspicious of every move.

"I don't think it was treasure," Barbie stated with more confidence than I expected. "I think this was personal." When I looked at her, she made a valid point, "A treasure hunter wouldn't stop to carve up your clothes, Patty. Also, no one knows about the treasure."

When the complaints about me first appeared, I said it had to be someone with a personal vendetta. I knew the stories filed against me were all lies, but they were lies being told by a seemingly unconnected bunch of former passengers. Then there was the email hacking and the attempt to drive a wedge between me and Barbie. Now I found myself at odds with Alistair, Jermaine had been attacked and seemingly everything I owned had been destroyed.

It was all connected. It had to be. My feet stalled.

"Patty?" Barbie gave me a questioning look, probably wondering what was going on in my head and what I was going to say next.

"There's another stowaway," I stated. Barbie raised an eyebrow. "She wouldn't dare use her own name – she would be too worried that I would find her."

Barbie engaged a tone I might reserve for asking questions of a crazy person holding a knife. "Who are we talking about, Patty?"

I shook my head – I wasn't ready to share yet. I had things I needed to check first, but the clues aligned in my head, and it was going to take some convincing to get me to change my mind.

"Patty?" Barbie's voice now sounded more like a warning.

I took out my phone, flicked an apologetic look at my Californian friend and sent a text message. With that task complete, I started moving again.

"Come on, Barbie, let's check on Jermaine."

28

UNHINGED

Settling in front of the mirror, the person responsible for Patricia Fisher's pain fingered the sapphire necklace now hanging around her neck.

Breaking into Patricia Fisher's suite had been her riskiest play to date, but the one that brought the most satisfaction. Taking away her friends, ruining her relationship with the captain - a man far too good looking for her anyway - embarrassing her and exposing her as the amateur hack detective that she was - these things were just necessary steps towards a greater goal.

Patricia Fisher needed to suffer, and it had to be public. There was no joy in it if the person behind it all didn't get to watch.

"Do you need me to do anything else today?" asked Jordan. He was hovering by the door to her cabin, agitated by what he had just been coerced/bribed into doing and feeling bad about it.

Looking at her reflection in the mirror, the woman behind Patricia Fisher's pain smiled to herself. Jordan had not wanted to take part in the destruction of the Windsor Suite. He positively begged her to leave him out of it, but she knew there was too great of a chance that the butler would recognise her. It had to be someone else at the door when he opened it, so she gave the young hacker little choice.

She also gave him an extra ten thousand pounds to shut him up.

He did as she demanded, firing the stun gun the moment the door opened. She was flat against the wall outside, ready to shove Jordan through it once the weapon was deployed. Had the butler not been rendered unconscious, she was resolved to stab him with the knife she held, but it proved unnecessary.

In retrospect, she could not decide whether she was pleased about that or not.

Jordan took little part in destroying the contents of the suite, but she was fine with that - she wanted to do it. Shredding the awful woman's dresses, snapping the heels off her shoes, dropping her electronics into the toilet ... all these actions came with a cathartic release akin to euphoria. Patricia's jewellery went overboard – all except a sapphire necklace. It was just too pretty to throw into the sea.

Fingering the trinket now, she stared into the mirror with a smile curling the corners of her mouth. She had achieved so much already, and she was only just getting started. Patricia had such a long way to fall. Patricia had to become nothing more than a ruined, wretched wreck of a human. Only then would she consider stopping.

Hennessey's report about how she humiliated Patricia and threw her to the deck was a priceless account she wished she had on camera. Oh, how she would love to see the pain etched on Patricia Fisher's face.

It meant that Hennessey had largely fulfilled her purpose and needed to vanish before the ruse could be exposed. The captain would deny the affair, but she knew Patricia Fisher well enough and was convinced her recent past would make her too suspicious to ever trust him again.

Jordan had found Hennessey, proving his worth early on – the boy was a whizz with social media and such. But she could never have imagined Hennessey would jump at the chance being offered.

It made Hennessey perfect for the role – literally no one else on the planet could have performed it as well.

According to the tall redhead, the deed was done. The captain of the ship was considered a cheat and that would hurt Patricia deeper than any knife wound she could inflict. It was simply delicious to imagine how the awful woman now felt.

From behind her, Jordan made a noise – clearing his throat in a purposeful way. Oh yes, he had said something, hadn't he?

"Yes? What is it?" she demanded.

Jordan was terrified of his employer and had already resolved to escape her company and the ship the moment he got paid. He was in too deep, that was his problem. She hooked him with an early payment that was enough to get him involved, and once he was onboard the ship, it was too late to back out.

Now though, he was waiting for the big payout she promised was coming his way and she kept adding to it. He knew she had the money, she had showed him her bank accounts and used them to rent the suites and pay the bills he and Hennessey were running up. She wasn't paying them though – not until the job was done.

Could Jordan wait that long? Should he? Was it a better idea to cut his losses and escape before the madwoman got some bad news and stabbed him in a fit of rage? She was clearly unhinged; he held no doubts on that matter.

Sheepishly, he repeated his earlier question, and slipped out of her cabin the moment she said he could go.

With the door closed once more, she turned back to the mirror, touching the necklace again. It truly was a beautiful piece.

"Did he buy this for you?" she asked the air. "I bet he did, Patricia. Well, now it is mine. If I were a younger woman, the dashing captain would be mine too. Alas, that is a task too great for me to achieve yet I have taken him from you, nevertheless."

A flicker of a frown creased her brow. She wanted to kill the dogs and Jordan had finally shown some gumption when he stepped in to stop her. He was making so much noise about it, she almost used the knife to shut him up.

He had grabbed them away from her when they attacked the moment she went through the door. Rotten, horrible little mongrels recognised her, that was the problem. Well, Jordan had saved them once, but there was opportunity yet.

29

FOURTH MURDER VICTIM

Jermaine had been taken to the medical centre on the top deck and then transferred to the main sick bay way down in the crew area. There they had an operating theatre and ward containing twelve beds.

On our way I had conversations with Baker and Bhukari. They were just arriving at the brig where they planned to interview Luis Velasquez. They expected me to join them until I told them what had happened in my suite.

I asked Baker to delay the interview for now - they could let Luis stew for a while, and I would get there soon enough. I also spoke with Schneider who had Sam and Pippin with him. They had responded to a possible Andrea sighting which came through just as they were packing the last of the treasure into my safe. It turned out to be nothing – mistaken identity, but meant they were not in my suite when Jermaine was attacked.

It was no surprise to the doctors when we arrived at sick bay. Drs Davis and Nakamura were both there, still busy with the work we sent them this morning, and now more so because they had a live patient to deal with.

A least they gave him priority over the corpses.

Immediately scaring away the doubts and fears in my mind, Jermaine lifted a hand to wave at me and Barbie. I paused to tie the dog leads to a table by the door. Strictly we were not allowed to bring them into the medical centre, but neither doctor made a comment.

"I'm perfectly alright, madam," he called out. "The good doctors are merely being cautious in monitoring me."

Dr Hideki Nakamura rolled his eyes and gave a small shake of his head.

"You have a nasty blow to your skull, Jermaine. Checking you for concussion is wisely prudent."

By the time Hideki had delivered his line, we had crossed the room to get to Jermaine's bedside. He was sitting up in bed, his butler's tunic absent, as was his bow tie. His bottom half covered by a sheet, there was no outward sign of any injury, until I saw the two small spots of blood below his left pectoral muscle. They had stained his perfectly white shirt.

Tracking my eyes, Hideki said, "That's where the electrodes punctured his skin." He had moved around to stand next to Barbie, the two of them linking hands in greeting.

Anticipating that I had questions for him, Jermaine began supplying answers.

"I did not see my attacker I'm afraid, madam. I answered the door to a person wearing a mask. I believe it was a man, and from what little I saw I would hazard a guess that he was of Asian descent. However, I based that assessment purely on hair colour and skin tone. I could only see the tips of his ears and then only for a second. He fired his weapon the moment I opened the door."

Placing a hand on his forearm, I said, "Never mind all that, sweetie. I'm more concerned about you. Are you sure you are alright?"

Jermaine gave a small incline of his head. "Yes, madam. The doctors assure me that I should suffer no lasting ill effects, so I have nothing more than an itchy patch of my skin where the electrodes left behind a small burn, and a bump on my head where it would seem I collided with the wall upon losing consciousness."

He tilted his head to show me the wound. I did not like that he had been hurt, but had to agree that it looked superficial.

Jermaine had a question for me. "Were they after the treasure?"

"Treasure?" repeated Hideki.

Dr Davis, who was sitting at a desk a few yards away also turned his head. "Hmmm? What was that about treasure?"

It neatly summed up the problem with the word. There was a crowd of treasure hunters outside the ship this morning because that one word captures mystery, romance, opportunity, and more. Treasure: it does not have a value. If you say ten million dollars, peoples' eyes will light up, but treasure goes many steps beyond that.

Jermaine realised what he had done, his cheeks burning as he closed his eyes in shame – there were now two more people in the loop.

I explained in very limited detail, saying that we found the albino's knapsack and with it his passport. The doctors were pleased to have a name for the man in their morgue. Since the word had been employed, I admitted there were some more items of value in Finn Murphy's knapsack and swore them both to silence.

Task complete, I then had to deal with the truth about why someone had forced their way into my suite. I glanced at Barbie who met my gaze with sympathetic eyes. I had to tell Jermaine the truth – it wasn't like I could hide it from him unless I never let him back into the suite, but Barbie and I both knew what impact the truth was going to have on our friend.

I chose my words carefully, attempting to ease him into the awful revelation to come. "It seems whoever it was, broke into the suite with the intention of causing me more distress."

Jermaine's brow ruffled, as he wrestled with the cryptic manner in which I was explaining things.

"Sweetie you have to promise me that you will not blame yourself. There is nothing you could have done."

His eyes narrowed slightly. "Nothing I could have done about what, madam?" he tried to drag an answer from me and shifted his gaze to Barbie. "What is it that I don't know, please?"

"They trashed the suite," I tried to break the answer down into bite size chunks. "The paintings have been gouged, someone went a little berserk on the curtains and soft furnishings. It's all stuff that can be replaced."

Astute enough to read between the lines, Jermaine asked, "What is it that cannot be replaced, madam?"

I sighed and let my shoulder droop. I was going to tell him, but Barbie supplied the answer before I could.

"Whoever broke in carved up all of Patty's clothes, broke her shoes, and destroyed her electronics. Anything they could ruin, they ruined."

Jermaine's eyes widened as the horror of the news overtook him and he looked so guilty one might have thought he was behind the vandalism.

Barbie slapped his face.

"Hey!" she snapped in his face.

Her blow hadn't been a hard one – it wasn't intended to cause pain, but to jar him and get his attention.

Next to her, Hideki rolled his eyes, muttering, "Yeah, sure, slap the head of my suspected concussion patient. Why not?"

Now that Jermaine was listening, Barbie said, "You didn't do anything wrong, babes."

"She's right," I agreed. "And the most important thing in that suite was you." My statement was one hundred percent true, but that didn't stop me from feeling the enormity of what had happened. A tear slipped from my eye and Jermaine reached out to place a hand on my arm. Barbie dropped Hideki's hand to reach across to cup Jermaine's head. With her other hand she found mine, interlinking our fingers.

The three of us remained like that – a frozen tableau until Jermaine broke the spell by swinging his legs out of the hospital bed.

"Sweetie, are you well enough to leave yet?" I tried to block his way with my body.

Hideki said, "As your doctor I advise against leaving at this time. Concussion can reveal itself in unexpected ways long after the event that caused it."

Jermaine picked up his bow tie and started to straighten out his shirt. "Then I shall be sure to watch for any symptoms, sir. There are miscreants to apprehend, and I will play my part."

That single sentence summed him up to a tee. Jermaine lived his life to a simple set of rules – a code of conduct if you will. He put his own interests and needs behind those of the people in his life. Playing his part, knowing he did his bit, was a guiding principle.

Barbie came around the bed to help Jermaine with his bow tie. He could do it himself, but the darned things are tricky to get right without a mirror. The jacket hid the small blood spots on his shirt so that within moments he was once again looking like the butler appointed to the ship's royal suite.

"There are clues, madam?"

Barbie narrowed her eyes at me. "Yes, babes, but Patty is doing that sneaky thing where she doesn't tell us what she has figured out yet."

I shot them an apologetic grin.

"Sorry. If I say too much it sort of confuses things in my head and I'm not sure what I have figured out yet."

"Okay then, Patty," Barbie needled me to start spilling. "What and who is on the list? You always have one. Let's get whoever is behind this."

"Not so fast," I held up both hands to slow her down and looked at Hideki. "First I have murders to solve. The person behind the vandalism of my suite is the same person who organised a bunch of passengers to make complaints about me, the same one who leaked my document about the gems we found in Finn Murphy's gut, and possibly the same one creating a rift between me and Alistair."

"You mean the redhead?" Barbie questioned, unable to follow what I was saying.

I shook my head, looking her way again. "No, but I'll try to explain that in a little while. I need to talk to Alistair because there is something I don't understand."

Barbie gasped, excitement and hope filling her face. "You think maybe he didn't cheat?"

Hideki didn't know about this bit. "What? The captain's been playing the field?" He got an elbow in his ribs for his question.

"Shhh," Barbie insisted. "Don't interrupt."

I huffed out an exhausted breath. "I don't know. He lied to me, I'm sure about that. The rest of it … I don't know." I caught myself focusing on the wrong thing again and waved my hands in front of my body as if fighting off any further questions. "Look, there's someone onboard with a vendetta against me. That's old news, right?"

"Right," Barbie and Jermaine replied together.

"It's news to me," remarked Hideki grumpily, this time blocking the elbow when Barbie jabbed it toward his ribs. She shot him a cheeky smile.

I pushed on, wanting to get things done. "We'll get to the bottom of who is trying to wreck my life shortly. First, I have three murders to solve and that has to take priority."

"What about all your things?" Barbie wanted to know.

"Soon," I promised. We had gone around in a circle, but I was back at Hideki. Including Dr Davis in my question, I raised my voice a little. "Have you ascertained the cause of death for each of the victims?"

Dr Davis was sitting at a desk writing up notes, but stopped and swivelled his chair around to face us.

"Vincent Pompeo was strangled from behind and most likely pinned to the bed while it happened. I found premortem bruising consistent with having his arms held."

"A third person then," I concluded. It was exactly as I suspected.

I got a nod. "Yes. One of his killers might have been a woman. It's hard to tell but the bruising suggests the hands around his neck were smaller than the average man's." He got out of his chair to indicate how he believed Vincent Pompeo had been killed. One person was on his back, using their weight to pin him down and a second had hold of his arms, probably also pinning them down so he couldn't easily fight back.

It was brutal and calculated.

"Dr Nakamura conducted the autopsy on Nicole Tibbett," Dr Davis handed off to Hideki.

With a nod of thanks, Hideki reported, "Killed by a single blow to her skull. The wound was consistent with being struck by a blunt instrument with a rounded edge."

"A dumbbell?" I wanted to be sure what he was saying.

"Almost certainly. I believe one was missing from the fitness suite?" Hideki sought confirmation.

"It was. The cause of death?"

"Bone fragments penetrated her brain tissue leading to massive internal haemorrhaging. She was most probably unconscious before she hit the floor and died shortly thereafter." He was softening the news because he knew Barbie was friends with the victim.

"Ok. So what about Sanjeev Bhaskar?" I wanted to hear about him because the third victim was the most interesting of the three.

Dr Davis said, "I will admit I was at something of a loss to explain what could have happened to him." Upon seeing my surprised expression, he quickly added, "I don't mean from a medical standpoint; the cause of death was easy to determine. What I mean is, I saw him in his cabin and there was nothing in there that could have killed him."

Barbie shook her head as if trying to clear it. "Wait, what are you saying? How did he die?"

Dr Davis walked through a set of translucent plastic curtains at the back of the medical centre indicating with a hand that we should follow. It led to further hospital beds and then to a door at the back which connected the operating theatre to the right and the morgue to the left.

We traipsed after him without asking further questions until we reached the morgue. There Barbie hesitated by the door.

"Is this something I want to see?" she asked.

Hideki said, "Probably not."

I didn't want to see either but how much worse could he look compared with earlier?

"You stay here, sweetie." I touched her arm and left her outside when I followed Dr Davis into the cold room. Of course, there was a small, minor, little, insignificant fact I had forgotten.

I requested Lieutenant Kashmir bring the day's fourth murder victim down here earlier and he was lying in a pile on the floor just inside the door.

I swore, ran outside while hyperventilating, and tried hard not to wet myself.

"Oh, yes," Dr Davis's voice echoed out from inside the morgue. "I forgot to thank you for our latest guest," he remarked dryly.

Barbie craned her head around the door, choked out a gasp and said a word much like the one I employed.

"Now that is a big snake," she remarked. "Wooo. I was not expecting that."

Nor had I been. Mr Snakey was just as dead as he had been the last time I saw him, but no less terrifying for it.

"Why did you send me the snake, Mrs Fisher?" Dr Davis asked.

I didn't have a good answer for him. The truth was that at the time I was being obstinate and wasn't going to back down to Commander Philips. There was more to it than that though. There was something about the snakes escaping that just wasn't adding up.

To give Dr Davis an answer, I told him, "I needed to put it somewhere. I'm not sure that it has anything to do with what's going on or not at this point, but I couldn't risk its body being disposed of."

Dr Davis raised his eyebrows, considering my comment for a second before saying, "Well, you certainly guessed right, Mrs Fisher. Your reptilian friend is Sanjeev Bhaskar's killer."

Barbie poked her head around the doorway and into the morgue again.

"I'm sorry what?" she echoed my thoughts with her words.

Dr Davis crossed the morgue to one of three stainless steel beds where he pulled back a thin white sheet to reveal the top half of Sanjeev Bhaskar's body.

His skin was now blotchy and purple in places. Without his clothes to cover him, I could see the terrible damage inflicted upon his body. All of a sudden, the doctor's comment made sense, and a piece of the puzzle fell into place.

There had been no obvious sign to indicate how Sanjeev was killed and now I knew why. We didn't find a murder weapon because there wasn't one. Not in a conventional sense. Sanjeev had been crushed to death by the giant boa constrictor.

"What a terrible way to go," I murmured, trying hard not to imagine what must have gone through Sanjeev's mind when the snake came out of nowhere and attacked him. He would have been in his cabin, minding his own business when it slithered out from under his bed. His cabin was on the same deck as the storage room, I knew that much. Like the conduits running down behind the bulkhead in cabin 1215, there had to be connecting pipes and spaces through which the snake made his way from A to B.

It meant the second snake was as likely to find its way into the crew accommodation and we needed to warn them. Oh, well, I wanted to talk to Alistair anyway.

30

THE CLUE THAT CHANGED EVERYTHING

"Do you want me with you?" asked Barbie when I announced my intentions. It was generous of her, but lovers do not quarrel in front of other people – it's just not how things are done. I was going to ask her to be close by though because, depending on what he said, I suspected I might need her once he and I were done.

I shook my head anyway. "No …" My mouth stopped moving just as I was about to ask her to not go too far when I met with Alistair. The cause of the seizure was the thing the snake was lying on. "What's that?" I asked, extending an arm to point while taking a step back so my arm didn't get any closer to the dead reptile (I've seen zombie films).

"The duvet cover?" Dr Davis wasn't sure what I was trying to ask.

I already knew what it was, of course, that was why it stopped me mid-sentence. My skull was itching like mad because I had just figured out a big part of the mystery. Swallowing a mental brave pill, I approached the dead snake, crouching to inspect the material on which it lay.

"Where did it come from?" I asked, fingering the fabric while not touching the snake (just in case it moved).

Dr Davis came around to my side, grabbed the duvet cover in both hands, and with a mighty heave rolled the boa constrictor to one side.

"Mrs Fisher?" his voice echoed after me. He had to raise his voice for me to hear because the snake had touched my hand and I was now twenty yards away and back in the main part of the medical centre where there were at least two doors between me and the giant reptile.

Barbie arrived a moment later, laughing in my face when she joined me.

"I have never seen you move that fast, Patty. The next time we do shuttle sprints in the gym, that's the amount of effort I want from you."

I was so pleased she found my discomfort amusing. I had a rude response for her but kept it to myself. Drs Davis and Nakamura came through the plastic curtain behind her with Jermaine on their heels. Dr Davis had the duvet cover in his hands.

"You asked about this?" he reminded me, holding the duvet cover in his hands. "It's what they used to transport the snake. It's rather heavy and unwieldy, you see."

I did see. I also remembered that the covers in cabin 1215 had been messed up and were on the carpet. At the time I put no thought to it. Vincent Pompeo was stretched across the mattress and that made it look as if the covers had been shifted during the struggle of his murder.

That wasn't it though. At least, I didn't think so. I would have to check, but I expected to find the Boatengs' duvet cover was missing.

It changed everything.

Andrea and Luis had found out about the snakes and went down to the storage room to find them. The answer to my riddle had been hiding out of sight because I thought the deaths were unrelated. Nicole and Sanjeev were both victims of the same evil couple. Andrea stole Sanjeev from Nicole, and I was certain that when I dug into it, I would find Nicole held something over Andrea that resulted in her death. However, having made the decision to kill Nicole, it wasn't much of a leap to also kill Sanjeev.

Why she wanted him dead I had no idea. According to Barbie they were still dating, yet that was either no longer true – possibly a recent development – or at the very least Andrea had found someone new since she spent the previous night with Luis. There would be a why behind Sanjeev's death, but shockingly Andrea and Luis managed to successfully employ the snake as their murder weapon.

It was both ingenious and despicable. Now that I knew the truth of it, pumping Luis and Andrea for answers - assuming we could find her - would be so much easier. They would see that I knew the truth and though I would not call it pleasurable, there was a certain satisfaction in knowing killers had been caught and would face justice.

Vincent played a part too, though I was yet to figure out how or why he was part of the team. Maybe he was a snake expert. Maybe he was involved with Nicole. I told myself it was okay to still have a couple of unknowns; they would come out in the wash.

When I explained all this to Barbie, Jermaine, and the doctors, they were amazed.

"How on earth did you figure that out, Patty?" Barbie wanted me to reveal.

I offered her a half shrug. "It's how my brain works. I just needed to see enough clues."

"What must we do now, madam?" Jermaine was ready to leave the sick bay, probably anxious to get back to the suite and get it straightened out.

"We check the bedding in cabin 1215 and in Sanjeev's quarters and then we grill Luis until he confesses. If Andrea is still onboard," my gut told me she was, "someone will find her soon and between the two of them the truth will out. First though, I have to speak with the captain.

31

THE PAIN OF BREAKUP

I sent Alistair a text message in which I expressed a need to report in person on the murder cases. Had I chosen to lead with a need to discuss our relationship, the task would not have reached the top of his priority list. However, for his passengers and crew, I knew he would hand over whatever he was doing.

That I asked him to meet me in a briefing room on deck seventeen was sufficient code to announce that we also had personal matters to discuss - I knew he was astute enough to read between the lines. Barbie took the dogs from me, keeping them out of the way so I could focus on what I needed to do.

He arrived to find me staring out to sea. Windows along one side of the room provided a panoramic view of the ocean. The sun twinkled on the wave crests, sparkling like a moving sheet studded with diamonds above which sea birds swooped and soared. It was enough to entertain my eyes while my brain sifted the clues I had seen and the facts I believed I knew. I was doing it to yet again distract myself from the conversation to come.

"Patricia," he announced his presence and closed the door, the returning silence cueing me to turn and face him. We were on opposite sides of the room, about three yards apart and making no move to get closer.

Until today this would have been strange behaviour, but he could sense the frost emanating from my cold eyes.

"Who is Hennessey Gates?" I asked, my words bold and clear. Watching for his reaction, I expected to see guilt, or shame … surprise at least, but I got none of those. There was a slight narrowing of his eyes, but otherwise his expression didn't change at all.

"Of course," he remarked. "I should have expected that you would learn her name."

There it was. Even if he didn't make it sound like one, it was an admission of guilt, nevertheless. He lied to me this morning when he claimed to have no idea where the strand of red hair came from.

"I'm sorry that I lied to you, Patricia. I have not consciously done that before, nor would I have done so this time had you not caught me by surprise. That is a poor excuse, I realise."

I had a lump in my throat that felt like I had swallowed a puffer fish and my eyes were filling with tears as the emotions that had been trapped behind a barrier all day broke forth with more energy than I could hope to resist.

I wanted to hear his confession. It would be done then, and I could free myself and move on without any doubt that I might have been wrong. Pushing myself to get the words out, I asked, "Have you slept with her?"

I couldn't see what his face was doing because I was staring at the carpet and could not bring myself to look up. However, I didn't need to see him to be able to hear his voice.

"Yes, Patricia. Many, many times."

It was like being stabbed in the heart repeatedly to hear the words come from his mouth. It was all true. Everything she said … laughing in my face when she claimed him as her prize …

"We were engaged to be married. I thought I was in love with her, but until yesterday I hadn't seen her in more than a year."

Wait, what?

Alistair continued, "It threw me completely and though I will not hide the fact that I lied to you, I did so because I wasn't ready to talk about it." Alistair was filling the room with words, but I wasn't hearing them anymore. I was still stuck on the bit about not having seen her for a year.

Finding my voice, though my throat felt like someone had taken an axe to it, I said, "You're saying you haven't been cheating on me?"

Alistair stared at me, blinking once then twice as he processed my question.

"Oh, Patricia, is that what you thought?" He started forward, intending to sweep me into a hug, but my automatic reaction was much the same as if someone were attacking me. I backed away a pace, raising a hand to fend him off.

"You're lying," I accused him. "You went to her cabin last night."

He stopped moving and dropped his hands to his sides. His expression held a question he wasn't going to ask: How I knew where he was last night? I hadn't been the one spying on him but that hardly mattered. He couldn't deny visiting her cabin without lying again, but admitting it was true meant he was lying about not cheating.

To answer me, he said, "I did."

"Why?"

Alistair pursed his lips and puffed out his cheeks a little, his expression changing as he attempted to work out what he wanted to say. The sceptic in me argued that he was buying time to concoct a story, but when he started speaking, his words rang with truth.

"She caught me off guard when she appeared, and I wanted to know why she was on board. I checked the log – she is travelling alone and has an open ticket, so she clearly had a purpose rather than a destination in mind. I wanted to know what it was, so I went to her cabin last night. I lied to you because I didn't believe what she told me – that she was here to win me back. It's not her style for a start, but I wanted to get to the truth of it before I spoke to you and when you found the red hair this morning, I panicked."

I looked up at his face.

"You don't panic, Alistair." This was true and we both knew it.

He nodded, accepting my accusation, but said, "This time I did. I cannot explain it other than to say I am in love with you, Patricia. I wanted to convince Hennessey to leave the ship and to leave us alone and for you to never know about her."

"Why? Why do you want me instead of her?" I needed to hear his justification for rejecting the flaming-haired beauty.

"Hennessey is everything that you are not, Patricia."

This was not a good start.

"She isn't kind or courageous. She doesn't put other people first."

This was better though.

"Her heart understands the concept of love, but she will always be far too in love with herself to ever give fully to another."

Alistair's eyes were locked on mine as he spoke directly to my soul. The pain in my throat was yet to subside, and if anything, there were more tears slipping from my eyes now than before. I could feel them dampening my chin and was sure I had a drip of mucus hanging from the tip of my nose. I felt dislocated from my body, my brain floating freely on a surge tide of emotion.

"I broke it off long before I met you, Patricia, and had resigned myself to remain single. Until you came along, that is. Hennessey is elegant and beautiful, but the fire that gives her passion also makes her erratic, jealous, and difficult to love. This morning she appeared in front of me while I was on my rounds."

Alistair made a point of mingling with the passengers and crew every day. There were questions shouting inside my head to be heard, but they were going to have to wait. Alistair was telling me everything, and as if interrupting might break the spell and make it all lies, I kept quiet.

"Last night she claimed to have sought therapy and begged that I consider rekindling our romance. She reacted badly when I refused her advances, cursing and swearing. In so doing she proved the Hennessey I knew was just the same as she had always been. When you found me with the red hair on my jacket, I panicked. That's the truth of it. I fear she might have placed it there deliberately for you to find. Her presence onboard the Aurelia threw me. I am truly sorry I lied to you, Patricia. I will not do it again, but I beg that you believe I have remained true to you."

I'm a strong, independent woman and I don't need a rock to cling to. Regardless of that fact, I am also still a living, breathing human being and I crave affection as much as the next person. Alistair gave me that in a way that my ex-husband never had. Far from making me feel lesser for being a woman, he made me feel empowered.

I wanted to be with him. I loved him.

I couldn't manage to say any of that though because my throat was now so tight and painful that words just wouldn't come. Instead, I sobbed, my shoulders shaking as relief, confusion, anger, and hope all fought for dominance.

Alistair didn't stop this time when he started toward me, and I made no attempt to ward him off. He swept me into his arms, crushing me to his chest as he wrapped his arms around my back. I felt his lips deliver a light kiss to the crown of my skull and then we stayed that way, my body supported by his weight and my tears soaking into his tunic for more than two minutes.

When Alistair finally broke the silence, it was so he could say, "I do not deserve you, Patricia, and you do not deserve the lack of trust I have displayed. I have treated you terribly, believing you could be capable of such foolish acts when it should have blatantly obvious there was someone operating against you in the background. Can you ever forgive me?"

He was handing me the opportunity to tear a strip off him. I would be justified to do so for everything he just said was absolutely true. He *had* treated me badly, and I did deserve a greater level of trust than I had been afforded.

However, I could also see things from his perspective. Alistair wasn't the person behind my pain. The torment I was being forced to endure was at the hands of another. The way he reacted was probably much the same as anyone else might have given the circumstances. I believed Purple Star were putting him under pressure and it would be just as unfair for me to treat him harshly for his lack of trust.

Bringing my emotions slowly back under control, I said, "There's nothing to forgive."

We were quiet again for the next minute or more, revelling in the warmth and support each gave the other. That our closeness had come so near to being broken made me angry … vengeful even. I was going to get my own back the first chance I got.

Drawing in a deep, shuddering breath, I murmured, "Hennessey …"

Alistair knew precisely what I was going to ask. "I am sure you would like to see me eject her from the ship. I'm afraid she is a paying passenger."

"She's involved in the conspiracy to ruin me," I stated bluntly, leaning my head back from his chest so I could see his face. It was time to tell him everything I believed I knew.

Alistair's mouth flapped open, but closed again without saying anything.

"The complaints made against me, the document from my computer that was leaked to the press?" I reminded him of just two problems we had argued about recently. "These are not random events from the maelstrom that is often my life."

"You think she is behind them?" Alistair was having trouble believing my claim.

I sniffed in a deep breath and readied myself to explain. I did not, however, attempt to move. I was quite content being held.

Mumbling a little because my throat still felt raw, I said, "No, but I believe the person who is, chose to seek out someone who might ruin our relationship. There are a few things I have yet to tell you."

Alistair cocked an eyebrow. "Such as?"

I laid my head back against his chest and told him my theory about the email hacking and how someone had tried to influence my relationship with Barbie. I was repeating much of what I told him this morning, but this time he was ready to believe me.

"The same people broke into my suite, hurt Jermaine, and trashed my possessions." I leaned out again to look up at his eyes.

"You know who it is," he remarked. "Don't you?" There was a laugh in his eyes.

I gave him a half shrug. "No. I have an idea though. I need to do some work to be sure and I need to deal with the current murder cases first."

Alistair cradled my head and kissed it again.

"You see, Patricia, this is what I mean. Your life is in turmoil and your focus is on catching the people behind three murders. I bet you have that all figured out too, don't you?"

He got the half shrug again. "Maybe." Willing to come up with any reason to remain where I was in his arms, I told him all about the snake and the whole love triangle thing between Nicole, Sanjeev, Luis, and Andrea.

"How does Vincent Pompeo fit in?"

Alistair's question was a good one, but also one I didn't have an answer to. It prompted me to slowly push myself away from the comforting spot I occupied. With a hand on Alistair's chest, I levered myself off his tunic and stepped back.

My mascara had left an inky black mark. There were no mirrors around, but I had to look a mess.

Alistair tracked his eyes to where I was looking. "I have other jackets, Patricia. I will change on my way back to the bridge. I only have one of you. Are the people behind this conspiracy to ruin you dangerous? Can I assign additional guards?"

I considered it for a moment but shook my head.

"I have plenty of security at my disposal." We both knew how dedicated and capable Jermaine was.

"Perhaps you should make a point of travelling with your butler until this matter is resolved."

"I will," I promised.

"Can I escort you back to your suite?" Alistair offered me his arm. "I've had people in there working hard to restore it to its former glory."

I was pleased to hear my accommodation might be more liveable than when I last saw it but my answer to his question had to be a firm 'no.'

"For now, at least, just in case we are being watched, I want the person responsible for my woes to believe they are winning. You should leave first looking angry, and I will depart a short while thereafter in tears once more."

I got a nod of understanding, Alistair checking his watch to see the time – there would be many tasks waiting for him. There always were.

He kissed me once more, on the lips but with affection rather than passion, then said, "Good luck in concluding the murder cases."

"Case," I corrected him.

"I'm sorry."

"Murder case. It's all one case." I checked with my head. "At least, I think so. I promise to tell you everything as soon as it is done."

With that, I got a peck on my cheek, and he slipped out of the door. Left alone in the meeting room, I gave myself a shake. I felt utterly drained. I needed something to eat, a stiff drink, a shot of caffeine, and probably a shower and change of clothes.

I figured I might manage to get one of those.

32

GIN. THANK GOODNESS

Barbie appeared seconds after I left the meeting room. She had been loitering around a nearby corner and watching for me to exit. Seeing the misery etched into my face – I was faking it now, but looked a state from the recent outpouring of emotion - she hooked an arm into mine and walked silently by my side.

Once I believed we were safe to talk and not being followed, I steered her into an alcove.

"Patty, are you okay?" she asked, wheeling to face me and taking a firm grip on my arms as if I might need her strength to keep myself upright. "Break ups are always just so … awful."

"He isn't cheating," I told her with a smile. She was going to argue, ready to point out that I must not be thinking right. She tracked him to Hennessey's cabin last night after all. "Trust me," I assured her. "The redhead is a former fiancée, and I think she is here as another part of the plan to mess with my life and make me look bad." I tugged at her arm to get her moving again.

"You're serious, Patty?" she questioned. "The captain really isn't sleeping with the redhead?"

"Hennessey. You told me her name is Hennessey, and no I

genuinely believe he is innocent. She went to some effort to make me believe otherwise though."

"Why?" Barbie struggled with the concept. "She doesn't know you. What could she possibly have to gain?"

I steered her down a passageway. "Money. I think she is being paid." Before Barbie could challenge my latest claim, I let go of her arm and took out my key card. We were heading for my suite. "I need to clean myself up and get a change of clothes."

No sooner had the words left my mouth than I remembered all my clothes were trashed. There had to be something that was still wearable, right? I opened the door to my suite to find Jermaine inside. It was refreshing to see him back where he belonged.

The dogs strained at their leads; the cabin filled with new smells to explore. I let them go, watching as they shot across the carpet to leap onto the couch. It was a new one, though not unlike the one that occupied the same spot before – and for the first time in hours things felt normal. Ever since I found the red hair, my head had been swimming with an overload of emotional turmoil.

Jermaine was in the kitchen, the door to the refrigerator open and a notepad in his hand – he was taking inventory. The suite was back to looking almost as it had. The curtains were not the same, but if anything, they suited the décor better. The oil paintings had been replaced with new items, a team no doubt dispatched to take all the broken and damaged items away as another team arrived with new ones.

These were the things that could be easily fixed. The damage to my clothes and whatever else they had chosen to destroy I would get to shortly. First, I needed to check on Jermaine.

"How are you feeling, sweetie?" The dogs trotted after me as I focused my attention on him. Barbie had already crossed the room to ask the same question.

"I am fully recovered, madam." Of course, I knew he would say that even if it wasn't true.

Barbie said, "Patty thinks the redhead is part of the conspiracy to mess with her life. The captain hasn't been cheating after all."

Jermaine cocked an eyebrow at her, prompting her to say more.

"Hennessey Gates is the captain's former fiancée and Patty thinks someone lured her onto the Aurelia just to mess with her."

Jermaine swung his gaze to look at me. I had joined the two of them in the open-plan kitchen end of my suite where I hoped to find the gin had not been tampered with.

With a knowing look on his face, Jermaine said, "You know who it is, don't you, madam?"

I threw my hands in the air. "Why does everyone think I have all the answers?"

I got deadpan expressions from them both.

"Okay, well maybe, but it's just a guess and not worth sharing. I have asked a question and will know if I am right when I get an answer."

Barbie looked cross. "Patricia Fisher you tell us who it is right now!"

I shot her an apologetic look. "I can't, sweetie. It will just be distracting. Maybe tonight if we can sew up these cases, then I will tell you. I might have an answer by then anyway."

Barbie narrowed her eyes at me. "You'd better had, Patty. You're far too good at keeping secrets."

All I could do was shrug and flop wearily onto one of the breakfast barstools. Jermaine knew me well enough to reach into the fridge for the gin, showing me the bottle and getting a slight dip of my head in thanks.

Barbie chose to join me, and Jermaine laid out three glasses – one for each of us. I accepted the cold glass of Hendricks gin and Fevertree slimline tonic with another nod of thanks, and gulped half of it with my eyes closed. Any positive effect it might have on me was entirely in my head, but as the cold liquid flowed across my tongue it took away the sting of tears and left behind a determined sense of purpose.

If I was right about the identity of my tormentor then I was in more trouble than anyone realised. Their actions were out of character or, at least, beyond anything I had previously thought them to be capable of. The undertaking to ruin me hinted at a level of insanity I could not have predicted and that scared me.

What else were they capable of? What else might they have in store for me or my friends? The attack on Jermaine was an escalation from forging complaints and hacking my computer, and I thought myself lucky neither he nor my dogs were badly harmed.

Draining the last of my gin, I swivelled around on the barstool, dropping to my feet whereupon I announced my intention to get a shower and change.

Barbie called after me, "What are you going to do about clothes?"

33

SHIPS THAT PASS IN THE NIGHT

Ten minutes later, after a hurried shower with the head set low so my hair stayed dry, I kissed the dachshunds goodbye and stepped out of the suite with Barbie and Jermaine on my shoulders. I was wearing form-fitting Lycra or, more accurately, I was wearing Barbie's Lycra which fit her form perfectly, but just made me look a little ridiculous.

Her clothes had see-through panels on them and hugged her skin to show off how perfectly toned her limbs and all her other bits are. The same clothes made me look like a blancmange.

I could buy new clothes. There were boutiques on the ship, and we would stop somewhere cosmopolitan soon enough where I could spring for a whole new wardrobe. That didn't help me much now though since I didn't even own a pair of clean knickers. Barbie gave me a pair of hers – new ones she hadn't worn yet. However, my twenty-two-year-old friend wears skimpy thongs that a person could swallow without the need for a glass of water. They avoid the obvious panty line across one's derriere – desirable in tight Lycra, but I was used to something with a little more support and had to focus hard not to fiddle around with my bottom which felt like it was being abused.

We went to the brig – my second visit of the day, and more successful this time since I made it past the outer door. There, Baker still had Luis Velasquez waiting to be interviewed. Andrea was still to be found, but I doubted I would need her to prove my theory.

"How did you find out about the snakes?" I posed my first question before I was even sitting in my chair.

Luis had been escorted to one of the interview rooms by the guards working in the brig and settled into his chair by Lieutenant Bhukari. She and Baker were in the interview room with me, the three of us facing him as we drilled down to get the truth behind his crime. He looked guilty, that was for sure, the paramedic squirming in his chair and wishing to be somewhere else. Jermaine and Barbie were waiting for me in the main part of the brig, chatting with the guards there over a cup of coffee. Schneider and Sam were in the operations room chasing down information on Vincent Pompeo and trying to find a connection somewhere between any of our victims.

Pippin had been drawn away to investigate another Buddy sighting that would probably prove to be accurate, but historic. The ape didn't stay in one place for long. If I ever got finished with the murder enquiry, I would organise a feast for him and take great pleasure in shooting him with a tranquiliser dart.

Slapped with his first question – one I deliberately chose to throw him off balance, Luis frowned and blinked.

"I'm sorry? What was that?" he questioned. "Did you say snake?"

"Yes, Luis," I feigned boredom. "It is the most extraordinary murder weapon I have ever heard of let alone come across."

He blinked again, looking from me to Baker, onto Bhukari and back to me.

"Wait. You think I know something about a snake?"

It was a valiant attempt. Convincing almost, but I offered him a confident smile.

"We can do this for as long as it takes, Luis. Andrea appears to have abandoned you to face the music alone. Did you know that? We are looking for her, but unless we find her, you are facing the charge for all three murders." He recoiled from my accusation, horrified and rightly so.

"Murders! What on earth are you talking about?"

"What part did Vincent play?" I pressed, ignoring his act.

"Who the heck is Vincent? Vincent who?"

"Drop the act, Luis!" I snapped, startling him with my sudden change in volume and attitude. "Three people are dead, your lover and partner in crime, Andrea Bassinet-Blatch, is on the run, and when we analyse the physical evidence taken from the three scenes, we are going to find your fingerprints and DNA. Your only hope at reducing the sentence you face is to confess and tell your side of the story."

"But I don't have a side of the story!" he protested, and for the first time I began to doubt my conviction. There was something about how terrified he looked. There was guilt in his expression and in his body language, but something wasn't adding up. "And I'm not even sure she can be called my lover." I had been considering a new line of questions – coming at him from a different angle when he made his comment about Andrea and that changed things.

"You spent last night with her," Baker pointed out. "Are you proposing to claim the two of you played Scrabble all night?"

Luis gave a defeated sigh. "I don't know what we did."

His remark caused me to frown. "How long have the two of you been dating?" I wanted to know. That they were dating at all contradicted Barbie's information and needed to be clarified.

Luis' eyes had been firmly locked on the floor, the guilty man unwilling to make eye contact. Now he lifted his chin to look at me and I saw honesty on his face for the first time.

"We haven't been dating. I asked her out once a long time ago and she knocked me back. I figured that was that, but she came over to me in the bar last night and was all over me. I haven't spoken to her or thought about her in months."

Baker jumped in. "You still spent the night with her though, right?"

Luis shrugged. "She whispered some things to me in the bar …"

"What sort of things?" I wanted details.

Luis blushed. "Sex things. What she wanted me to do."

I blushed as well, changing my mind about how much detail we needed.

Luis continued talking. "She told me she needed a man's hands on her body and apologised for turning me down when I asked her out months ago. Andrea said she hadn't stopped thinking about me since."

I wasn't going to say it, but there was something about his story that didn't feel right. Andrea had to be fit, lean and toned just like Barbie. So too is Sanjeev, another member of the fitness fraternity. Luis is an okay looking guy, but he sports a belly and lacks that … je ne sais quoi. Andrea could go for him, he wasn't unattractive, but if he wasn't lying about her suddenly jumping him, then … what? My skull gave a little itch.

Pushing the suspect about his shared alibi, Lieutenant Commander Baker pressed on.

"Whose cabin did you go to?"

"Mine."

"What time did you arrive?"

Luis wasn't sure, but thought it was around ten thirty the previous evening. When pursued on the subject he became defensive.

"Look, I don't know, okay? I don't remember much about it. I guess I'd had more to drink than I thought because I felt quite light-headed when we got back to my cabin. I remember her taking off her clothes and when I woke up in the morning, she was still in my bed and naked."

Baker asked, "What time was that?"

"Just before seven this morning. I remember because I was supposed to get up at six and was almost late to start my watch." Luis could see that we were listening, so he reiterated an important point from earlier. "Look, I don't know Sanjeev. I certainly didn't know Andrea had a boyfriend, and I don't know anyone called Vincent. I didn't kill anyone last night and I'm sure Andrea will vouch for me as my alibi."

We continued to quiz him, but the certainty I'd entered the

room with was gone. I had allowed myself to believe Andrea and Luis were the kind of star-crossed lovers who went on a murder spree. They would not be the first in history.

Now I wasn't sure what to think. To give myself some time, I left Baker and Bhukari to it, exiting the interview room to tackle a different task. I had promised Reece Mefford I would let him know how the hunt for his snakes was going and right now that meant telling him one of them was dead.

I doubted he would take it well.

34

BERTIE OR BRIAN

"Dead?" Reece Mefford answered the door in a dishevelled state. He had been drinking – the pure alcohol on his breath left no question in my mind, though how much and for how long I could only guess.

Despite his state, he still took a moment to take in my appearance. I was expecting him to question my outfit, which was why I cut him off quickly by announcing the new development.

"I'm afraid so," I continued. I was standing in the passageway outside his cabin just as I was the last time I visited. Barbie and Jermaine were still with me, lurking a few yards away where they could watch but would not come across as imposing.

I'm not sure what I thought Mr Mefford might say in response to the news, but, "What happened to its body?" wasn't it.

It struck me as an odd question, but I gave him an answer. "It was taken to the morgue."

Reece reacted with a hopeful tone. "So, it wasn't put in an incinerator or anything?"

I shook my head slowly from side to side. I didn't know if the ship even had an incinerator. "No, sir. I saw it myself. It is in the morgue. Do you wish to ascertain whether it was Bertie or Brian?"

"Who?" Reece blinked a couple of times. "Oh, sorry, yes. I see what you mean. Yes, I would like to see him, please. They do have individual markings. I doubt anyone else – other than my wife – could tell them apart." Reece's face morphed into one heavyset with sadness and when he spoke again, it sounded like the weight of the world had landed back on his shoulders. "I need to collect it, Mrs Fisher. My wife will want to bury it with me. Has there been any sign of his brother?"

My skull was itching again, but I was putting it down to the strange connection to the murder case. I hadn't told Mr Mefford that his pet had been targeted so it would commit murder on someone else's behalf – I didn't see any need, but there was something about the way he was acting now that was confusing me.

"Do you know Vincent Pompeo?" I asked, watching Reece's face to see what reaction came.

He thought for a moment, consulting his mental contact list before answering. "No, sorry. I cannot say that I do. Who is he?"

"How about Sanjeev Bhaskar or Andrea Bassinet-Blatch?" I ignored his question to fire off another of my own. I got the same pause and negative answer for them.

"Nicole Tibbett?"

Still a negative and I believed he was telling the truth. Whatever the hind part of my brain was trying to tell me, it wasn't anything to do with the murders. That didn't surprise me – I couldn't come up with a tangible reason why the man transporting his two pet snakes would have any knowledge of my victims. But how did they know about the snakes?

The mystery meter was still in the red and I wasn't getting anywhere. I promised Alistair I would have answers for him, but all I had was dead ends and a dead snake.

"How about it then, Mrs Fisher?" Reece's voice dragged me back to the present. "Can I get his body back?" His hopeful tone had returned.

I promised to ask the question and figure out how that would happen. I figured the dead snake could be loaded back into the glass tank and left on ice in the morgue. If that was what the owner wanted, I wouldn't get in the way, but had no idea what the health and safety people, not to mention Dr Davis might have to say about the matter.

Leaving Reece Mefford behind, I started back toward the elevators. I was going to catch up with the other people involved in the investigation, visiting the operations room on deck ten.

From my handbag, my radio squawked. "Lieutenant Schneider for Mrs Fisher."

The handbag really didn't go with my Lycra clothes, which by-the-way, were no longer hugging my skin but beginning to gather in places as I moved. They looked great on Barbie, and it was all she had in her wardrobe that would fit me, but where I was distinctly not the *right* shape for them, they were bunching at the knees and riding up over my belly.

All fingers and thumbs, I dug around until I found the noisy device, finally answering Schneider when he called me for a third time.

"Schneider, have you found something?"

"Yes. I can't do it over the airwaves though. Can you come to the operations room?"

His request altered our route, but only slightly. Going to the operations room was next on my agenda, but what I hadn't announced was a plan to sneakily visit a boutique on the eighteenth deck first. A new outfit was in order. In fact, anything that didn't make me look like one of those women who wore their daughter's clothes and told themselves they looked just as good in them would do.

It would have to wait though. And so would Schneider and his information it transpired because Barbie caught hold of my arm to whisper in my ear.

"That's Andrea."

I looked around, unable to see where Barbie was looking. There was no one in sight.

In the end, I had to ask, "Where?"

I hadn't seen her, but the lead suspect was walking right toward me. Coming along a passageway that intersected ours, Barbie had spotted her as we passed it. She was coming our way, and all we had to do was wait.

When Andrea reached the intersection and stepped out, she found Jermaine, me, and Barbie all staring at her. If she ran, my friends would catch her, but she didn't run. She didn't even seem to register that we were there.

In contrast to the mental image I had of her, she wasn't looking around furtively, checking her environment and looking for a way to escape the ship. Andrea Bassinet-Blatch just looked miserable. She had been crying – the impact of her decisions and the likelihood of imprisonment weighing heavily on her soul no doubt.

Only when she attempted to go around us, mumbling an apology, and Jermaine raised an arm to stop her, did she look up to see who it was.

"Andrea?" I spoke her name to bring her attention in my direction. "I need to speak with you about the death of Sanjeev Bhaskar." I could have listed Nicole and Vincent as well, but intuition was guiding me. She had an alibi for the time of their deaths in the form of Luis. Baker and Bhukari were still picking that apart, but whether Luis' story unravelled I could not guess. What I did know was that Andrea was yet to provide an alibi for when Sanjeev died.

To my great surprise, her face crumpled, and tears began to fall again. Huge racking sobs shook her shoulders, and she wailed his name.

Yet again, I was befuddled. If she was his killer, why was she so upset to hear his name?

We were unable to get any kind of a sensible answer from her. She was trying to speak through her tears, but the words were garbled and nonsensical. Keeping her where we were, I used the radio to summon Schneider to my location – we were heading back to the brig.

35
—————

NO CLUE

A ndrea offered no resistance as she was processed into the
brig. She didn't speak at all, and no one asked her any
questions save for those required to log her arrest. Luis
was still in the brig, but back in a cell where he would remain until
we had this all figured out.

While we waited for the guard to finish with Andrea and
allowing enough time for her to calm down, I caught up with
Schneider.

He'd kept Sam with him after they chased down half a dozen
supposed Andrea sightings, returning to the operations room where
they delved into the lives of the victims. I fervently hoped to hear
there was something worth finding, so imagine my relief when
Schneider got to the good stuff.

"Vincent Pompeo is a small-time crook from Miami," the
Austrian revealed. "He's got a rap sheet as long as my arm, but it's
all minor stuff." Before we could press him to expand, he added,
"Drug and gang related crimes mostly. His longest stretch inside was
for distribution. He got five years that time, serving three before he
got out. That was eighteen months ago."

"Okay," I tried the new information on for size to see if it meant anything to me. "So we have a small-time crook from Miami, known for involvement in drugs, and up to no good on a cruise ship." Everyone was staring at me, waiting for a giant leap from one clue to the solution. I pulled a face. "I have no idea what that has got to do with snakes, fitness people killing each other, or anything else."

Schneider said, "Well, it looks like his gang went to jail when you busted the Godmother and exposed the Alliance of Families. He was one of the few who escaped incarceration, probably because he was too far down the food chain to be named in any of the documents Barbie leaked."

It explained why he might have chosen to abandon his home turf for new pastures, but told us nothing about why he was on the ship or what he was doing.

Deepa helped out with a question. "Hey where are the other victims from?"

Barbie snapped her fingers. "Nicole is from Florida somewhere. I'm not sure where exactly …"

"It's Miami," stated Baker, his fingers flashing over the tablet he held. "This thing isn't going to tell me if they knew each other …"

"And Miami isn't exactly a village where everyone knows everyone," concluded Barbie.

I nodded along. "No, but a tenuous link is still a link. We need to check into that."

Before we could discuss it, Lieutenant Wong stuck his head back into the reception area.

"Miss Bassinet-Blatch is ready for you now."

It was time to grill our lead suspect, but was she a stone-cold killer or yet another distraction? I had three bodies, no proper leads or links, and the almost solved case of an hour ago was just as confusing as when I first walked into cabin 1215.

Half an hour later I was nowhere nearer to figuring it out.

"I'm telling you the truth!" Andrea wailed. "I don't know anything about any snakes. I was in bed with Luis Velasquez when Nicole was killed, and I don't know anyone called Vincent Pompeo."

Her story was that she and Sanjeev had broken up yesterday. In her words, he dumped her, ending the relationship because they wanted different things. She was in love with him, but he was just having a bit of fun. Wallowing in the grief of her rejection, she sought solace in the arms of a man she knew was interested in her. It was a foolish reaction, Andrea claiming she had never thought anything through less. But there it was - she and Luis provided each other's alibis.

Until I could prove otherwise, I had nothing to tie her to Nicole's murder or Sanjeev's death. She admitted that in the past she and Nicole had their differences, but they were long behind them now and the two had become friends. Her comments in the group chat supported her claim. I had to wonder if Sanjeev had dumped her to go back to Nicole – it might provide a strong motive for their deaths but still left me questioning how Vincent was involved.

"Sanjeev had no interest in Nicole," Andrea claimed. "You're barking up the wrong tree with that one. He ditched her because she was talking about settling down. Bless her, she was ready to move in with him after a week. That's why it didn't last."

I was left with nothing but conjecture about what might have happened between Sanjeev, Nicole, and Andrea. I couldn't prove anything, but Andrea's grief – inspired when she learned of his death – seemed genuine.

In her version of events, Andrea woke this morning confused about where she was and then embarrassed about what she had done. Leaving Luis' cabin in a hurry and with an apology, it was some time after that when she learned of Nicole's murder and was brought in for initial questioning. In her own words, she was glad to have an alibi. Only after she was released by Baker did she learn of Sanjeev's death. He might have rejected her, but that did nothing to change how she felt about him.

Unable to process her emotions, she couldn't even be sure where she went, only that she wandered the ship in a trancelike state until she bumped into us.

"I don't believe you," I concluded when she finally ran out of words. It was a verbal slap to the face that produced yet more water-works. "I think you killed Nicole and your night with Luis is nothing more than a clever manipulation to cover your tracks and create an alibi."

I was pushing her to see if she would crack. In truth, I wasn't sure I suspected her at all.

"That's not true," she cried, her tears falling to dampen the table on her side.

I wanted to accuse her of lying about the snakes and about Sanjeev and Vincent, but for the life of me I had no clue what was going on or why. I terminated the interview, but wasn't going to release her yet.

I was rescued from having to say anything more by a knock on the door. It turned out to be Lieutenant Pippin who came with mixed news. Leaving Andrea to stew as Baker and Bhukari escorted her to a cell, I listened.

"Well, I'm sorry to report that the ladies from the bursar's department have concluded their inspection and are adamant that nothing is missing. I made the mistake of dropping in to check on their progress and had to endure their desire to make others suffer as they had."

"They did not enjoy their outing?" I jested.

Pippin gave me a dour look. "I would say that was the case, Mrs Fisher. Anyway, they found nothing and claimed they opened as many boxes as they could without breaking any seals. The only thing that had been touched in that entire storeroom was the vivarium with the two snakes."

It wasn't what I wanted to hear, but it also came as no great surprise. It made me resolve to deal with a task I put on my agenda more than an hour ago.

Huffing out a breath as I readied myself for more hours of running and chasing, I started for the door, turning to walk back-wards so I could address the room.

"Anyone else coming?" I joked with a smile. "I need to check on Sanjeev's cabin and then probably cabin 1215."

36

A CLUE

You know how it is when you want to be right because then your confidence is justified and your claims vindicated, well that was how it was when we opened Sanjeev Bhaskar's cabin on deck six. I had a theory in my head that was all to do with the snake and about how he had come to be a victim.

But then, I bet you also recognise how being right can sometimes bite you in the bum.

Sanjeev's cabin was exactly as we had left it, the door sealed and locked to prevent anyone messing with any physical evidence before we returned, and a sign erected to make the need to keep out utterly unambiguous. I let Lieutenant Schneider open the door, following him in with everyone else on my shoulder. Pippin and Bhukari had their weapons drawn on Baker's command – he got that I was nervous about the other snake - but there was no sign of life within.

It was quiet inside the cabin, the sterile environment of a man most recently dead. I could not tell whether everyone was being silent out of respect, or simply because everyone else was being quiet, but I was the one who broke it when I spoke.

"That's the duvet cover we placed over Sanjeev earlier." I was standing in the doorway to the bedroom in his tiny crew cabin. It was a duplicate of the other crew cabins I had seen, including Barbie's. A foot from my feet was a duvet cover. It was crumpled into a heap on the thin weave, functional carpet.

Barbie, Jermaine, and everyone else crowded around me, peering over my shoulders to see the object in question. I was annoyed with myself because I hadn't spotted the incongruity earlier. To be fair, my attention had been on the body and the terrible state we found it in, but even so, looking down at the crumpled cotton now, the thing that was wrong about it was glaringly obvious.

It was Jermaine who said it first. "That's not from a single bed."

"Oh, yeah," snorted Barbie, her eyes now drawn to the excess of material.

Glumly, I agreed. "No. Proving it might be impossible, but I believe this is the double duvet from cabin 1215."

"Why is it here?" Sam couldn't figure that part out.

Bending at the waist and knees to crouch, I grabbed the duvet cover and yanked it into the air. I was about to demonstrate that it had been used to transport the snakes. However, I had not given any thought to what the crumpled cover might be hiding.

The second boa constrictor, undoubtedly choosing to be still when it felt the vibrations of our feet nearby, had remained undetected beneath the cotton duvet cover until I abruptly exposed it. Startled, it lifted its head into the air.

As a child, my mother would assure me that insects, spiders, and other bugs that gave me the heebie jeebies were far more scared of me than I was of them. Well, that might be the case even now, but if the snake was terrified, it was doing far less screaming than everyone else.

Achieving a note that would have made an opera soprano proud, Schneider leapt away from the giant snake, colliding with the bulkhead just a few feet behind him where he then clung.

Barker, Bhukari, Pippin, Sam, and Barbie all vanished from behind me as they took fright and ran for the exit. This gave me room to escape which was a good thing because I was attempting to master unpowered flight. Honestly, had I not collided instantly with

Jermaine's chest, I might have exited Sanjeev's cabin without touching the deck. As it was, my face smooshed against my butler's right pectoral muscle and bounced off. Tumbling backward - yes, toward the snake – I screamed again, my arms flailing.

I was going to land right on top of the angry/frightened serpent and become immediately ensnared in its coils. A terrifying image of the snake's jaw detaching as it opened its mouth to swallow me whole filled my brain and I would have fainted had Jermaine not caught hold of my arm.

Yanked back to upright, Jermaine deftly spun me around and away, swapping places with me and putting his body between me and the giant reptile.

The snake flicked out its tongue, tasting the air. Did it like it? Was it going to track me down and eat me? It wasn't attempting to attack Jermaine, who in contrast to everyone else seemed unphased by the presence of the reptilian predator.

Lieutenant Schneider had climbed onto the small dressing table next to the built-in closet. I could see him through the doorway. Looking less panicked, and actually kind of embarrassed now, he began to lower a foot to the deck.

The snake turned its head to look at him and two things happened. Firstly, Schneider withdrew his foot, whipping it back up to join the rest of his body huddled on the dressing table. Almost simultaneous with that, Jermaine gripped the open end of the duvet cover, scribing an arc with his arms as he took the material up, over and down to once again engulf the snake.

A second later, Jermaine stood up with a hand holding the large cotton sack closed. Fat at the bottom where the snake struggled and wriggled, and bunched at the top where he held it, the duvet cover now looked sort of like a semi-deflated Santa's sack. If Santa were an evil git who brought giant snakes to children at Christmas, that is.

My heart, which I swear hadn't bothered to beat for the last ten seconds, finally came back to life and I gasped a deep breath.

"I have the snake," announced Jermaine. "It is quite safe for everyone to return."

His invitation garnered eyeballs peering around the door, but no one was coming back into the cabin, and I was joining them outside.

We came to check a theory – that the snakes arrived in Sanjeev's cabin inside the duvet cover. Now I believe that to be true, I just needed to check on cabin 1215. If the duvet cover there was missing, I would know for certain that Vincent Pompeo went down to the storeroom to get the snakes. They were his target. The why of it still eluded me.

"The animal needs heat, madam," remarked Jermaine. The sack he held had gone still once more. "I believe it is too cool here and that might be why it was seeking warmth beneath the duvet cover. I believe you said something earlier about a vivarium?"

He was right, of course - the snake was an innocent party and deserved to be looked after. I would be able to inform Reece Mefford that we had found his other pet and it was still alive. He would be needed to make sure the remaining snake's habitat was correctly set up and that the animal had sustained no injury during its adventure.

That it might be hurt hadn't entered my mind until that very moment, and it changed my plan of action.

"Jermaine, can you take the snake to sick bay, please, sweetie?"

"Sick bay, madam?"

Hearing my request, Barbie and the others gave me curious looks.

"I must inform the owner that we have his snake, but I would like to confirm that we have taken its plight seriously and done our best to check it is healthy. They can put a heat lamp on it too." I was thinking that the vivarium might take a while to set up and get ready.

Lieutenant Commander Baker nodded his agreement. "That's good thinking, Mrs Fisher. I will accompany you, Jermaine, it looks like a heavy load."

Decision made, Jermaine slowly lifted the heavy cotton sack from the deck, manoeuvring it onto one shoulder like a giant hobo pack. As he did so, something fluttered down, catching the light, and twinkling as if lit from within.

No one else saw it – I was the only one close enough and facing the right way. It caused me to ask, "What was that?"

I got a few, "Huhs?" as heads poked around the doorframe again.

Jermaine backed up a step, seeing me advance and able to determine where I was trying to go. I had to get on my hands and knees to search for what I had seen, my odd behaviour luring my team back into the cabin.

"Did you find something, Mrs Fisher?" asked Sam, joining me on the thin carpet, his trusty magnifying glass appearing in his right hand. "Is this it?" he asked a moment later.

I twisted around as everyone gathered to see what was beneath the piece of convex glass.

It was a small piece of foil. Round and about a quarter inch across, it had a small tab protruding from one side to enable a person to grip it. Like the lid of yoghurt, but much smaller, I carefully plucked it from the floor and held it in the palm of my hand for everyone to see.

Using a fingernail, I flipped it over to find markings on the other side. Employing the magnifying glass once more, I read aloud, "CHT Micromed," and looked up to see if that meant anything to anyone.

"It looks like the top off a drug bottle," offered Deepa. "Like when they need to give you a vaccine." She tried to create a visual for us. "They have the little vial, and the needle goes through the plastic bit at the top, but there is a tamper seal on it – the little foil thing. That's what it looks like to me."

Barbie had her phone out. "CHT Micromed is a brand name for a medicinal painkiller." Her eyes were down as she read from her screen. "It's morphine," she announced.

They used it to pacify the snakes! I could see it instantly. The foil thing had been hidden inside the duvet cover. It had been missed during our initial evidence gathering and only came to life now because Jermaine turned the cover inside out when he grabbed it.

I even knew where it had come from.

37

ANOTHER CLUE

Jermaine and Baker chose to wait for a porter to arrive with a trolley – the kind they use to shift luggage. The snake was heavy enough that it was safer for everyone including the snake if they avoided carrying him by hand.

While they went to the medical centre, Schneider and Sam were heading to Reece Mefford's cabin. I wanted to do it in person, but would catch up with him shortly. The important thing was to make sure his pet was cared for.

With me, I had Pippin and Bhukari as armed guards, plus Barbie. She was too invested in the case now to walk away.

We needed to get to deck twelve, which is an easy elevator ride or, if you have Barbie with you, a torturous exercise mission.

"But you're in sports gear already, Patty," she pointed out, a broad smile on her face because she was excited about burning some calories.

"We're game, aren't we Pippin?" said Deepa, thirty years my junior and another fitness freak. Pippin started jogging on the spot.

"But I'm carrying my handbag," I pointed out in an apologetic tone. *Really, I love to run up multiple flights of stairs, but gosh darn it, I cannot right now.*

Barbie took my handbag, slipping it off my shoulder though I grabbed the straps and tried to hold onto it.

"I'll carry it for you," she flared her nostrils at me with a triumphant smile when she finally wrenched it from my grip. "Everyone ready?"

The problem is one of my own making, you see? When I first came onboard and Barbie helped me get fit, I foolishly announced that I had never felt better, healthier, or more confident, and instructed her – like an idiot – to always find ways to squeeze some fitness into my days.

If I'd been given a second, I might have thought up a new excuse, but the blonde horror set off, Deepa and Pippin looking at me as they jogged in place and waited for me to start running. With a sigh, I accepted my fate and set off.

Fifteen minutes later, and six decks higher, I wheezed to a stop on shaky legs protesting from all the stairs they were forced to ascend.

"That was great!" cheered Barbie, still jogging on the spot. "Shall we do it again?"

"NO!" My shout made her recoil. "I mean to say we do not have time," I explained more calmly. Now that we were on deck twelve, the task at the top of the list was to check in cabin 1215 to see if they had a duvet cover present or not.

Arriving back in the passageway that led to the Boatengs' cabin, I was surprised to find Molly still stationed outside the door.

"How long have you been here, Molly?" I questioned.

She was squirming and panting and looking desperately uncomfortable.

"Since we finished up down in the Engineering department, Mrs Fisher," she groaned. "I wasn't sure what else I should do so I came back to where I was before."

"But that was hours ago," I pointed out unnecessarily.

Molly agreed, "Yeah, and I really, really need to pee!"

"Why didn't you just go inside?" Lieutenant Pippin questioned. "Or radio for someone to replace you?"

"Never mind that," I grabbed a door card from Deepa and

swiped it at the cabin's entry panel. Sending Molly ahead of us, she ran for the tiny cabin's bathroom, slamming the door shut as we moved through and into the bedroom.

Sure enough, the duvet cover was missing. It was another fat clue I just hadn't seen. The toilet flushed behind us, and a much-relieved Molly appeared a moment later.

"I didn't think I could use the loo in here on account of it being a crime scene," she explained.

"Why didn't you use your radio?" asked Deepa, frowning slightly at the junior crew person.

Embarrassed, Molly shrugged. "I didn't want to call for help on my first day. At the academy they kept telling us we would be expected to manage for ourselves and operate independently."

"That's right," agreed Deepa. "But that doesn't mean you cannot take care of your personal needs. Maybe you should just come with us?" She twisted to look my way, checking my opinion.

"Yes, I think that would be best, you've been here long enough." Deepa was on her radio instantly, contacting the security hub to let them know they'd forgotten to replace Molly and requesting a replacement.

We had to wait around for the new person to arrive, so were still in cabin 1215 when Schneider's voice boomed over the airwaves. He wanted me, but Deepa reached up to the radio on her lapel long before I could think to dig around in my handbag.

"This is Bhukari. I have Mrs Fisher with me, over."

"We're at Reece Mefford's cabin, but he isn't here, over."

That Mr Mefford had chosen to go out was disappointing – I wanted his help to make sure the snake was well-cared for. However, there was no imperative for Mr Mefford to remain in his cabin all day and I had not suggested he should. What I ought to have done was take his phone number, then I wouldn't have needed to send people to his cabin in the first place.

"Have you checked inside?" I asked, remembering that he had been drinking. Deepa wasn't pressing her send button at the time, so I had to repeat my question, but the answer was the one I expected:

They hadn't opened his door despite having a universal key card to do so because they had no just reason.

Explaining that he might have passed out, Schneider went silent for a few seconds, his voice coming back over the airwaves a moment later to confirm Reece Mefford was not in his cabin.

Ensign Buckshaw, who I met at Nicole's fitness centre on deck eighteen first thing this morning, arrived at the doorway. He was puffing and out of breath, whoever sent him to replace Molly undoubtedly telling him to get to us at speed.

While Deepa dealt with him, I asked Schneider, "Can you wait around for a little while to see if he comes back?"

"Sure. You want for me to put an alert out for everyone to be on the lookout for him?"

I shook my head, muscle memory controlling the gesture Schneider couldn't see. "No, Schneider. He'll show up soon enough and we are just being cautious with the snake. Maybe this way we will have his snake warm and happy before he sees it."

There being no reason to hang around on deck twelve, we set off again, this time heading for the brig. I was about to put Luis back into the hot seat and this time I was armed with knowledge.

38

GENDER CONFUSION

L uis looked distinctly less guilty this time when I came into the brig's interview room. Baker and Bhukari were with me, just as they were before, but the haunted expression glued to Luis' face a few hours ago had lifted. I thought I knew why.

"You look happier," I remarked, settling into the middle of three chairs across the table from the paramedic. It was a simple opener that invited him to respond. A wise person would stay quiet, limiting the information they gave away for free, but Luis wasn't bright enough to know that.

"I'm looking forward to getting out of here," he looked from me to Baker, then to Bhukari and back to me. "You've figured out I had nothing to do with any of the murders, right? That's why you wanted to speak to me again, isn't it?"

I nodded my head in Deepa's direction, the lieutenant withdrawing a small evidence bag from a pocket. She placed it on the table, the three of us watching Luis to see how he reacted.

He just looked confused for a second or so, his eyes squinting as he leaned forward. The clear plastic evidence bag appeared empty until one looked closer.

Our suspect's head snapped up, his eyes meeting mine as the colour drained from his face. His first words condemned him.

"How did you know?"

Now here's the thing – I now knew he was guilty, but I didn't know what he had done. If I answered him and guessed wrong, I would expose how little I had figured out and in so doing hand the advantage back.

Instead, I said, "Why don't you tell us why you kept quiet about this earlier?"

Luis was back to looking miserable, his head down and his expression hopelessly beaten.

"Because I knew it would mean I was fired. You can't lose drugs twice and get away with it. The first time they had me fill out a stack of paperwork and gave me a severe reprimand. I had to go in front of the captain, that's how serious it is. I guess I hoped this time I could cover it up ... somehow."

What had I expected him to say? I thought he had used the morphine on the snakes deliberately, but the paramedic wasn't worried about being tried for multiple homicides, he was talking about losing his job.

Adjusting my next question as my brain reacted to the incoming information, I asked, "Are you covering for Andrea?"

I got a one shoulder kind of shrug, an almost imperceptible non-gesture of apology.

"I guess," Luis murmured. Looking up at me he said, "I mean, I guess that's what happened, right? I don't remember much after she came onto me in the bar, so I figured she slipped something in my drink. It would certainly explain why I don't recall whether we had sex or not. It was just so out of the blue. She's not interested in me and then suddenly she is – in a big way. I knew there was something wrong when I woke up. She was naked in bed with me, but she moved away as soon as I opened my eyes. Then she couldn't wait to leave."

This was great! Luis had started talking and now couldn't seem to stop. I couldn't yet tell if he was lying or telling the truth and it didn't matter too much. Somewhere in his words was what really happened; I just needed to sift through the fog of lies.

"When I got dressed … that was when I knew. The keys to my med bay were in the wrong pocket."

"Wrong pocket?" Deepa questioned.

Luis shifted his eyes to look at her.

"Yeah. I dress to the left so my stuff is in my right pocket." He said it like it should have been obvious.

Martin leaned around me to speak to his wife.

"That's totally a thing, babe."

She wrinkled her brow and squinted her eyes. "Men are so weird."

Ignoring them both, I pressed Luis. "Please continue. Your keys were in the wrong pocket?"

Luis glanced at my partners, waiting a second to see if they would interrupt again before he started talking again.

"Yeah, well I knew something was amiss, so I ran … like literally ran to the med bay. There were four vials of morphine missing. Nothing else, but the junkies always go for the pain meds. I tried to find Andrea, hoping I could convince her to give them back, but she wasn't in her cabin. I asked around but no one knew where she was. I even went to the watersports place where she works but it was crawling with these goons." He gave Baker and Bhukari a meaningful glance and seeing their glares, he apologised, "Sorry. I'm sure you mean well …"

"But inconveniently we interrupt people's criminal behaviour," Deepa finished his sentence, the snark in her voice impossible to miss.

There was no possible response so Luis chose to move on.

"I went back to the med bay, making sure I was there first and could shuffle things around so the missing vials weren't so obvious."

"It was going to be spotted though," I questioned.

He gave a sad nod. "There's a weekly inventory which has to tally against what we have administered. I might get away with a few missing paracetamol, but morphine tends to get noticed. It's not like you can give that out for a stubbed toe or some mild sunburn. I was still hoping I could find Andrea and … I dunno, maybe get them back or find a way to prove that she had taken them."

Baker asked the obvious question. "Why didn't you tell us this earlier?"

Luis sat back in his chair, making a scoffing noise when he said, "Would you have believed me? I thought you already knew and that was why you came for me. I had no idea you were going to start asking me about murders. Honestly, I felt nothing but relief when I realised you didn't know about the morphine. You were asking me about Sanjeev and Vincent – two men I have never heard of – and all I could think about was how to make sure no one ever found out about the missing drugs."

His explanation correlated to everything I witnessed in the previous interview. He *had* looked guilty, but then relieved when we accused him of conspiracy to murder. Now I knew why. I also had what I needed to push Andrea into a corner. It was time to prise the truth from her.

The do-si-do process of taking Luis back to his cell – if we could confirm all he claimed, he would be free to go soon enough – and putting Andrea into the interview room was going to take a few minutes. While the guards were doing that, we returned to the brig's reception area where we found Pippin anxiously waiting for us.

The second we came through the door to join him, he blurted, "Vincent Pompeo and Nicole Tibbett are cousins!"

He'd been trying to raise us, but our radios were not allowed in the interview room so with news too hot to wait, he'd legged it down to the brig to deliver it in person.

"How did you find that out?" Deepa questioned the randomness of his information.

Pippin wrestled the electronic tablet from his trouser pocket, touching the screen and then backing toward us so he could show us what he had as we looked over his shoulders.

"It was in the next of kin information." I knew we had details for every passenger who ever came on board. It was one of those just-in-case things that was on the forms passengers fill out. The crew must provide far more detail, but Pippin was explaining again as his fingers moved over the touch-sensitive screen. "We already knew they were both from Miami, right? That's not that big of a coincidence, but then I spotted that Nicole's next of kin is a Pompeo. Her mother is Vincent Pompeo's aunt!"

Young Lieutenant Anders Pippin was near bursting with excitement and well he should be. This was a big breakthrough. Unfortunately, I still had no idea what it meant, and the back of my skull steadfastly refused to itch upon hearing the new information.

"Nicole Tibbett knew the man who was killed in cabin 1215," Baker recited. "Vincent Pompeo was supposed to get off the ship in Gibraltar, but faked his departure …"

Deepa remarked, "I think we can be fairly sure Nicole had a hand in that."

"Yes," Baker agreed. "But why? The ship is heading across the Atlantic shortly. We will be in Miami in little more than a week. Why get off at all?"

Molly suggested, "Maybe Miami isn't where he wants to go."

I shook my head, unable to wade through the fog of confusion in my brain. "His destination doesn't matter," I muttered. "He was trying to create an airtight alibi. He came on board to commit a crime. He knew it would be detected eventually, but if anyone ever looked his way, he would be able to claim he wasn't on board. Chances are there is a trail in Gibraltar – a hotel reservation and such. No, we need to be looking at why he was involved in the first place."

"Well," Baker conjured a theory, "we know he's a criminal, and we know Nicole was in a relationship with Sanjeev that ended abruptly. It could be that she was planning the perfect murder."

I gave it a second to consider his suggestion, but it just didn't feel right. "A year is a long time to harbour a grudge for a failed relationship."

"Yeah, but women are crazy," Baker shot back without thinking. When Molly, me, Barbie, and his wife, Deepa, all glared at him, he took a pace back. "Well, some are," he argued weakly.

Pushing on, I said, "What we know at the moment is that Andrea took the morphine and Vincent climbed down to get the snakes. We don't have anything to connect Vincent to Andrea and no proof that Andrea did take the drugs – we just believe that to be the case. Someone planted the snakes in Sanjeev's cabin and that could only have been with the hope they would kill him. I don't think that was Andrea – her tears were real. It also couldn't have been Nicole because her time of death is too early."

Molly raised her hand.

Pippin laughed at her, getting angry eyes from the junior crew member. Adjusting his face, he said, "You can just speak. We are quite informal here."

Baker, the senior person in the room, added, "Just throw ideas around. Sometimes they spark a new thought that can lead us in an unexpected direction."

Relaxing, Molly said, "Could there be yet another person involved? Someone we don't know about yet?"

Her question silenced us all.

"She's ready." The statement came from Lieutenant Wong. He was hanging through the doorway, his hands gripping either side of the frame as he invited us to return to the interview room.

Pippin had uncovered a brilliant new piece of information. It linked two of the victims, one of whom was known to be a criminal, but what that had to do with Andrea, Sanjeev, snakes, or anything else, I had no idea. Resolved to grill Andrea until she cracked, or I figured it all out, I sucked in a deep breath and readied my first question.

Andrea Bassinet-Blatch bore the puffy, red eyes of someone who has been crying for hours and doesn't know how to stop. Sitting opposite the door on a lone chair behind the table, she looked up as we filed in and began talking before any of us were able to sit down.

"Are you here to let me go?" she snapped irritably. "I haven't done anything wrong, and it should be clear to anyone with eyes that I am in a state of grief. I just lost someone very dear to me and I ought to be allowed time to come to terms with it. Instead, you lot have me locked in a cell in the brig." She was railing about her treatment, trying to play the innocent card.

Baker opened with, "We know you stole the drugs from Luis, and we know why."

Andrea angled her head away from me to where Baker sat on my right.

"What drugs? What are you talking about?"

Deepa spoke next. "The ones you stole from the med bay on deck seventeen. You seduced Luis last night and slipped something into his drink. Once he passed out, you took his keys, stole what you needed and went back to his cabin."

Andrea's head turned to look at Deepa where she sat on my left. It was like watching someone who was watching tennis.

Before she could respond, I said, "We know about the snakes, Andrea. We know Nicole and Vincent were related. Tell me, was Sanjeev's death an accident?"

Andrea stared at me, her expression hard, but she waited too long before she denied knowing what I was talking about.

"You're all barmy, you lot. I haven't stolen anything, and I don't know anything about any snakes. I spent the night having sex with Luis and didn't leave his cabin until I woke up this morning and realised what I had done."

With deliberate motions, Deepa reached into her top left breast pocket, removing the evidence bag again. She placed it on the table, saying nothing.

Unable to stay silent, Andrea said, "What? What's this?"

When she leaned closer to squint at the tiny piece of foil inside, I said, "That is all the evidence we need, Andrea." Her head snapped up to look directly at me. Did I detect a flicker of worry in her eyes? "That piece of foil came from one of the morphine vials you stole. You used the morphine to subdue the snakes, didn't you?"

"No." Her answer was immediate, but unconvincing.

"You wanted to commit the perfect murder." I was pressing her, planning to hit my prime suspect with question after question until she finally caved, but the doubt I thought I saw evaporated in an instant. When I accused her of trying to craft a perfect murder, she tilted her head to look at me with a curious expression and a smile flickered across her lips.

When she spoke it was to say, "You've got nothing on me, have you?" The sadness hadn't left her face − I was right that she was upset about Sanjeev, but the amused confidence in her eyes told me I was wrong about everything else.

Mentally berating myself for overplaying my hand, I attempted to reset and try again.

"You killed Nicole with a dumbbell."

"She was my friend."

"Was she?" I challenged. "Isn't that a new development? I think you made friends with her because you were planning to kill her. Did you lie about her and Sanjeev? Were they getting back together? Did you kill them rather than face the humiliation of rejection? I think you planned the whole thing and killed everyone involved believing that would leave you in the clear."

This time Andrea actually laughed, a snort escaping her nose before she said, "Try proving it." It was a direct challenge, a confident statement to bring the interview to a close. We had nothing on her other than circumstantial evidence and conjecture. Worse yet, she knew it.

There was no point in continuing to quiz her − she had the upper hand, and I wasn't getting it back until I found something solid to use against her. Rising to my feet, I kept my eyes locked on hers.

"I'll be back soon enough, Andrea. Don't think for one minute that you will get away with it."

She laughed again. "Get away with what?"

Outside in the brig's reception area, my friends were still waiting for me, and I guess the anger boiling inside me was visible on the outside because they were all eyeing me cautiously.

Barbie asked, "Everything okay, Patty?"

I took a slow breath, pushing the stress of failure from my body when I exhaled.

"I'm nowhere," I admitted. "I cannot even work out what is going on. There are three dead people and I'm not sure what the motive was for any of them or even if Sanjeev Bhaskar was murdered or killed accidentally."

The moment the words left my mouth, the back of my skull itched. Sanjeev, who I assumed was the target of everything to do with the snakes … was he murdered or killed through misadventure? If I looked at the case from a completely different angle – including Sanjeev as part of the plot and not the intended victim – what did that mean? It meant the snakes got into his cabin because he took them there.

"Patty?" Barbie's voice invaded my thoughts.

"Madam?" Jermaine spoke softly from somewhere near my left shoulder. "Is everything all right?"

I ignored them both, focusing on the snakes and what I might have missed.

"Oi! Mrs Fisher!" Molly's shout, raucous and uncouth like the young woman herself, penetrated my brain, bursting the bubble of concentration like an anvil dropped on a watermelon.

Startled, I snapped my head around to look at her.

She lifted her arms, inviting applause. "That's how you get someone's attention."

"What's going on?" I asked, confused.

Barbie rolled her eyes. "You went into a trance, Patty. We were talking to you, but you weren't moving a muscle. It was like someone shot you with a freeze ray."

Shaking my head to clear it, I asked, "Anything from Schneider and Sam about Mr Mefford, the snakes' owner?"

Pippin, the one in the room whose radio hadn't left his side, gave the answer. "Only to say that they were still outside his cabin, and he hadn't returned."

The snakes. There was something about the snakes. I fished out my phone and called the sick bay.

Hideki answered, his voice booming over my speaker. "I have you on speaker …"

Barbie interrupted me to call out, "Hi, sweetie," to her boyfriend.

"… and I have Barbie with me among others," I finished my sentence. "How's the patient?" I hoped to hear the boa constrictor was warm and well. "Did you find somewhere suitable to put him?"

216

"The snake? *She* is doing quite well now that she is warmer. We had to employ an old baby incubator Dr Davis had in storage. Someone said something about a vivarium, but no one has turned up with it yet. We had to shove the heat lamp into the incubator and hope for the best."

I absorbed what he said, but was stuck on one point in particular.

"You said the snake is a she?"

"Yes. Is that a problem?"

Only if you are the owner and claim to have two boy snakes.

"How sure are you?" I challenged.

I heard him suck a little air through his teeth. "Well, my knowledge of female anatomy is rudimentary …"

Barbie's cheeks coloured and Pippin commented at a barely audible volume, "I doubt that's true."

Barbie's cheeks went several shades darker.

"Okay, it's a girl snake," I concluded. "How is she?"

"Pregnant," Hideki announced. "So is the other one. The one the ape killed. I'm afraid to report that I only thought to check the dead snake when I found the obvious lumps in the live one's abdomen – there's no sign of life from the babies in the dead one though."

I was about to comment on what a shame that was when Jermaine raised a pertinent point.

"Snakes lay eggs."

Hideki said nothing for a few seconds, then there were muffled words being exchanged at the other end as if Hideki had his hand over the phone.

When he came back on the line, he said, "I'll get back to you shortly. I need to check something."

The line went dead, leaving those of us in the brig's reception area all staring at each other. There was one simple and very obvious conclusion to draw, and it was Jermaine who said it first.

"There's something in the snake!"

217

39

WHAT IT'S ALL ABOUT

W e tore from the brig, running like a pack of wild animals with a predator behind us as we raced to get to sick bay.

I was cursing myself for the things I had missed. Reece Mefford claimed to be married and something had bothered me at the time. Off my game, it was only now that I realised he wasn't wearing a wedding ring.

That wasn't the only thing my befuddled brain had missed. Anna and Georgie had been going nuts when I was outside Sanjeev's cabin. They could smell something, and I was convinced now that it had been the snake. We hadn't found it when we tossed the place looking for evidence, but if I looked, I knew I would find a gap where it could have slithered under a closet or set of drawers. It had been mere feet from me the entire time I was in there, coming out again when we all left.

This had to be true because the second snake had escaped, finding a conduit under the floor that took it to where it met its untimely end courtesy of Buddy.

By the time we arrived back at sick bay, less Molly who announced her need for a "Number two" – her words not mine –

and stopped off when we passed a restroom, Drs Davis and Naka-mura had taken a scalpel to the dead snake and there before us was the answer to everything.

"Pills!" Baker's exclamation summed up my thoughts neatly. On the stainless-steel table in the morgue where they perform the autopsies, the belly of the dead snake lay open to reveal pouches of little orange pills.

I didn't want to get any closer than I already was, but I had to ask a question.

"How did someone get the pills into the snake?"

Dr Davis pointed to something I wasn't going to examine too closely. "They were inside what the snake ate. We recovered four pouches, each of which looks to contain maybe two hundred pills. I have no idea about street value, but I'm guessing it is enough to make this scheme worthwhile."

"Vincent Pompeo certainly thought so," I commented as my mind whirled. Smuggling drugs is a lucrative business; everyone knows that, but how to get the drugs through border controls must be a constant challenge. Using the snakes was ingenious. I knew people were used as drug mules, swallowing packets containing narcotic substances so they could carry it undetected through customs, but using the snakes was even better. No one would ever look at them and they were big enough that they could carry a significant amount.

Like everyone else, Deepa was staring at the packets of pills and shaking her head in disbelief. "Snakes as drug mules. I wouldn't have come up with that if you had given me a thousand years. I guess our need to find Reece Mefford just increased."

Having entered the autopsy room and fanned out just inside the doors, none of us wanting to get any closer to the table, we were all facing into the room. In fact, the only one facing the doors was Dr Davis and he had a curious expression on his face.

I was about to ask what he was thinking when he spoke. "Reece Mefford, you say?"

The question wasn't aimed at anyone in particular, but I replied, "Yes. He's the supposed owner of the snakes. He thought they were boy snakes and claimed they were his wife's beloved pets. I think we can now assume none of that is true."

Dr Davis' expression hadn't changed, and he was looking past my head rather than at me. "Is he a tall, thin chap in his forties with pasty, white skin and receding black hair?"

Unsure what had prompted this line of questioning, I said, "Yes, why?"

I wasn't the only one to wonder what Dr Davis was looking at – Lieutenant Commander Baker had taken his eyes off the autopsy table to track the doctor's gaze and it was he who answered.

"Because he's standing right outside." Baker was spinning around to face the doors, his attention on a figure now coming through them.

I gasped in shock as the door flew open. Baker was reaching for his sidearm, Deepa and Pippin too probably, but they were not going to be able to use them because Reece Mefford had a hostage.

I recognised her immediately.

"Sangita!"

Reece, with his left arm wrapped tightly around her neck and his right arm holding a knife beneath her chin, forced his way into the room.

"Get back!" he growled.

Wheezing as his arm squeezed her throat, Sangita managed to say, "He was outside the crew elevator when the doors opened. He knocked out Heike and grabbed me."

"Drop your weapons."

Nearest to him, Baker begged, "Just be calm, Reece. No one needs to get hurt."

"Drop your weapons!" Reece repeated his command, shouting the words with added force and digging the knife into Sangita's throat just enough to make her squeal in pain.

There was no option but to comply. I had taken too long to figure it out. Not that I had figured anything out really, I had stumbled and scratched my head and managed to look bewildered. I knew why the snakes were so important now, but I hadn't solved the case.

Baker nodded his head at Pippin and Bhukari, silently telling them to do as Reece demanded. Three weapons hit the cold tile with resounding clunks. As much as anything, I was scared for what someone might try. Would Jermaine, ninja that he is, attempt to disarm Reece?

I didn't think he would for fear he might put the hostage in further danger, but I could see the tension in his bunched muscles. More worrying still, Molly had stopped off at a restroom and was going to walk through the door behind Reece at any moment.

Staying in control of the room, Reece barked his next command.

"Back up!" He gestured with the knife again, coming another pace into the room as we all moved away.

I could see what he was going to do next – everyone else could too, but there was nothing we could do to stop it from happening. With an angry bellow, he shoved Sangita across the room, sending her to sprawl on the deck as he grabbed the nearest gun. With Baker's pistol in his hands, any chance we might have had evaporated.

He claimed the other two guns, crouching to pick them up but never once dropping his guard or taking his eyes off the people in the room.

Deepa and Barbie helped Sangita to her feet as she scrambled to get to the comparative safety our company offered.

"There's nowhere for you to go, Reece," Baker attempted to reason with the drug smuggler. "How do you propose to get off the ship?"

Reece pointed the gun he held at Baker's centre of mass, and I wasn't the only one who gasped in fright, thinking he might pull the trigger.

Mercifully, it was just a threat, and Reece sneered, "I'll walk off like anyone else. No one is looking for me. Now back away from the table and keep your hands in the air. I see anyone lowering their hands or doing anything I don't like the look of, I'll start shooting. With three guns I think I have enough bullets for all of you."

He manoeuvred us around, penning us in one corner by the

door to the morgue and for the first time he looked down as his fingers scrambled to grab the packets of pills.

"Where does that door go?" He demanded to know, staring through our midst to the steel door in the wall.

"That's the morgue," revealed Dr Davis, speaking calmly in the hope that his tone might help keep the crazy gunman calm too.

Despite the muck that covered the plastic pouches of pills, Reece lifted them to his lips and kissed them. He sounded proud when he boasted, "Four years I've been using this route to supply my dealers in America. Four years. Now I'll have to come up with a new way to get through border control." He twisted at the waist, his gun arm tracking through the air until it was pointing at me. "And it's all your fault."

"Me?" I questioned.

Reece came forward a pace, the muzzle of the gun never wavering. "Yes, you. You took down the Alliance of Families and ruined everything I had built. When you came to tell me about the snakes earlier you asked me if I knew someone called Vincent Pompeo."

"You do know him then," I concluded, annoyed with myself once again for not reading the lie when he spoke it to my face.

However, Reece said, "No, I'd never heard his name before you said it. I do remember there being a Pompeo working for one of my distributors in Miami though, so I made a call and guess what?"

"It's the same guy." I stated the obvious.

Reece motioned to Jermaine with the hand holding the pills. "You. Open the door."

He was going to put us in the morgue and lock the door. It was refrigerated so we would get cold, but it wasn't below freezing.

To me Reece said, "Yes, it's the same guy. My guess is he found out about my unique method of delivery and chose to intercept the drugs en route. Quite how he knew where to find them I have no idea, but it hardly matters now."

As the morgue door swung open behind us and we began to file inside, I could see exactly how the pieces went together. Vincent had approached his cousin with a plan. He must have known Nicole was on the same ship as the smuggler and seeing opportunity align with ability, he chose to steal the pills for himself.

Nicole was in on it, but she couldn't do what was needed by herself, so enrolled her former boyfriend, Sanjeev. He in turn told Andrea and the two of them had cooked up the plan to kill their accomplices and keep the drugs. It could have been Andrea or Sanjeev who killed Nicole, but probably both who saw to Vincent – I remembered the bruising around his wrists where he had been held.

They were set to get away with it, but with the snakes now in his cabin, Sanjeev came to a terrible end. Vincent knew the drugs were in the snakes and Nicole would have been able to find out where they were and how to get to them.

I wanted to smack myself in the head!

The schematic on the wall in Nicole's cabin! Now I knew what it was for. She needed to figure out how to access the storage room. Had she used her feminine wiles to obtain it, seducing an unsuspecting engineer? I was never going to know, but the clue to her involvement had been there almost at the start. Had I not been so distracted by my drama with Alistair I might have been thinking clearly enough to have seen it.

Their plan was bold and ingenious. Were it not for the fact that they were all criminals, I might have been willing to applaud them.

Backing into the morgue, I saw Reece lift something from the autopsy table. It was a scalpel.

He lofted it, saying, "Perfect. I need to get the other set of pills." He meant to cut open the remaining boa constrictor!

Sickened by the thought, and that there wasn't a thing I could do to stop him, my eye caught a flash of movement just outside the door to the autopsy room. It was brown hair – Molly returning!

Did I shout a warning to her? Would that improve her chances or weaken them? If I said nothing and Reece shot her when she walked in, would I blame myself forever?

Advancing with the gun pointing through the morgue's door, Reece snarled, "Back up!"

In two seconds, we were going to be locked inside!

Unable to stand the thought of anything happening to my former housemaid, I screamed her name.

"Molly! He's got a gun. Run for it!"

Reece spun around, twisting on the balls of his feet to face back toward the autopsy room doors. Without hesitating, he fired three shots through them.

Bang! Bang! Bang!

The sound was so loud I could feel it in my internal organs. Though I was closest to the drug smuggler, Jermaine, Hideki, Pippin, Deepa, Barbie, and Baker were all trying to get to him. It was the first time he had taken his eyes off us since he walked in with Sangita.

I tried to get out of the way, I truly did, but I was the last one in and now stood blocking the exit. I dodged right to make way, sensed Jermaine coming toward me and dodged back the other way. Had I just stayed still, people would have gone around me like a rock in a stream. Instead, I confused everyone, causing them to sidestep twice to avoid me as I moved and moved again.

The net result, just when we had a chance to overpower Reece, was that I got in everyone's way and caused them to collide with each other. Baker slammed into me, knocking the breath from my lungs. He then grabbed my arms in a hopeless attempt to keep us both upright. We fell, wedging in the doorway because it was two of us and we completely filled the space only to pop free a nanosecond later when Jermaine, Barbie and everyone else piled into Baker's back.

I tumbled to one side, a push from Baker sending me clear at the last moment though I believe his intention was to get clear himself. He went down beneath a jumbled mass of arms and legs as no one else was able to make it out of the morgue on their feet.

All hope of grabbing Reece was lost unless I tackled him, and I was too terrified to even make my feet move. With my friends scrambling to find their footing and generally impeding each other in the process, Reece could have killed them all.

He swung his head in their direction, loosed off a few choice swearwords and made a run for it instead.

You couldn't convince me to chase a man with a gun under any circumstances, but that was what I did. Molly was on the other side of the autopsy room doors and was either already shot or was about to engage in a gun battle.

I had to help!

Reece fired his gun again, putting more holes in the doors as he ran at them. No sound came back, no shouts of pain or terror and no shots. Ahead of me, he kicked the doors open and charged through.

I feared the worse – that Molly had been shot in his first volley and was lying dead or incapacitated on the floor in the sick bay.

Ahead, the sound of something crashing to the floor reached my ears. Behind me I could hear racing feet as my friends ran after me, but I would get to the doors first. It didn't matter if Reece got away, I was only thinking of Molly.

I guess that's why the sight of Buddy threw me so completely.

40

COINCIDENCE

"Freeze dirtbag!"

I careened through the autopsy room doors and into the sick bay to find Molly standing over Reece Mefford. He was lying on his back with a trolley on his chest. Surgical tools, kidney bowls, and boxes of bandages and gauze were strewn across the floor.

Molly had her sidearm drawn, holding it with both hands as she stared down at the drug smuggler. Her left foot pinned his right hand to the deck, immobilising the gun he held, and crushing his fingers if the noises of protest he made were anything to go by.

Buddy was sitting on the cold tile, one little ape hand pressing against a wound on his side. There was a smear of blood on the tile – Reece had stepped in it and lost his footing.

I had come to a stop just inside the sick bay, my friends piling through the doors behind me and this time able to fan out as they too took in the crazy scene.

It wasn't Molly's brown hair I saw through the glass panel of the autopsy room door; it was Buddy's. Reece had shot him, and the resulting pool of blood proved to be his undoing.

"Buddy is hurt!" I cried, twisting around to find Dr Davis as he came through the door behind everyone else.

I got a questioning face in return. "Who's Buddy?"

Hideki was already moving. "That's the ape. Looks like he's losing a lot of blood."

Barbie darted forward to join him, the ape unresisting when they lifted him from the floor and onto a hospital bed. I felt genuine concern for the poor little thing. Of course, a lot of that evaporated when he spotted me watching him and flipped me his middle finger again.

"You're crushing my hand," wailed Reece, bringing my attention back to him.

Looking down at him still, Molly sneered, "Shut yer face." Baker came around me, heading for Molly and closely followed by Pippin, and Bhukari. "This is a bad guy, right?" Molly asked, looking up to check she hadn't got it wrong.

I nodded, a disbelieving chuckle making its way from me. "Yes, Molly. That's a bad guy."

She grinned. "I thought he probably was with the gun and the bags of pills. Sorry I took so long in the toilet. All this travel has given me terrible constipation."

It was typical Molly, always saying the words in her head without the slightest filter.

Rather than comment on her bowel movements, I said, "Molly your timing was impeccable."

Hideki announced that Buddy needed surgery and there ensued a short argument between the two doctors regarding the sick bay and it being reserved for human patients. I know Dr Davis could have pulled rank as the senior physician, but when I begged him to save Buddy, he sighed and told Hideki to make sure the sick bay was cleaned more thoroughly than usual once the procedure was complete.

Reece was hauled onto his feet and placed in cuffs, Molly getting the honours as her colleagues commented on what a crazy first day she'd had. He was heading to the brig obviously, the mystery behind the snakes and the dead climber now finally solved.

Today's work wasn't over though. Reece was in custody, but I still had three dead bodies and I only knew how one of them died. Sanjeev met with a fate one might say he deserved. I was sure I had it right, but knowing something and being able to prove it were two different things.

Leaving Hideki to work on Buddy, I made my way out of the sick bay. Ahead of me, Baker was speaking into his radio, informing Commander Ochi, the deputy captain, of the shots fired and that we had a passenger in custody.

Heike had been found and was being brought to sick bay with a suspected concussion. Sangita elected to remain behind to be with her friend when she arrived, and Baker left Deepa and Pippin with her. Both ladies would need to give statements and had suffered a hard shock in being attacked – now was not the time to send them back to work.

My phone rang as I traipsed along the sterile steel passageways one finds below the passenger areas. Taking it from my handbag, I was pleased to see Alistair's name displayed. I gave a tired snort, laughing at how the day had been filled with such highs and lows. A few hours ago, I thought my relationship with the handsome ship's captain had come to an end. Now I knew differently.

I thumbed the green button and placed the phone to my ear. "Alistair?"

"You are unharmed?" he asked. "Commander Ochi informs me that there has been a shooting."

"And naturally you assumed I would be at the centre of that?"

Alistair said, "Weelllll."

How I loved having someone who cared and worried about me. "I am fine," I replied with a smile. "It was Buddy who got shot. He's going to be fine though."

"Buddy? You mean the ape?"

"Yes, dear. Buddy the ape."

"So you've sewn up the murder cases, I assume."

My smile faded. "No, not yet."

"But I was told you have a man in custody. The one who was shooting." Alistair wasn't bothering to hide his confusion.

"Sorry, darling. The man Ensign Lawrie just disarmed is a drug smuggler. He was taking drugs to America using snakes as mules." I got stunned silence from the captain. "I'll explain it all in detail soon, I promise. The three deaths on board today were all to do with the drugs and an attempt to steal them."

"Riiiight," Alistair drawled. "That's about as clear as mud. Where are you now?"

"On my way to the brig. I'm still trying to figure out how to prove my prime suspect is lying."

"Okay. I'll meet you there."

Alistair's announcement was not what I expected.

"You're coming to the brig?"

"Yes, dear. The captain really ought to know what is going on and today's events have proven me to be in the dark about far too many things. I'll see you soon." He ended the call and I let Baker know we were about to have the captain's company. Forewarning would give the security officers a chance to make sure their uniforms were on straight if nothing else.

While I was on the phone, Baker had recalled Schneider and Sam, the two of them still hanging out near Reece Mefford's cabin for his return. They were going to join us in the brig too.

Unexpectedly, I felt an even greater urge to solve the case now. Alistair wasn't coming to scrutinise me, but somehow his presence added a new level of pressure. I hurried my steps, wanting to get to the brig and be locked in the interview room before he arrived. That way, and armed with new knowledge – I finally knew it was all about drugs – I hoped I might catch Andrea in her lie before I next spoke to Alistair.

Impatiently, I tapped my foot as the guards inside the brig went through the laborious process of letting us in.

Lieutenant Commander Baker led the way, Molly following behind with Reece Mefford in front of her.

"Cooool," Molly looked around as she came into the ship's jail. "I didn't get to see this place last time I was on board." The last time she was on board, she was a passenger staying in my suite and had no reason to even know the ship had a jail.

Spotting the young woman, and recognising her as one of the new ensigns, Lieutenant Wong shot her a grin.

"You want a tour?" he asked, the subtext that he was flirting not missed by anyone except Molly.

"Coo, yeah." Remembering her prisoner, she quickly added, "When we've dealt with this one, eh?"

Baker clicked his fingers to make a noise, dragging Wong's eyes away from the pretty, young ensign. "Bring Miss Bassinet-Blatch to the interview room again, please."

He got a nod of acknowledgement, the guards in the brig splitting up to perform different tasks. Wong stayed with Molly, gamely showing her the process of logging a prisoner. Others left to fetch Andrea.

Reece Mefford had nothing to say, and I was fine with that. I would have to type up a report later, but he was only going to be in our brig for a short period. Before nightfall and the ship left the dock, he would be transferred to the local police. They would hold him until he could be repatriated. Maritime law is complex stuff, there being so many interested parties involved when a person from one country commits a crime in another.

Suffice to say I was glad all I had to do was write a report. Baker and the others would compile evidence and such.

Wong completed the paperwork and announced that the final step was to place the prisoner in his or her cell and then made a joke about throwing away the key.

Molly sniggered at his joke, the flirting now going both ways until Baker cleared his throat in a meaningful manner.

Dropping his smile in favour of a serious expression, Lieutenant Wong asked, "Do you wish to escort him the last few yards, Molly?"

"Absolutely. Move it, dirtbag."

I watched with mild amusement as my former housemaid, who had been a bit lazy, and a bit rubbish at her simple job, escorted a prisoner twice her size through the door that led to the cells. She was about to turn right when Wong stopped her, making her back up a foot.

I saw why when two guards escorted Andrea past the doorway on her way to the interview room.

"Andrea!" blurted Molly. "Oh, wow I hope you didn't do whatever it was they have you in here for. I still owe you that drink."

My forehead became a stack of furrowed wrinkles as a frown formed. My feet were already moving, carrying me across the brig's reception area as a question formed on my lips.

"Molly how do you know this woman?"

Baker was coming across the room too, the same question undoubtedly on his mind.

Andrea made a panicked 'shushing' sound, imploring eyes begging Molly to keep quiet.

Molly wasn't taking the hint though. Rather, she was eyeing Andrea with scepticism.

"Remember I said I got horribly lost trying to find my cabin in the small hours this morning and would have stayed lost if I hadn't bumped into someone?" Molly reminded me of our conversation in the passageway outside cabin 1215.

Andrea closed her eyes as if that would help to avoid the horror incoming.

Holding my breath and praying I was about to get the right answer, I asked, "What time was that?"

"A little after three or thereabouts." Molly's answer sealed the deal and Andrea knew she was caught.

"There's never anyone around at that time of night," my prime suspect snapped. "I was three yards from Luis' cabin when this little brat found me. Five seconds. That's all I needed. Five stupid seconds." She was raging. Gripped by her anger, she lunged at Molly, hands looking to grab her throat and wring the life from her.

The guards all reacted, stopping the murderous fitness instructor before she could get to Molly's skin.

Reece tried to take advantage of the bedlam and make a break for it, but Molly's foot snaked out (see what I did there?) to trip him, sending him to the deck where Baker advised he should stay.

The buzzer sounded, the captain's face appearing on a monitor above the reception desk to show who was outside wanting to get in.

Alistair was here and I could not have been happier to see him. I would have gone to the door to meet him, but pinned in place by two meaty guards, Andrea was sobbing and giving away the whole story.

"Sanjeev said we would have enough money to set ourselves up. He was taking me back to England, but a share of the money wasn't going to do it. We needed it all, don't you see? Nicole didn't deserve any, she didn't even help out. She said the snakes were too scary."

"So you killed her?" I asked the direct question, hoping for a direct answer, and I got one.

"Damned right I did. She wouldn't stop flirting with Sanjeev. She had her chance with him. Besides, when we killed Vincent, we could hardly leave her alive, now could we?"

She spoke about killing two people as if it were just business.

Wong asked, "You ah … you still want us to put her in the interview room, Mrs Fisher?"

I shook my head. I had all I needed. Alistair was coming through the door when I turned around. Andrea was being taken back to her cell. Luis, who was back there somewhere, would be released, and Reece would occupy a cell until he was taken away. Whether Luis kept his job or not was not down to me, though I thought it would be a little harsh if he was punished given that he was drugged and robbed.

I was keen to get back to the sick bay to check on Buddy, and there were other tasks that required my attention yet. For now though, I went to Alistair, surprising him and embarrassing everyone in the room by standing on my tiptoes to kiss him.

When I broke it, he asked, "Darling, what are you wearing?"

41
___

CONFRONTATION

L eaving Baker and Bhukari behind to mop up the details, I made my way back through the ship on the captain's arm. I felt good. Even though I looked ridiculous, I didn't care one jot.

I had my friends around me and with them by my side it didn't matter who was trying to bring me down because they were not going to succeed. If anything, Alistair and I were stronger now.

We were going to confront Hennessey. Alistair believed it would cause her to leave the ship, abandoning any further plans she might have to mess with me. I wanted to get changed first – I had been in Barbie's clothes for long enough and my undercarriage was smarting from the thong I wore.

At a boutique on deck eighteen which sold everything I would need for the next day or so – I could get more items from other shops later – I went into a changing room armed with a full outfit. Everything from underwear and stockings, to shoes, a gorgeous dress, and even a matching hat. I'm on a cruise, people, hats are allowed.

"Patricia, darling, you look ravishing," growled Alistair, a glint in his eye.

Pleased with his comment, I spun around to check the mirror again. I was never going to look like Hennessey – few women ever would – but Alistair didn't seem to care, so why should I? I had a few wrinkles, my bum was a little saggy, my boobs had seen better days, but I was confident to be who I was and that was something he did for me.

We found Barbie and Jermaine waiting for us outside. They had coffee in travel cups and were chatting happily.

"Hey, Patty," Barbie waved. "You look better in your clothes," she admitted.

I handed her a bag containing the things she had loaned me, but Jermaine intercepted it.

"I will get this laundered, madam."

I thanked him with a smile. "What are you guys, waiting for?"

Barbie narrowed her eyes at me. "Oh, no you don't, Patricia Fisher. Don't try to pretend you have forgotten about the promise to tell us who has been causing all the recent drama. You said you would tell us all about it once you had sewn up the murder cases."

I nodded and replied, "Actually, I said I was waiting for an answer," I paused to check my phone, expecting to confirm I was still in the dark. I wasn't though, the reply I knew would come – one way or the other – was right there.

Barbie tried to sneak a look, forcing me to clutch the phone to my chest playfully.

"I need to speak with Miss Gates. After that I propose we all gather in my suite for gin and nibbles," I aimed my eyes at Jermaine to confirm that was okay and we had provisions to match my suggestion. When he dipped his head, I continued, "Then I will tell you what I know. I promise."

Barbie's eyes remained narrowed.

"Okay, Patty, but don't keep us waiting too long."

Crossing deck eighteen with Alistair as Barbie and Jermaine went back to my suite, I caught a glimpse of myself in the reflection of a glass storefront. It made me smile, but not because I liked my outfit; it was how I looked with Alistair on my arm that caused my chest to swell.

We were going to see Hennessey and I was going to pay her back for all the cruel lies she twisted.

Alistair, ever the captain, greeted passengers and crew by name as we passed them, riding the escalator down to deck seventeen and then deck sixteen merely because he liked to be seen in public.

The ship was filling with people again, the passengers making their way back on board as we readied to sail. I didn't know it, but I was being watched, a tanned man with blonde hair and a moustache riding the escalator just a few yards behind me.

On deck sixteen, Alistair escorted me to an elevator and once inside he pushed me against a wall and kissed me. Deeply, tenderly, and with a sense of urgency that spoke of events to come. He broke it only when the bell pinged.

We were at deck eight. Had I been heading to Hennessey's cabin by myself, I would have felt nervous, unsure how she would react. With Alistair at my side to throw in her face, I felt nothing but anticipation.

You can imagine my disappointment when she didn't answer the door.

We knocked and waited and knocked again. Frustrated, Alistair did something he ought not to and used his universal card to open her door.

We didn't need to go inside though; one glance was sufficient to confirm she was gone.

I felt a bit like singing, "Ding dong the witch is dead," yet managed to refrain.

On the way back to the elevator, Alistair contacted gate security and was able to confirm she had left the ship less than thirty minutes ago – right when I was buying my outfit. Had I gone straight to her in Barbie's ill-fitting sports gear, I might have found her, but what would I have gained?

A sense of triumph? It was a petty, childish emotion I was better off doing without.

There was no kiss in the elevator this time. We just held hands and stayed quiet, content to be in each other's company.

Before we went back into my suite, I checked the message on my phone once more.

42

FINAL CHAPTER

"So come on, Patty," demanded Barbie with mock rage in her voice. "Who is it?"

I was on my second Hendricks and tonic, the first having vanished rather quickly, and sitting on the new couch with my dachshunds positioned either side of me.

In response, I prodded the seat of the couch as if testing it.

"You know this thing really is a lot more comfortable than the last one."

Barbie cracked her knuckles and mimed strangling me. It drew a laugh from the room.

My team was present, all of them including Sam holding a gin and tonic. Somehow Molly had gotten included, tagging along with everyone else though she couldn't stop yawning. Alistair was relaxing in one of the chairs, and even Jermaine had doffed his jacket – literally the first time I had ever seen him do so in company.

They were all waiting for me to do the big reveal, but I wanted to have a little fun.

"Most of you know her," I teased.

Wrinkled brows considered my first clue.

"So it's a woman," stated Barbie. "It's not the Godmother though?"

I shook my head.

Jermaine asked, "Who was it that you sent a message to, madam? You said you were waiting for an answer."

It was a good question.

"It was Mavis at the post office back in East Malling."

"East Malling?" The name of my hometown was repeated by almost everyone in the room. Molly and Sam were from the same place, and everyone else had been there. Even Alistair.

Suddenly, Barbie started slapping Jermaine's arm in an excited fashion. She grabbed his sleeve and twisted him around to face her.

Their eyes met and they both blurted in unison, "It's Angelica Howard-Box!"

The name resounded around the room, and I did my best to rationalise Angelica's actions.

"Angelica has never really accepted that anyone else can be in the right. Her ability to convince herself that her actions are justified have always been a problem, but I never thought she would go this far."

"How can be you be sure it is her?" Barbie challenged me.

"Hand soap." I spoke the single word and sipped at my drink again.

"Hand soap?" Barbie repeated.

Putting my empty glass down, I said, "Angelica uses a brand of hand soap that she buys from Fortnum and Mason in London. It is expensive stuff, and I know that because she loves to tell people about it. She takes her soap with her so that she doesn't have to use a *lesser* brand and because she likes to show off. I once tried to touch it when we were both in the ladies' restroom at the village church. She slapped my hand away, but not before I had some. Hennessey touched me earlier and the scent coming off her was the same expensive soap."

I was being eyed sceptically. "Patty, hand soap is not a lot to go on," Barbie pointed out.

She was right, obviously, but so was I.

"It's Angelica," I assured them both. "After Robbie's wedding, when I uncovered her lies and schemes, I fooled myself into believing she would go home and let it pass. I was leaving the village again and would be out of her hair."

Okay, so I had caused the bride and groom to address their feelings and in so doing exposed that the only reason they were going through with the ceremony was because the groom's mother was a scheming cow. It was a celebrity wedding being covered by a bunch of glossy magazines and I ruined it. In Angelica's opinion anyway.

To allay any final doubts, I said, "I asked Mavis if Angelica had been in the post office recently. What do you think she said?" The answer being obvious, I supplied it for them, "She set up a drop box for her mail a month ago and said she did not know when she would be back. She's here on this ship and she will stop at nothing to ruin me."

Baker was already moving. "Central registry will have her cabin number."

I called out to stop him as he pulled out his tablet.

"She'll be here under a fake name. I believe she has a hacker in her employ – she doesn't have the brains to get into my emails herself. And it wasn't her or Hennessey who tasered Jermaine earlier."

Jermaine asked, "Then what do you propose, madam? Surely we need to stop her as swiftly as possible."

"Yeah, Patty," Barbie joined in. "What if she does something else?"

"Oh, I'm counting on it," I replied with a smile. "At this point she probably knows she failed to create the rift she wanted between Alistair and me." I nodded my head at Barbie. "She will also know her attempt to ruin our friendship failed. Plenty of people saw us together today and I think it's wise to assume she has spies on the ship." I looked at Alistair. "There will be one from the crew at the very least."

He swore under his breath, but didn't argue.

"So what's our next move, Mrs Fisher?" Sam wanted to know.

Well, I was going to get her. I was going to get her good.

EPILOGUE

Silvestre could not remember a more frustrating day. There had almost certainly been some, but they were not coming to mind now. Usually, patience is all he needed to achieve that which he desired. However, his plan to quickly find Patricia Fisher and extract information from her, by force if it proved necessary, had not come to pass.

The ship had sailed without a single opportunity to get her alone. At the next destination, he would leave the ship, change his disguise and buy a new ticket. Using a new appearance – one she wouldn't recognise – and staying in a new cabin so no one would notice the change, he would start again.

He had time. The result was what mattered.

Carefully, he had asked a couple of the crew about the report of a stowaway and the gems found in his gut. It was public information, so he played the role of a curious passenger attempting to establish if it was even true.

Neither of the persons he asked knew the answer. One complained that nobody ever told him anything and the other speculated that if there were a body, it would be in the morgue – an obvious answer any fool could have figured out for themselves.

Standing a few yards from the door to the Windsor Suite where he knew Patricia Fisher lived, Xavier Silvestre felt an irrational urge to break the lock and enter. It was after one in the morning, and he would find her in bed.

She had dogs though; tiny noise makers that would alert her butler - a giant brute of a man. Silvestre didn't fear him, he would kill the Jamaican easily enough, but now they were at sea, the option of hastily leaving was denied. He needed to play it safe.

Withdrawing with a silent promise to return, Silvestre walked away.

The End

AUTHOR'S NOTE

Hello Dear Reader,

Congratulations for getting all the way to the end of the book and still having enough energy left to read my notes.

This is the longest Patricia Fisher book I have ever written and one of the most convoluted, though confusing messes of mysteries appears to be my specialty. I had to write several pages of notes just to keep clear in my head what different parties were supposed to be doing.

It didn't help that I was writing this in the run up to Christmas. With two small children in the house, aged six and eighteen months, there was much to distract me, and I made sure to cut my hours to spend more time with them. Over the holiday itself, my laptop remained untouched for several days, a practice which always throws me. When I am in the story – something that happens when I am writing every day – picking up where I left off is easy. After a period of not writing, I find myself staring hopelessly at the screen until I can once again pick up the thread.

To add to the length of time this book took to write, technical woes erased a bunch of words several times. Typing the author's note now, I still haven't gotten to the bottom of what is wrong with my laptop and worry it might do the exact same thing at any moment.

In this book I make a wonderful faux pas when I utilise a clue to do with the snakes having babies in their bellies. Jermaine states that snakes lay eggs, but in fact Boas and few other species of snake do produce live young. Known as viviparous or ovoviviparous, these snakes either hatch the eggs inside their own bodies or give birth like a mammal.

I could have easily changed the story to make it factually correct, but decided that I rather liked the mistaken manner in which they uncover the truth. It felt more realistic because I bet there are lots of people out there who would have never known I had made an error were it not for me claiming it here.

It is a Friday night at the start of January as I write this final note. I have a bunch of emails to answer from eager readers looking to score a free audiobook – that's just one of the benefits of signing up to receive my free newsletter – I give stuff away.

In the morning, I am taking my son, Hunter, to a monster truck event at an arena in London. At six, such things enthrall him, and I paid extra to get a backstage pass so he can see the machines up close. Father and son will have a fun day, and it will be a pleasant diversion from the many hours I spend hunched over a keyboard.

It is cool here, but could not be described as cold. The garden is barren, devoid of greenery save for the evergreen shrubs I planted to combat that very issue. Some snow would be nice – the kids would love it, but in the southeast corner of England such weather is rare. Most years, we see only a few flakes.

On Monday, when I settle once more into my chair, I will be crafting the fourth story in my Felicity Phillips series. I have been looking forward to it since I finished story three and left a tantalising promise of a series crossover event. I have several of these crossovers coming, melding the characters together into a disorganised mass for a storyline that begs to be told.

The people who read my newsletter know all about this. So too my Facebook patrons. I won't bore you with it here though. Thank you for reading.

Take care.

Steve Higgs

WHAT'S NEXT FOR PATRICIA FISHER

Reaching the British Unions Isles, the passengers and crew arrive in time for the annual pirate festival. It's party time! But when Patricia and friends leave the ship, they find an eccentric millionaire waiting to hire them …

… and his fireside spooky ghost story is too good not to investigate. Patricia expects to figure this one out before happy hour arrives, but when the sun goes down and her client goes missing, the game gets downright scary.

Are there ghosts on this island? Has the client been snatched by vengeful spirits?

The locals certainly thinks so and they seem to know why.

Facing an unknown adversary, and the very real possibility that they trying to catch perpetrators who died hundreds of years ago, Patricia and her team need help. This kind of mystery calls for a specialist, so it's a good thing Patricia knows one.

I wonder who that could be?

STEVE'S BESTSELLING SERIES

BAKING. IT CAN GET A GUY KILLED.

When a retired detective superintendent chooses to take a culinary tour of the British Isles, he hopes to find tasty treats and delicious bakes …

… what he finds is a clue to a crime in the ingredients for his pork pie.

His dog, Rex Harrison, an ex-police dog fired for having a bad attitude, cannot understand why the humans are struggling to solve the mystery. He can already smell the answer – it's right before their noses.

He'll pitch in to help his human and the shop owner's teenage daughter as the trio set out to save the shop from closure. Is the rival pork pie shop across the street to blame? Or is there something far more sinister going on?

One thing is for sure, what started out as a bit of fun, is getting deadlier by the hour, and they'd better work out what the dog knows soon or it could be curtains for them all.

BLUE MOON INVESTIGATIONS

The paranormal? It's all nonsense but proving it might just get them all killed.

When a master vampire starts killing people in his hometown, paranormal investigator, Tempest Michaels, takes it personally ...

... and soon a race against time turns into a battle for his life.

He doesn't believe in the paranormal but has a steady stream of clients with cases too weird for the police to bother with. Mostly it's all nonsense, but when a third victim turns up with bite marks in her lifeless throat, can he really dismiss the possibility that this time the monster is real?

Joined by an ex-army buddy, a disillusioned cop, his friends from the pub, his dogs, and his mother (why are there no grandchildren, Tempest), our paranormal investigator is going to stop the murders if it kills him ...

… but when his probing draws the creature's attention, his family and friends become the hunted.

MORE BOOKS BY STEVE HIGGS

Blue Moon Investigations
Paranormal Nonsense
The Phantom of Barker Mill
Amanda Harper Paranormal Detective
The Klowns of Kent
Dead Pirates of Cawsand
In the Doodoo with Voodoo
The Witches of East Malling
Crop Circles, Cows and Crazy Aliens
Whispers in the Rigging
Bloodlust Blonde – a short story
Paws of the Yeti
Under a Blue Moon – A Paranormal Detective Origin Story
Night Work
Lord Hale's Monster
The Herne Bay Howlers
Undead Incorporated
The Ghoul of Christmas Past
The Sandman
Jailhouse Golem

Shadow in the Mine
Ghost Writer

Patricia Fisher Cruise Mysteries
The Missing Sapphire of Zangrabar
The Kidnapped Bride
The Director's Cut
The Couple in Cabin 2124
Doctor Death
Murder on the Dancefloor
Mission for the Maharaja
A Sleuth and her Dachshund in Athens
The Maltese Parrot
No Place Like Home
What Sam Knew
Solstice Goat
Recipe for Murder
A Banshee and a Bookshop
Diamonds, Dinner Jackets, and Death
Frozen Vengeance
Mug Shot
The Godmother
Murder is an Artform
Wonderful Weddings and Deadly Divorces
Dangerous Creatures
Patricia Fisher: Ship's Detective
Fitness Can Kill
Death by Pirates

Albert Smith Culinary Capers
Pork Pie Pandemonium
Bakewell Tart Bludgeoning
Stilton Slaughter
Bedfordshire Clanger Calamity
Death of a Yorkshire Pudding
Cumberland Sausage Shocker

Arbroath Smokie Slaying
Dundee Cake Dispatch
Lancashire Hotpot Peril
Blackpool Rock Bloodshed
Kent Coast Oyster Obliteration

Felicity Philips Investigates
To Love and to Perish
Tying the Noose
Aisle Kill Him
A Dress to Die for

Real of False Gods
Untethered magic
Unleashed Magic
Early Shift
Damaged but Powerful
Demon Bound
Familiar Territory
The Armour of God
Terrible Secrets
Top Dog

FREE BOOKS AND MORE

Get sneak peaks, exclusive giveaways, behind the scenes content, and more. Plus, you'll be notified of Fan Pricing events when they occur and get exclusive offers from other authors because all UF writers are automatically friends.
Not only that, but you'll receive an exclusive FREE story staring Otto and Zachary and two free stories from the author's Blue Moon Investigations series.

To get to this, you will need to copy the link below into a web browser.

https://mailchi.mp/fd47a6eb4ae5/patricialist

Want to follow me and keep up with what I am doing? I have a very active Facebook group with a fast-growing community of reader fans who want to talk about the books. You'll find me there most days talking about what I have coming up and letting people know about bargains. To get to it, carefully copy the link below into a web browser.

https://www.facebook.com/groups/1151907108277718

Made in United States
Orlando, FL
14 March 2023

31029923R00143